T0266258

DUCK POND EPIPHANY

DUCK POND EPIPHANY

TRACEY BARNES PRIESTLEY

SHE WRITES PRESS

Copyright © 2013 by Tracey Barnes Priestley

All rights reserved. No part of this publication may be reproduced, distributed, or transmitted in any form or by any means, including photocopying, recording, digital scanning, or other electronic or mechanical methods, without the prior written permission of the publisher, except in the case of brief quotations embodied in critical reviews and certain other noncommercial uses permitted by copyright law. For permission requests, please address She Writes Press.

Published 2013
Printed in the United States of America
ISBN: 978-1-938314-24-7
Library of Congress Control Number: 2013900131

For information, address:
She Writes Press
1563 Solano Ave #546
Berkeley, CA 94707

To BDP.
There really is happily ever after!

1

*T*here are moments that forever change our lives. I just didn't realize this would be one of them.

It began with an unexpected bit of bright spring rain and was followed by a simple event that derailed me from completing my endless list of errands. Instead of tracking down the missing dry-cleaning or checking to see if the hardware for the downstairs bathroom remodel had arrived, I found myself standing inside the edge of Lithia Park, sketching a pond full of playful waterfowl. They frolicked in the drops, stretching, hopping, flapping wings through a bird ballet—a bunch of ducks, with brains the size of cherry tomatoes, all of them never happier. Sidetracked by the comical sight and unable to resist, I had given way to creative temptation and was now thrown completely off schedule. My pencil stopped mid-line as I realized the consequence of such self-indulgence: pulling up late to the school to find my four sopping wet, tired, and hungry children. The oldest would be indignant he'd been made to wait, while his younger brother wouldn't even register the maternal misdeed. Their first little sister might already be in the grips of worry mania, unfortunately a place she knew too well for someone so young. The youngest would greet her mother with a huge smile and tumble awkwardly into the backseat of the minivan, her daily report about life in the first grade bubbling forth with nary a pause for a breath.

The image of my bedraggled offspring, and the hell I would pay, propelled me into action. Stuffing pencil and paper into the oversized bag hanging off my shoulder, I leaned into the cool, fresh drops and headed for the deserted sidewalk. But after just one block, my concentration was broken again, this time by a flash of color in the corner of my eye. Turning quickly, as a bull to the cape, a solitary crimson chair was revealed standing elegantly, proudly in the window. Draped with an imported silk curtain panel, it was simply lit by an antique floor lamp. The shadows cast by the overstuffed wingback intrigued me, and there was mystery in the subtle shades of burgundy and scarlet.

Every detail of the chair landed deep within my brain. As the gentle spring drizzle fell on my back, I knew it would be mine. It made no logical sense, of course. Where would it fit in our old farmhouse? And what about our budget, already stretched to the limit? None of that mattered. Something about the rain and the red chair added up to an epiphany, and I knew better than to question the significance, preferring to trust my history of meaningful moments that had the nearly mystic capacity of altering my life.

My first real epiphany occurred nearly fifteen years before the red chair sighting, when I dropped an entire kettle of beans on the kitchen floor. Pregnant and feeling much like a beached whale, I had completely misjudged how much room would be required to navigate both my belly and the brimming kettle from the sink to the stove, the kitchen in our first apartment not much larger than an airplane bathroom. The Bean Pot Epiphany (I always named my epiphanies) spoke to the stupidity of making Cuban black beans, from scratch no less, for the twenty-five people coming to our apartment that night to organize a fight against the new zoning regulations being considered by the City Council. But standing there with cold, slimy beans all over my swollen bare feet, it became clear that the true meaning of the Bean Pot Epiphany was really about my failure to take care of myself. I had to wonder why, at eight months pregnant, I was still working four days a week at the grocery store as well as tutoring the kid downstairs in hopes he'd pass his GED. Even worse, here I was, hosting a mass of loud, angry, idealistic students who didn't even pay taxes yet but had opinions as big as the state itself over something that was pretty much a done deal. The very pregnant, overworked young wife of Ashland's up-and-coming Southern Oregon University engineering professor clearly wasn't taking care of herself.

When *that* lightbulb went on, I left the beans on the floor, called the dogs into the apartment, jumped into our rusty 1952 Chevy truck, and drove into town to buy fifteen cans of black beans, five tubs of salsa, and four large cans of tomatoes. I wisely skipped the fresh cilantro. Not enough time, and really, would the impassioned activists even know?

When I returned, the floor only needed mopping—not shoveling—and the dogs were smiling. The canned concoction was simmering within minutes, and no one was ever the wiser.

The red chair sighting was a similar kind of "take care of yourself" realization. As I stood and stared through the wet glass that April day, thoughts about the chaos that my life had become ricocheted through my brain—four kids, one husband, three dogs, two cats, a potbellied pig, one nearly blind and certainly deaf horse, cranky chickens, a smelly hamster with a skin condition, and even a llama. The one common denominator? It seemed as though everything I owned had to somehow be shared with each and every one of those beings. Kids clamored for a bite of my toast. They crept into my bed weeping from nightmares or ready to throw up. The hamster required my time for a trip to the vet. Piles of two-legged humanity and four-legged critters spilled over every seat in the minivan. Sure, the kids stayed out of my underwear drawer (except that time the boys decided a 34B would make a great double slingshot), but mostly, everything I owned seemed as though it was up for grabs. (The only exception was my precious treasure, the violin I'd owned and played since the fourth grade. Children and spouse alike knew it was completely off-limits. The kids weren't even allowed to touch the faded black case, so convinced was I that this could somehow damage its contents.)

So on that wet afternoon, while visually tracing the seductive curves of the lush chair, I decided then and there that I would not share it with one living soul. It would be the one possession in the entire house that I would lay claim to, and it didn't matter what my family thought. This was not a matter of selfishness. It was simply a matter of having one tiny yet luxurious space all to myself.

On this particular day, so many years after that soggy Red Chair Epiphany, not one soul was demanding to share my beloved, four-legged refuge. More significantly, there would not be anyone around to share it with until the next holiday, months down the road. And that was the beauty of the moment. I, Lee MacPhearson, age fifty-three, was completely and utterly alone in my house. For the first time in twenty-six years, no one was going to run into the living room crying, walk through burping the alphabet, or throw him- or herself at my feet, certain they were about to die, screaming, "I'm staaaaaarving!" No husband would pass through without a word, no teenage daughter would race by at breakneck speed, scattering the newspaper I had been trying to read, in a contest to beat her siblings to the ringing phone. No. I was all alone, beautifully, peacefully, delightfully alone. I thought, "Surely, if there is a heaven, this is it. My red chair, the wind in the trees, the sun through the windows, and not another living soul in sight."

The situation shocked this middle-aged mother of four because feeling good was the last thing in the world I had expected to be feeling. Just five hours before, I had been in excruciating pain, the kind of pain only a mother knows—the kind that's black and steals your breath and makes you want to close your eyes and open them and have everything be all better, but it never is.

Five hours before, my sort-of-husband Brian (I'd taken to calling him that because technically he wasn't my ex-husband. Although we hadn't lived together for nearly a year, for some reason we hadn't made it official yet) and I had said good-bye to our youngest child, the one who it seemed just moments before had been that breathless first grader. I could hardly bear seeing my tiny, beautiful Ellanora in that dorm room. It was no bigger than a cell—convicted felons got bigger accommodations. I was incensed, just as I had been over the size of each of my children's dorm rooms. How do colleges and universities get away with calling the closets they offer up for the big bucks a room? Yet little Ella, as was her way, was thrilled to be there, happy with the view of the quad and the proximity to the stairs, wasting no time getting to know her obviously overwhelmed and rather timid roommate. Our shiny-eyed daughter unpacked her multitude of boxes with the same enthusiasm she had had throughout her entire life. It boggled my mind: How could anyone have a zeal for unpacking? Yet Ella did, and that's why people adored her.

It had been an excruciating experience for me to give that buzzing little body one last hug. It was the moment I had been dreading, for years really, that last squeeze when all I wanted to do was turn back the clock and start all over again. Instead, I put on my best poker face (which that morning I had literally practiced in the bathroom mirror, dripping wet from my shower, only to have huge tears start streaming down my face). Once again playing the steady and reliable mom, my goal was to not embarrass either Ella or myself. So I did a lot of hugging, cracked a couple of lame jokes, made a passing reference to my watery eyes, speculating that the cause was the off-gassing carpet, and tried hard not to think about the first time I had held this sweet beauty seventeen years earlier in a dilapidated but seemingly happy orphanage in Guatemala.

Seeing my face, Ella patted me and stood on tiptoe to whisper in my ear, "I'll be fine Mom, really, I will." I knew that, too, but it didn't help in the slightest. Of course she would be fine; she would be better than fine. If anyone was ready to set the world on fire, it was this kid.

No, *I* was the one I figured wouldn't be fine. The end of an era—four children, all gone off to make their way in the world. Parenting was what I had loved most about my life, and now, in some ways, it was really gone. Well, it would never be totally gone. I knew that. But the chance to giggle with my kids about the weird neighbor down the road who fed his horses gigantic, homegrown zucchinis for breakfast? Gone. Sitting in the shade after a roaring game of baseball in the back pasture, listening to them tease each other, laughing at the terrible throw I had made? No more. Having them scattered around the house, calling out for something? Bye-bye. Looking at Ella, I felt alone and odd, as if I'd been cut completely adrift. There was only one thing left to do. I threw out a final joke, grabbed one last hug, and quickly left the room.

As soon as we got into the Cherokee, my sort-of-husband blasted his favorite CD, a remix of Frank Sinatra, and began his customary stream-of-consciousness jabber. (My friends had always been jealous, one of them observing that "Brian is the only man on the planet who actually talks when he gets behind the wheel of the car. You should be grateful. My husband approaches driving as if we are on a mission from God and as though any verbiage, including all three kids screaming from the backseat, in deafening decibels, 'I have to peeeeeee!' will not break through his silent and determined assault on the road.")

No, words tumbled out of Brian's mouth at the speed of light. They careened around the interior of the vehicle, bounced off the dash, and smacked me in the face, right and left, up and down. He'd stop for a nanosecond for a brief intake of oxygen, sucking the air right out of the car. I gazed out of the window and wondered how bad it would hurt if I quietly slid out of my door onto the pavement. A sixty-five-mile-per-hour landing on hot asphalt didn't seem so bad considering my current circumstances.

But instead, I did what I had always done: stared out the window and imagined I was in a bubble, protected from the semantic missiles roaring by my head. I sat inside my soft, transparent bubble and tried to think happy thoughts. It was a little easier now that it was just the two of us. It had been a thoroughly challenging exercise all the years we'd had four children strapped into their respective traveling positions, seating that was typically determined by who had outfought whom for what seat. During those countless miles, my time in the bubble was a little crazy making. I was in. Then, "Sam is looking at me." I was out. Three seconds later, I was in. Then, "Sean farted. Make him stop." Out. The most fascinating thing about Brian's filibusters was that his ears completely stopped working when his mouth opened up. Every single complaint the kids made went whizzing right by him. While I was mildly intrigued by this phenomenon, I ultimately decided that he couldn't hear anyone else because it was already so damned noisy inside his head and there just wasn't any room for sound to penetrate his wall of words.

I managed to stay in my bubble for most of the drive home, wondering if Brian even noticed my silence, knowing that he never had before. When we stopped for lunch, he was rambling on about what we could do "now that the nest was empty." I looked up at him over my spinach salad and finally tuned into what he was proposing.

"We can give it a real *go* now, Lee. Like the old days, before the kids and all the other crap I brought down around our ears. Really, what's the first thing you want to do now that the house is empty?"

"Not have you move back in." It came out too fast, shooting across the table like a poison dart. Brian choked briefly on his lunch. "I'm sorry. I'm just tired and I want to try all this on for a while," I added. His color slowly returned to normal, as did my sanity. "Bri, you know it's what we have been talking about."

Brian knew all too well what I was talking about. We had spent months, years, talking about the sad reality that had become our lives. By now, he also knew he had screwed up the best thing a man could ever have, and for what? The freedom to go fishing when he wanted and to have sex with women stupid enough to have sex with a fifty-six-year-old, slightly balding, mini-paunched, separated father of four? This could have been the best time of our lives. But it wasn't, and even though he still thought of me as his wife, apparently he had yet to come to terms with the fact that I was determined to move on.

Brian's face had gone sour. I could tell he was heading straight into that dark place he had come to know too well, and his mood was the last thing I wanted to deal with.

We finished our lunch and drove the rest of the way home in cold silence.

It was a productive drive for the woman in the bubble because I was able to finally and clearly think about what I wanted, now that I had only myself to think about. And even though my heart felt bruised by the day's events—driven over by one of John Deere's finest—I began to try on the bewildering opportunity to decide for myself and myself alone. It had been a struggle to make my way to this point, and Lordy be, here it was. I dared not smile, lest Brian react the wrong way. Instead, I chose to travel deeper and deeper into the safety of my bubble and give thought to all things wonderful.

We finally, blessedly, arrived at the farmhouse. With the practiced gentility of a veterinarian tending a mangled puppy, I made it clear to my sort-of-husband that I needed to be alone. I couldn't bear to look at him and his desperate hunger to put all the pieces back together again. Instead, I gave him a hug, the kind you give someone you need to be polite to, and ducked quickly into the house.

Just one short hour later and here I sit in my luscious red chair, soaking in the familiar sounds of my life. The ducks splash about out on our pond. Two of my dogs lie at my feet, sleeping and breathing deeply, and the third is out on the porch, his rhythmic, flea-scratching thumping a comfort to my ears. My grandmother's clock ticks steadily away on the mantel. I discover that I feel surprisingly content.

I'm thinking granola might be a fine dinner, maybe with the last of the blueberries from the garden. Maybe not. Perhaps I'll just eat mango sorbet straight out of the carton and look for an old black-and-white movie on the tube. Of course, a long bubble bath is on my agenda, every last drop of hot water for my very own consumption. There won't be five other showers to consider or a dishwasher to run. No husband will be complaining about the propane bill. The thought of all those bubbles makes me smile. I decide to take the entire pint of sorbet into the bath.

On the edge of town, Brian sits on the balcony of his apartment and looks out across the street. It's a lousy view, nothing but more apartments. A peace-symbol flag hangs from a distant window; he can see a poster of J Lo through an open sliding glass door. He wonders why men drool over her. Sure, she has a pretty face, but he's always thought the woman has a big butt. Music blares, the bass turned up so high that it rattles the walls and shakes the entire complex. Houston, we have liftoff. The sun is setting on student housing, and here he sits.

He takes a sip of his beer and thinks about driving away from Lee, from his home and his life. The beer tastes flat, much like he felt after surveying the damage he had done to his life. He considers spitting out the bitter liquid, but where? On the balcony below him? He looks over the railing and sees his three young, beefy neighbors hammering down their own brews. Shit. He has no other choice but to swallow, and the foul, cold sludge slides down his throat, once again reminding him of his stupidity.

If someone had told him four years ago that he'd be sitting all alone on the balcony of this plastic apartment, he would have called that person a fool. Back then he felt he had it all—a job he could hardly wait to get to each day, a beautiful, smart wife, and three kids who showed great promise and only one who left him sleepless, a good ratio nonetheless. He had a huge old farmhouse he had completely restored that sat on twelve acres of the most beautiful piece of earth imaginable and his very own natural pond that made for great times for everyone in the family. Who could ask for anything more?

It had been that pond that had been his demise. Bullshit. He had been his own demise—his foolishness, his middle-aged, dumb-ass stupidity. It seemed to make so much sense a couple of years ago. The restlessness, the need to think for himself and himself alone—to be free of the mundane chores of the family man, the endless requirements of child rearing, something Lee had always been better at than he. The freedom to take off on a Saturday morning to fish or spend the entire day in his office without any thought of who needed what. And women. They started catching his eye in a very different sort of way. For the first time since he had known Lee, he wanted to go beyond just looking. He wanted to touch.

Jim, his best friend for as long as he could remember, had recently divorced and was having the time of his life. Brian had watched Jim go through some desperate times, much like Brian was going through himself. But eventually divorce proved to be the right decision for Jim. Brian knew he and Jim had very different marriages. Jim's wife, Pam, was a clingy, sour, miserable woman who couldn't have been more different from Lee. But so many things marriage required plagued both men.

For months, Brian, the controlled, contained engineering professor, tried everything he knew to ignore the thoughts, the frustration. He told himself daily that he had a wonderful wife, which he knew he did, because it wasn't really about Lee. It was about Mr. Responsible being very tired of being responsible. When he was absolutely honest with himself, he knew he didn't want to have to put his dirty clothes in the hamper or call home to see if Lee had forgotten anything for dinner. He didn't want to pay a stack of bills and move money from one account to another to cover the property taxes. He was sick and tired of being responsible because it was all he had done for as long as he could remember. "It's the Scottish way," his mother would pound into him. And although they were about ten generations away from those ancestors who left the island behind in search of a new life, it was the way his mother got everyone in the family to behave. She shot the orders at them. They all worked their asses off. He never once heard his father complain. Instead, the man just volunteered for every possible mail shift that came up. The quiet, beaten-down father of six said it was to provide for his family. But by the time Brian had reached adolescence, he thought his father was a genius, for he had figured out the perfect way to distance himself from his demanding, controlling, and very critical wife.

As the dutiful son, Brian had done what was expected of him and more. Though he worked a part-time job all the way through high school, he managed to graduate with honors and get a handsome scholarship to college. On the home front, he helped his five younger siblings with their homework and their chores, and he even ferried them to activities when their mother was up to her elbows in her own chores. It seemed like all the MacPhearsons ever did was work. There were no vacations. "Can't afford them," his mother would say. "Besides, what in the world would we ever do?" Not even a Friday night Disney movie for the clan. Brian grew up believing that relaxing was a sure sign that the devil had taken your soul. God forbid you ever actually played!

And that's how he approached his adult life—providing twenty-four-seven for his wife and kids. Not that it was what Lee expected, or what she particularly wanted. His wife was the one to tell him, on a very regular basis, that he needed to work less and play more. In fact, that had been one of the reasons he had fallen in love with her. She knew how to play, big-time. A simple meat loaf and mashed potato dinner could turn into a party for two; mucking out stalls became a race, with the winner receiving a blue ribbon that Lee would somehow magically produce on the spot. Brian had been happy to let Lee lead him and the kids through years of fun and play, until one day it wasn't enough.

No, he was trapped. He knew it, felt it, didn't really understand it, and was embarrassed to acknowledge it. Talk about cliché. What middle-aged man didn't feel trapped? When such thoughts broke through into the real world, Brian would simply bury himself in more work, more responsibility, hoping the tried-and-true ways of managing his life would carry him through until some point when it would all make sense. But it never did, and the swirl of conflicting feelings and thoughts and guilt would inevitably return.

Even when they did, they hadn't been enough for Brian to broach the topic with Lee. It had taken much longer for him to tell Lee what was happening because it had taken a couple of years for him to stare it down and decide that it wasn't going to go away, no matter how many times he went fishing or hung out in the bar with Jim.

The conversation had been the ugliest they had ever had in the entire twenty-eight years they had known each other. But really, it wasn't a conversation at all.

He stood at the kitchen counter, as he had done a thousand times before. Lee was making bread. It was something she had always done, and it was something he liked. Brian took a deep breath.

"Lee, I've been thinking," he began.

Lee looked up briefly but kept kneading the bread with her strong hands.

"Sounds serious," she replied.

"It is," was all he managed to get out before Lee burst forth.

"Well good, you're finally going to talk. You've been moping around here for months. The kids have been asking me, 'What's wrong with Dad?' and I've been telling them, 'He'll tell us when he's ready. That's just how your father is.'" Slapping the dough, Lee inhaled sharply, then finally asked, "So, what's up?"

With that, she stopped cold and looked him eyeball to eyeball. He hated it when Lee did that. Those were the only times he wished his wife weren't six feet tall. His knees felt slightly weak. He pulled out a stool, slid onto it, took a deep breath, and continued.

"I guess you've sensed that I've been unhappy. I know I've pulled away from you and the kids. But I've come to realize, well, it's this way. Here it is. I think I got married too young, that maybe I took you and the kids on out of some misguided sense of responsibility. I love you all, I do. I just feel trapped. Trust me, this isn't about you, really, it isn't—I find you attractive and smart and… "

Lee cut him off.

"Let me guess? You need to find yourself, like Jim did. Leave your wife and kids so you can go fish and barhop with the students and maybe even score with some little chickie-poo who thinks Dr. MacPhearson walks on water right next to Jesus Christ himself. That about sums it up, doesn't it, Bri—this domesticity stuff sucks, this 'til death do us part' deal is for other people.

"You think I didn't know this was coming? Yeah, I'm smart, but it doesn't take a genius to figure out that when a fifty-five-year-old man stops coming home on time for dinner for the first time ever or when he stops kissing your cheek when he walks by, like he's been doing for over a quarter of a century, or when he leaves the house first thing Saturday morning and doesn't come home until dusk, that something major and very stinky is about to hit the fan."

Lee returned to kneading the bread dough. Brian stared at her strong hands muscling the dough into submission. He knew there'd be no air bubbles in that loaf. It occurred to him that he might have something in common with the mass of flour and yeast.

His wife raged on.

"I did what I could on my end. Did you even notice? I stopped asking for your help with so many things. Have your precious recycling bins ever been so organized and well maintained? I never said a word about your countless fishing trips. Better yet, I didn't pressure you to talk to me, because Mr. Motor Mouth talks nonstop, until it's something important. I lost those thirteen pounds I'd carried around for the last couple of years, bought that ridiculous lingerie last year, and even had my hair highlighted, figuring it might bring you back to me. But nothing was working and I knew it."

Lee threw the bread dough down on the counter. It landed with a dull thud.

"You foolish man. You stupid, stupid man. You have no idea how good your life is. Too much responsibility? What the hell is life about except responsibility? It's the deal we all make or else we lead lives that are empty, lacking purpose and direction. That's why we have to play. You never could figure that out along the way, could you? But now you get it, don't you? You really think old Jimmy has it licked—his bachelor pad, the coeds who adore him, the kayaking trips on the weekends. Well, Mr. Dumb Shit, I'm not giving up as easily as Pam did. You know me—we made a deal and you're going to honor it." She sliced the dough in two with one swift stroke of the butcher knife.

They began marriage counseling. He hated every minute of it. Lee was right. He could talk a monkey out of a tree, but talk about serious crap in front of a weird little pissant man with an irritating habit of clearing his throat every three minutes? No way. They sat there, week after week, not getting anywhere. On some level, Brian knew that he didn't really want to leave his wife and family, but he sure didn't want to be married and be a full-time father anymore. He wanted the comfort and security of the life he had built, but he wanted the freedom of the twenty-one-year-old he had once been even more.

What made it even worse was that his wife was trying 150 percent, which only made him feel guiltier. Lee miraculously somehow managed to keep her anger in check… most of the time. More often, she'd try to reassure them both, saying stuff like, "All marriages have ups and downs, and people work their way through them. We're not going to bail just because we're on a down."

During their counseling sessions, they took their marriage apart, one painful detail after another. They discussed the pressure that Sam, their second son, had brought on the entire family—the endless behavior problems, the frustration of his alcohol abuse, how responsible Brian had felt for that, how relentless Sam's problems seemed. They pored over each and every remodeling job. Brian admitted that he had hated most of them. This one surprised and shocked Lee, and her temper flared. "I wish you could have told me at the time instead of pushing through. How can I combat damage that's already been done?" They pored over the pressures his career had foisted upon them, the endless hours he had felt compelled to give to his position, his advancement. No stone was left unturned.

But what he hated the most was when they talked about their "relationship." He hated it because a part of him knew it wasn't all that bad. He really did still love Lee. In fact, he secretly wished it was just the two of them again, wondering if those were their best years, when being responsible hadn't been such a drain, when they'd had the most fun. Not that he didn't love his kids, but being a father had required so much of him, and he was tired. He kept saying that this "wasn't about" Lee. He really couldn't imagine his life without her. But he knew that Lee was wrapped up in all the responsibilities he was trying to get untangled from. Given that, how could he possibly stay with her?

And the fact was, which he finally had to admit, he fantasized about other women. The idea of a new naked body to explore, to pound away at—what man wouldn't find that appealing, he asked? Pissant Man said he couldn't relate to that. Brian wasn't surprised. It had been those fantasies that finally forced him into telling Lee what was troubling him. Much as he wanted to secretly cheat, he knew an affair would be a crushing blow to his wife. He wasn't ready to cause her that much pain, no matter how good the new secretary in the Biology Department looked to him.

So they made countless deals—*agreements*, the shrink called them—dates on Saturday nights, weekends when he had total and complete freedom, answering to no one but himself, nights when he wouldn't be expected home until late. They all seemed to work for a while, but really, when put to the wall by Pissant Man, Brian had to admit that they just felt like Band-Aids, that nothing was really going to stop the hemorrhage. He felt he had simply waited too long. The damage was done.

But then Lee had another one of her epiphanies.

Brian found her that morning on the porch drinking her coffee. It was where he often found her on weekend mornings, the only mornings she would get up before him, all wrapped up in one of her homemade quilts, happily swaying back and forth in the bench swing he and the kids had made for her one Mother's Day. He walked out onto the porch, but Lee didn't stop looking down at the pond, that sweet little body of water that had sealed the deal so many years before. Twelve acres with a natural pond—what better place to spend a life together? Finally, Lee broke away from the pond and looked him straight in the eye. A chill ran through him.

"I owe you a huge apology, Bri," Lee began. Her words hung between them. Moving over on the swing, Lee patted the wood next to her. He sat.

She continued.

"I was sitting here this morning, and you know what, the ducklings have hatched. Look." Brian checked out the water's edge, and sure enough, seven little ducklings were bobbing on the water with their parents. Each year, the hatching of the ducks was a much-celebrated event. Lee and the kids had been known to throw huge birthday parties for the ducklings. "I looked at those ducks and thought about how many times I've sat here waiting for them to hatch. Then it hit me. The last time I saw Pissant Man" (they each had individual sessions with him, something Brian hated), "he asked me why I was afraid to be alone. I told him it was a stupid question, that this mess wasn't about me being alone. But this morning, I realized that I've been fighting you about the separation all these months, making it all your fault because, in fact, a huge part of me is afraid. I couldn't imagine being alone out here, with just the girls to cook for, to take care of, to laugh with. The thought of sleeping all by myself made me sick to my stomach. Facing my future without someone to share it with? Bone chilling. Having my life and my life alone to manage? Daunting.

"And then this morning I looked at those ducks, and for the first time, I wondered where I had gone. I'm not who you married. I was the free spirit, the one who got you to loosen up, to have fun, to step out of your stupid, tight-ass engineering suit and enjoy life. Wasn't I the one who said we should live life without regrets? So why haven't I ever gone back and finished my MFA? I was always the one to jump into the middle of a challenge, the crap heap, and find that pony. I was the one who said be passionate about your beliefs, yet over the years, my passion slowly fizzled into thin air. We've both been completely defined by our responsibilities, driven in a way, not able to see any other options."

Lee stared down at the pond, as if the water might hold the right words. Finally, she spoke.

"I am so sorry, Brian. I get it now. I know exactly what you have been trying to say all this time. You're right, a separation would be a good thing. I'm not about to live the rest of my life being afraid. God— why have I been so dense? Sure you love me, just like I love you, but I guess not in that 'happily ever after' kind of way. And in spite of what you've said, I know we both adore this brood of ours. But where is it written that two people have to spend fifty years together? I know I haven't wanted to let go of the familiar, the family that has given me so much. And yeah, I've been devastated by the discovery that I'm not the be-all, end-all for you. But I'm seeing that there's a lot more to all this than I ever thought, and it has my name written all over it. I'm sorry to have put us through this. You just figured it out before I did. And I thank you for having the decency to not act on any of it before I caught up with you. Always the gentleman. I've just been sitting here this morning trying on all the possibilities both of us can have by being apart." She filled her lungs with clean spring air. "It's kind of a little exciting, isn't it?"

Brian stared at his wife and tried to breathe. Lee went on.

"Sure, we have the girls for a couple more years and everything that goes with them. There will always be Sam to deal with, but hey, that doesn't mean we have to be tied to old definitions, to the ways we've always done things. So, yeah, I'm finally on board. Where do we start?"

Brian still wasn't breathing right. Lee reached over and took his hand. "I hope you think of me as always owning up to my mistakes. Well, that's what I'm trying to do now, tell you that I was a little slow on the uptake but I have been mistaken about this part of things, and I'll happily work with you to decide the best way to go about a separation."

Brian felt like one of the many fish he had landed after it flopped around on the bottom of the boat for a few minutes and then took on that gray, gasping-for-breath, fear-in-the-eye kind of look.

Fighting panic, Brian stood up and walked the length of the porch. He stared down at the pond and watched the ducks swimming all around each other, oblivious to the human drama being played out just a few short yards away. Lee and her damned lifetime of epiphanies flooded his brain. He looked back at her now, her simple elegance, so beautifully poised in the swing. For the millionth time since he had known her, the sun caught in her hair. Lee's hair. It had always been so amazingly shiny. It was something that managed to keep him curious about her—how come his hair was dull, how come so many people had flat, lackluster hair? But never Lee. And now, he was about to lose her. His eyes filled with tears.

"Oh, shit," said Lee. "I've called your bluff, haven't I?"

And now here he was, nearly two years later, alone on his crappy little concrete balcony, surrounded by youth and their age-appropriate stupidity. It struck him that his own indecision and fuckups were far more distressing than those of his young neighbors. After all, he was supposed to be old enough to know better.

2

*T*he phone rang just as I was moving the couch to the other side of the living room. I knew it had to be Barb, and I was a little surprised my friend of nearly twenty years had managed to wait this long before she called. Of course, what was even more surprising was that Barb would be up this early. Noon was her usual time to rise but rarely shine.

For a brief instant, I worried that it might be Brian, morose after parting the night before, wanting to talk when I had nothing to say. I waited to hear a voice coming through the answering machine.

"I know you're there." It was Barb. "Pick up or I'll figure you aren't alone and I won't bug you again, except… " I grabbed the phone, relieved I didn't have to deal with Brian.

"I'm here," I gasped, breathless from heaving the couch into submission.

Barb didn't miss a beat. "Sounds like I'm interrupting something good. Should I call back?"

"If shoving a sleeper sofa to the opposite wall is good, then my life can only improve. No, you're not interrupting. I just woke up this morning wanting my entire life to be different, so it made sense to start with the couch. Do you know where I can buy those slidey things advertised on television at three in the morning, where a petite woman single-handedly pushes her SUV into the garage and never breaks a sweat? If I'm going to be single, I think I may need a dozen or so of them."

In her usual fashion, Barb cut to the chase. "Yesterday, how was it? Are you really single?"

I had to smile—women were refreshing, so efficient. Do not pass go, out with it, dish me the dirt. That's what women do.

"How was what? How was the 'I've left my last-born child three hours away in a prison cell and she was cheerful and I was bleak'? Or the 'No, you may not move back in now and play house with me just because there aren't any kids left to get in the way'?" I realized a lot had happened in the last twenty-four hours. No wonder I was having trouble with the couch.

"Well, both of those. All of it. I couldn't stand waiting a minute longer. Silly me. I thought you might be a good friend and at least leave me a message last night. I couldn't decide if no news was good or not. Were you out there on that lonesome hilltop trying to figure out how to commit suicide in an electric oven, or were you fucking your brains out with your sort-of-husband, which you swore you wouldn't do, but hey—the house was empty after all, and you always told me that the best sex you guys ever had was when all four of the kids were farmed out." I could hear Barb bite into something and then continue with her mouth full. "So, is he there?"

"No, he's not here, and he won't be here, and I am thrilled to be able to say that." I plopped down on the couch and surveyed the room from the very middle. It had some promise.

I decided to put her out of her misery.

"You can relax now. You're right, I was more than a little nervous about the moment I'd have to look him in the eye and tell him to take his sorry ol' ass down the road. But did I crash and burn? No. In fact, it seemed so easy. Well, that's not exactly right. It wasn't easy at all. I mean, I know in some distinct ways I still love him and all that crap, but really, all I could think of was how I was going to rearrange the furniture and what did I want to have for dinner. Isn't that strange? I wondered a lot about how Ella was doing and when I would talk to her again, but I sure as hell wasn't thinking lovey-dovey thoughts about Brian."

I caught my breath. "That's kind of awful, I think. If he knew, he'd be heartbroken. He'd undoubtedly be so pissed off that his head would spin around like a roulette wheel and poisonous arrows would come shooting from his eyes and I'd be looking at an eternity in hell. Perhaps, if there is a God, I already am. But here's the strangest part, Barb—I don't give a rat's ass about that. I woke up this morning feeling better than I have in a couple of years." The line went quiet for a minute. I whispered, "Shit, we decided this wasn't hormonal, right?"

"No, no, no. Don't go there," Barb howled. "You and I both know this isn't about your damned hormones. Remember how good you felt when you finally ditched all your reproductive organs? You've been sailing hormonally steady ever since. I wish I could say the same thing about myself—I'm like the Wicked Witch of the West one minute and freakin' Mother Teresa the next. And you know me: Mother Teresa is a real stretch. Promise me this will go away when my little baby muffin pops out of the oven?"

I contemplated the somewhat alarming image of forty-year-old Barbara popping out a baby muffin. At five feet even, Barb was exactly one foot shorter than I was. She also outweighed me, though neither of us knew by exactly how much, but we were both certain it was by a lot. There had been that one time years ago when we had made ourselves a huge pitcher of margaritas, drinking it all down like college girls. Somehow we ended up on the bathroom scale because Barb bet she weighed more, and good, very drunk friend that I was, I insisted that it was impossible. Lo and behold, Barbara was right. Fortunately, we were both so far gone that the next day neither of us could remember by how much. And neither of us really wanted to know, so it became one of our little jokes that could throw us into riotous chuckles for no reason at all.

And now Barb was tremendous, surely weighing nearly twice what I did, because all she had done for the last six months was eat, and she still had three months to go before popping out her first baby muffin.

But it wasn't just her weight that had me a little concerned about this pregnancy. How in the hell would my friend ever make her way through labor, Barb being perhaps the most out-of-shape citizen in the entire state of Oregon? She willingly, loudly, and regularly shared her opinion on the national fitness craze and my most favorite activity.

"Why would anyone in her right mind want to run until they are sweating and completely breathless? Even animals know when to find a good shadow to hang out in and patiently wait for the unsuspecting dinner morsel to wander by."

No, personal experience told me that muffin popping was no easy feat. I knew that Barb was the last person to be physically ready for the task, and worse yet, she showed no apparent interest in getting ready.

Of course, there had been a few times over the years when Barb got up on her high horse and decided to "try to get healthy, just for the hell of it." Once, after a particularly inspiring all-nighter sitting in front of an exercise cable channel, she called to announce her intentions.

"Oh my God, all I have to do is walk. That's what they said, just walk away the pounds!"

I was happy to support the idea, suggesting we walk together on deserted back roads. But it wasn't just Barb's meager motivation that sabotaged this particular trespass into health. It was also her very short legs. After no more than ten minutes, she lagged at least fifty yards behind me.

She yelled out to me and all the grazing cows, "We look like a giraffe and a possum out for a stroll." Trying to catch her breath, she continued. "There's no way I can *possibly* keep up with you. You're a freak, a mutant. You have the femurs of a dinosaur." After two more days of walks, Barb sat down by the edge of the road. "The way I figure it, I'm most likely to end up road kill." She took a long drink of water. "Go get the car. Our days as exercise partners are over!"

Then there was the time, right before she got pregnant, when Barb was of the mind to "embrace her curves," which she admitted she'd recently read in some feminist book. "I think that theory was laid out in chapter 7—and I'm pretty sure the only reason I remember that was because I was on a sugar high, having just consumed an entire pint of

Ben & Jerry's Chunky Monkey. Damn it was good." She celebrated with food until she made herself sick. It had been a particularly difficult phase. We both seemed equally happy when it eventually came to a quiet halt.

Now here she was, my very best friend in the world, six months pregnant, rounder than humanly possible, chewing on something yet again and talking about popping out muffins. All I could muster was "Baby muffins... ?" before I burst into laughter.

Barb pulled me up short. "Okay, it wasn't that funny. Let's leave my screwed-up life out of it for the moment and just talk about yours. So you managed to hang tight with him. Good girl. But enough about the adult drama for the moment. How tough was it with Ella, my sweet little godchild?"

It had been a little odd to make Barb Ella's godmother, beginning with the fact that she had requested the honor. "Always a little unorthodox, that Barb," was how I presented the request to Bri.

He thought it was beyond unorthodox. "We're not even Catholic or Episcopalian, or whoever it is that signs up godparents. Worse than that, we're nothings in the religion department, big zeros to be exact. And what about the other kids? They'll all be jealous. They'll want their very own godparent, maybe even two. And, well," he tried to find the right words, "I know Barb's your best friend, but you're always saying she doesn't understand the first thing about kids. You know how she can throw herself into things—what if she does that with Ella? The poor kid would be screwed up before her third birthday. Naw, it will never work."

I had bristled at his honesty, but I also knew he was right. Barb was a little goofy, a little too "out there" for most people's taste. "Eccentric" was an understatement.

And now she was going to have a baby, a thought somewhat more chilling than Barb as a simple godmother to a child whose parents kept a close watch. I brought myself back to our conversation. "So what was the question again?" I asked.

"Ella, Baby Ella—do you think she'll survive out there in the big bad world? I thought about her all night, nearly prevented James from taking his curtain call. Fortunately, he's the only person in this production who is fatter than I am, so he just muscled his way past and murmured something despicable under his breath. But I was stalled, right there in the wings, thinking about what it must be like to say good-bye to a kid. I guess because I haven't even said hello to mine yet. She didn't cry, did she? You did, I'm sure, but tell me she didn't?"

This pregnancy business had softened some of Barb's edges—her tender sentiments were usually well guarded.

I filled her in on how the kid drop had gone, owning up to my own tears and reassuring her that Ella was well on her way to becoming the most amazing godchild to ever attend Barb's alma mater. "It was pretty clear she was ready for us to hit the road. Not that she was rude or anything, just bursting with enthusiasm for her new life. We took the hint and made our exit."

"Good, good. I figured that's how it would go." She paused for the slightest moment, then charged on.

"Okay, I can check that obsessive thought off my long list and concentrate on the remaining four hundred and twenty-seven. Now, let me get this straight: Your first day as a free woman and you're rearranging the furniture? Not very exciting. Could be thought four hundred and twenty-eight for me. Come on now, tell me you have something a little more compelling scheduled for your first day of liberation."

I thought about her question. It threw me.

"I don't exactly feel liberated. True liberation would mean a remote beach, endless money stashed in international accounts, a number of loyal young men, all devilishly handsome, poised, waiting to take care of my every whim. I only feel twenty percent liberated at best—make that fifteen percent. I think my smartest approach for today is to concentrate on all things small. I might freak out if I actually let the magnitude of what I am doing creep into my consciousness. That being said, I need to get a walk in before I head down to the gallery. Tom left me a terribly excited message yesterday that 'Mike Tyson' came in and bought three pieces, including that one horrendous sculpture we've had sitting on the shelf for months. Mike Tyson, it can't be that toothless nitwit boxer, can it? Maybe it is. He also took one of Robert Hoteman's monster canvases that I regretted ever hanging in the gallery. Can you believe it? I won't have to sell another piece until you're a mother! Anyhow, it was good news to come home to, and I want to make sure Tom gets them shipped out."

Barb's tone shifted ever so slightly.

"You and your stupid walks. Couldn't you just once fall off the exercise wagon and join me and the rest of the peons down here in fat land?"

It didn't happen often, but once in a while Barb could push my buttons, and this was one of those times when all of her two hundred–plus pounds felt as though they had landed on my chest.

"Barb, you better watch your mouth! You sure don't want your little girl growing up with all the crappy messages about weight that you have floating around inside your head, do you? She will if she's always hearing those kinds of things come out of her mother's mouth." I caught myself and managed to bring my speech up short. "Sorry. You know I just can't stand it when you put yourself down."

Barb's response was quick and pointed.

"Apology accepted. You know, I still can't imagine having a little girl of my own. Besides, I didn't get any fatty messages from my mother. She was always a tad too tipsy to notice my thunder thighs, let alone to say something about them." Barb was back in the driver's seat, and we both knew it.

"So, we're on for Monday night dinner, right?"

"Right. I'm there! Okay, rearrange your furniture, you freak, then go do your walking thing. Make it a good one for the both of us, and, as they say in Hallmark card land, enjoy the first day of the rest of your life." We both laughed. Barb added, "God, that expression sucks! Anyhow, have a great day, and I'll see you tomorrow night about seven o'clock. Call me in the meantime if you want. I'm just sleeping in tomorrow and doing absolutely nothing except lying around and getting kicked by this little beast."

"Take it easy, Barb." I took a chance. "You know I love you?"

"Yeah, yeah, love you too," she replied. And two of the dearest friends imaginable hung up.

3

*M*onday morning arrived long before I was ready to face the week and my business, let alone the rest of my life. But there was no escaping. If nothing else, I needed to check in at the gallery and at least pretend I cared about things.

Pulling my hair into a ponytail, I stared at my image in the mirror, silently acknowledging that since the separation, my business had become something of a bad topic between Brian and me. But truthfully, it had never been a great one. No, when it came to my livelihood, the road had been rocky at best.

The ancient storefront had come on the market over ten years ago. I saw the For Sale sign in the window as I was taking the girls to their ballet lessons. While I waited for my little tutu'ed sprites to fumble their way around for an hour, I sat in the bakery next door to the studio, sipping my tea and staring across the street at the building. It had been a junk shop for as long as I could remember, and the store itself was junk too. The overhang was waiting to land on the doorstep; the wooden windows were all rotten. The last time I'd been inside, it had felt like a haunted house at a bad Halloween carnival... the floor actually sloped to one side. The kids had been delighted, while I had felt a little seasick.

But that morning, staring at the ramshackle building, taking in all the old girl's flaws, I started to go a little nuts. Suddenly, I saw nothing but possibilities. Certainly raising the kids was my first priority. But there had to be something more, a way to get outside of my family life, to try, in some small way, to have a life of my own, something that was challenging, creative. At the very least, the thought of having a place to go that wasn't home was nothing short of thrilling.

Bri wasn't convinced it made any sense for us to pour all our savings into something that old, and, more importantly, he seriously questioned the wisdom of my retail fantasy. "Really," he asked one day, "why do you want to run an art supply store? You'll just get bored. Think of all the dumb questions: 'What color is vermilion?' You'd hate that." He had a point. I had little tolerance for life's minutiae.

But over time, I convinced both of us that it was a good deal. What else was I going to do with just a BA in art and four little kids to take care of? Sure, I was a frustrated painter, but at least with the shop I could express a little creativity and be around other people who loved making art. And besides, given the location, the real estate investment alone was a surefire winner.

It took a while to negotiate the lease—I didn't figure I should be the one to have to foot the bill to have the foundation leveled and the windows made watertight—but once the space was mine, a grand restoration began, and that tiny space was transformed into warm and inviting, even on the grayest of wet winter days.

The thrill of the store lasted all of a year. I spent the entire second year rearranging the stock and daydreaming a lot. By the end of the third year, I was bored beyond belief. Though I'd envisioned myself to be a creative, inspired, and high-voltage shopkeeper, I had completely failed to anticipate how mundane it was to order products or how frustrating it was to sort through the paintbrushes after particularly careless and thoughtless customers had rummaged through them. Then there was all the bookkeeping. Had my checkbook balanced even once since opening the store?

I started having a recurring nightmare about IRS agents, who for some reason were raccoons that wore nothing but Speedos and New

York Yankees ball caps, boarding up my shop and standing guard in the tiniest kitchen I had ever seen, while I baked thousands of oatmeal raisin cookies to work off my debt. I always woke up in a sweat and could rarely fall back to sleep.

But I didn't dare tell Brian about how I felt. He would panic and say, "Now what the hell are we going to do?" He might even gloat. It didn't happen often, but if he went so far as an "I told you so," I promised myself I'd move all the way over to the far side of our bed and stay there for a good long time.

Then one day, seemingly from the heavens, it all fell into place. My friend who ran the bookstore in the building next door said the owner was going to retire and shut down. For once, my brain fired on all six cylinders. I hatched an even wilder scheme—I'd rent the space and turn it into a small, high-end gallery. It was perfect. There weren't that many galleries around in those days, and the good ones were on the other end of town. I knew the area could support another—there was the theater crowd who came to town every year, plus all the tourists who came to Ashland three seasons out of four. Looking at, talking about, and selecting art could never bore me. And genius Tom, my clerk, could be promoted to store manager and be entirely responsible for all things boring. I'd host little openings and bake lovely treats, serve local wine. I'd even name it Mad Dog Gallery in honor of my delightfully goofy kids, who were known to race around in the midday sun like dizzy Englishmen straight out of the now politically incorrect Noël Coward song. It was perfect, a gold mine waiting to happen.

I did my homework and then presented the plan to Brian one night after I'd fed him his favorite pot roast and vegetables. I bathed and put all four kids to bed without even once asking him to help. He never suspected his sitting-duck status.

"Brian, I've been doing a little research," I began. He loved it when I talked "research." "I think we are in the position to diversify the business." (Aha! He was a sucker for academic lingo. I had him on the hook. Now all I had to do was reel him in.)

Brian looked up from the papers he was correcting. "What do you mean 'diversify the business'?"

I quickly and expertly explained my plan, making it sound like I had just finished up at Harvard Business School. After dropping phrases like "profit margins" and "improved cash flow," I went over all the contacts I had made with local artists, those I knew had the potential to sell. "And really, Bri, you've always said I have a good eye for art."

I wished I had been able to put money on his next question because it would have paid off well.

"What's it going to cost to get going? How can we afford to buy paintings and then turn around and sell them?"

I explained how all the artists were willing to begin on a consignment basis, and they'd split the profit, giving me time to generate enough income to work on commission. And, in case I needed it, Henry down at the bank was willing to give me a small business loan at "a very reasonable interest rate." Tom said he'd manage the store for six months before demanding a raise.

"I've also run some numbers." (Brian's eyes twinkled at that phrase. It was like foreplay to him.) "And there won't be much to do to the space. That's the nice thing about a gallery—good lighting, a paint job, one desk, and a chair, and we'd be in business."

Brian said he'd think about it and went back to correcting his papers. I felt pretty damned flat—all the buildup and then nothing. Of course, that's just how Brian was, and I knew it. He'd come back in a couple of days with more questions. A few days after that, we'd talk about it again, and within the week, we'd have made a decision. It was just that this time, I really wanted him to be different, to jump on the idea and tell me I was brilliant, that another gallery was just what Ashland needed and I was the woman to do it. That wasn't going to happen, so I took a bubble bath.

In the end, the final decision took nearly four weeks. We might have made it in the customary seven days, but Daughter Number One, lovely little Sophia, came home with the chicken pox. Within forty-eight hours, the rest of the kids started dropping like flies. I felt like I was working a hospital ward in some Third World country—the air was thick, and the kids were scabby, oozy little souls of bitter woes. Every night after work, Bri arrived home with more Popsicles and another box of oatmeal to be used for soothing baths. It was a dark time.

Tom, a retired high school basketball coach and my only employee, ran the shop single-handedly for days. But one man, no matter how talented and competent, can only do so much. I had him shut down a few times, making a sign for the window that read "Closed due to plague. Sorry for any inconvenience." Tom took one look at it and gently pointed out that perhaps it was "a bit over the top. You don't want to make national news." He assured me that a simple Closed sign would do, and then he tried to get me to take a nap on the couch in the back room.

For days, the carpet was littered with scabs. It was disgusting, and daily vacuuming was pointless. The children howled at their discomfort while I prayed the water heater could produce enough warm water for yet another oatmeal bath.

Very slowly, one by one, the children got better. And then one day, their plague was over. I was giddy the morning I dropped off all four kids at school. I headed straight to work, just me and Aretha singing at the top of our lungs. It was as if some kindhearted governor had just commuted my death sentence.

For the first time in months, I was happy to be at the store, and as soon as I put down my bag, I remembered the gallery plan. Before doing anything else, I left a message for Brian: "Can we please talk about the gallery tonight?"

I threw out tradition and served up pizza for dinner. Sam was thoroughly confused, risky business for that poor little boy. "But Mom, it's not Friday night," he noted. I reassured him that we were celebrating their recovery from a brush with death. It had been a fun evening with our frisky, healthy kids—not even one tear over homework. After baths, stories, and a final tuck-in, Brian's first words were, "What are you going to name your gallery?"

Renovating the new space went surprisingly well. The gallery took off! My mother would give me the evil eye for saying this (prideful thinking was right up there with child abuse in her book), but I think my sense of art was the key—that and my ability to get the artists to trust me and my instincts. More than one unknown artist found himself with money in the bank after a show at Mad Dog Gallery. It was the up-and-coming gallery, written up in the *Seattle Times*, even featured in a piece on *Good Morning America* about rural artists.

Within a few years, Mad Dog Gallery had become one the most successful galleries in town. It helped that Barb made so many connections through her position as artistic director for the Oregon Shakespeare Festival. It helped even more that she was quite happy to direct the rich and famous to my doorstep, where, upon arrival, these well-heeled out-of-towners seemed genuinely pleased with my selections. In turn, they told all their San Francisco, Los Angeles, and Manhattan friends about what one national art publication had called a "charming little storefront full of exquisite, one-of-a-kind art."

A few years after we opened Mad Dog, we were able to buy the building. Bri had been dragging his feet on that decision for so long that I considered forging his name on the loan papers. We fought about it on more than one occasion. He seemed to resent my enthusiasm. But Brian's promotion to full professor happened to come through right about then. For some reason, this increased his confidence in my business sense just long enough for me to get him to sign the papers. (Okay, it took another pot roast too.) After that, he stayed out of my way except to grumble about any major expenses I had to make to improve either of my businesses. At times, I'd find myself annoyed that he was so tight, or I'd wonder why he seemed irritated by my creativity and energy. Mostly, we maneuvered around each other in a distant kind of dance.

It took nearly four years for the business to get me back in a choke hold. But that time, it wasn't boredom that had me by the ankles; it was responsibility. By then I had teenagers, one of whom was either going to end up in prison for grand theft larceny or on the side of the road, a burned-out druggie. Our Sam was a precious but troubled lad who drove me crazy nearly every single day. Meanwhile, his older brother, Sean, was cruising through life, every parent's dream, full of quiet direction and constant demands for rides to everything from football practice to his Saturday jobs on farms throughout the county. The girls both played soccer and then basketball—short but fast, that's how they were known—and I was the team driver.

Just getting the four of them to wherever they had to be on any given day was enough to leave me senseless. Funny how Brian managed to stay pretty clear of this part of our parenting. Many times I'd ask him to take one of the kids somewhere, and he'd have "work to do" or a "meeting to attend" instead. Like I didn't? I should have wised up a whole lot sooner. Instead, like millions of other women, I was a "working mother" (now there's a head-spinning understatement) who barely kept her head above water.

4

*I*t wasn't wise to revisit a lifetime in one's bathroom mirror. I surveyed my face one last time, aware that my mood felt like a poorly chosen outfit, too tight and drab. It was going to be a long day.

After pulling myself together, I began the drive into town. As I made my way up and down the familiar hills and through the fading pastures, I tried to focus on what was right in front of me—a day at work. No more, no less.

Parking my car behind the shop, I noticed the washed-out paint on the building. Chiding myself for not painting it, as I had planned to do, I made a half-hearted attempt to cut myself some slack. After all, a few other things had gotten in the way. At least the garden was looking fresh. Bri had always given me a bad time about putting flower boxes in the back: "What, so the homeless who sleep in the alley can have something nice to wake up to?" he had asked. I'd made myself a promise: Next year the homeless would have both a painted building and beautiful flowers. Staring at the board and batten siding, I wondered how tough it would be to paint a mural on it.

Now, as I made my way to the front of the store, Tom was cleaning the glass on the door. That was just one of his many habits that I valued—I hated cleaning with a passion, always had, which drove Bri nuts. The shop and gallery were spotless. Now he turned to face me as I came in through the storeroom. "Well, how'd it go?" he wanted to know.

"I guess that's the question of the day, isn't it?" My answer was fast. Too fast. "I'm sorry. There's just a part of me that wants today to be a normal day, another Monday when I arrive to find you feverishly cleaning the front door and all I have to do is walk in here and appreciate my good fortune."

Tom resumed cleaning the glass. "Okay. Tell me about it when you want." Ah, the male response to all things emotional. "In the meantime, did you get my message?"

"Yeah, what's that all about? Did that lug suddenly grow a brain?"

"It wasn't the stupid boxer Mike Tyson," he corrected me. "No, it was the 'I'm one of the most successful telecommunications guys in the Western world' Mike Tyson. You remember, I showed you the article on him in *Forbes* a couple of months ago?"

It sounded vaguely familiar.

"Oh, crap, I knew you wouldn't remember, and I'm the seventy-one-year-old who checks daily for any signs of dementia. Anyhow, he is one rich fellow. He comes in late yesterday and takes a slow lap around the gallery. Then, he starts asking me a lot of questions—thoughtful, educated questions. He knows art, that's for sure. Next thing I know, he's picked out three pieces, including that junk Hoteman canvas—okay, so maybe he doesn't know that much about art—and wants to know if we can 'negotiate' a fee for all three. The retired basketball coach in me got right into the game. I played it cool, ten-seconds-on-the-clock-and-down-by-three cool. I apologized that I couldn't accommodate his request, since he had selected pieces by three different artists and we had to honor our financial agreement with each of them. And, just like that, he's hoping we take American Express, otherwise where's a bank so he can get a cashier's check. I about dropped my choppers."

I laughed and looked at his perfect teeth. I'd always thought they looked a little too straight, a little too white, like the after picture of a kid who's spent two years in braces, complete with headgear and a lifetime of fluoride.

He continued, "So I packed them up this morning. I told him we didn't have UPS on Saturdays and he said it was no big deal, send them out on Monday. That's all we're doing now, just waiting for the pickup."

I hugged him. "Thanks for hanging tight on the money thing."

"Yeah, I was glad you weren't here. You would have folded in a heartbeat, screwed up the whole thing." He was smiling.

"Then I'll be on my way, I think, if you don't mind." I headed for the door and stopped to look back at Tom. "Would you call Bri?" I asked. "Don't tell him I told you to, but I think he'd like to hear from a friend this morning."

"No kidding? Lost two of his best girls in one day. I bet he's stinging pretty bad."

"Don't go there, Tom, okay?"

He walked over to me, the only woman he had ever had to look up to. "Sorry. That was a lousy thing to say." We shared a brief hug, and I left.

◆

I saw the flowers on the back porch as soon as I pulled in behind the farmhouse, a simple bunch of wildflowers in a mason jar. Brian had been here. He'd been giving me wildflowers since our first backpacking trip a lifetime ago.

I read the note he had tucked in with them. It was classic Brian-speak. "Been thinking. Call me. Bri." Call him? Was he kidding? The last thing I wanted to do was call him. Hadn't he understood anything I'd said on our ride home? It was all of forty-eight hours later and he wanted to talk? My entire body tightened. What was there to talk about? Hearing his dreary voice on the other end of the phone sounded about as fun as a root canal. I groaned. Call him? I threw my bag down on the kitchen counter and headed straight for the fridge. Not one to drink too often, I was definitely in need of my favorite edge trimmer, a cold Juniper Ale.

With dogs at my feet, tails wagging, our mighty parade of four made its way into the living room. Kicking off my shoes, I started to turn on the television, hungry for some distraction. But instead, I did the grown-up thing. Settling into my chair, I faced the situation I found myself in. Call Brian. The mere thought of picking up the phone sent me into a tailspin.

Call Brian?

Two of my dogs sat perfectly erect, tails wagging slowly, both waiting for any shred of attention I might throw them. (The third, never known for her enduring attention span, had already passed out at my feet.) I looked at my loyal beasts, recognizing yet again one of the things I've always loved about dogs—they're such great listeners. (Ever tried to have a heart-to-heart with a cat? Forget it.)

The conversation that followed—yep, me talking earnestly to my dear mutts—was a little crazy making.

"Call Brian? Why in the hell would I do a harebrained thing like that?"

"Because I should. I owe him that much. How can you turn your back on the man you've spent over twenty-five years with?"

"Nope, we're over, I don't owe him anything. He probably just wants to get all moony-eyed and teary and beg me to let him come back home."

"But he's the father of your children. You both said you'd try and stay friendly, at least for the kids' sake."

"Well, that damned note doesn't sound all that friendly. And those flowers—he's trying something from his old playbook. That's cheating."

My black Lab mix, known as Nightmare since the day we got her, slid to the ground. Boredom had overtaken her. But Peaches, the standard poodle mix with the IQ of a college freshman, hung tight, sensing I was one step short of a meltdown. With just the very tip of her tail wagging now, she put her head into my lap, and the most natural thing in the world followed. My hand found its way to her head. Petting the familiar fur, my breathing slowed. I took a sip of the sassy ale and finally began to relax.

It was time to follow the advice I'd given my children countless times: "Speculation is a supreme waste of time and energy." I took another swallow of the chilled ale and dialed Brian's phone number.

The speed with which he answered threw me back into the tension I had just managed to slide out from under. Had he been sitting there, all this time, just waiting? Guilt loitered at my back, but mostly I was pissed. Might this be a two-beer night?

"Hi Lee, thanks for the call."

"Sure, what's up?"

"I was wondering if I could come over?" His question hung in the dead air between us. "I think I've figured out some stuff and, well, I'd like to, uh, kick it around with you. What do you think?"

I tried to sound normal when all I wanted to do was crawl through the phone line and (God, can I say this out loud?) smack him. What was wrong with me? I started petting Peaches again, hoping the familiar contact with my furry friend would somehow keep me securely in my body.

"Uh, it's really not a good time, Brian. I just got home from work and I'm really tired tonight. Maybe some other time?" I held my breath, fearful that if he said just one wrong word I might spontaneously combust. And right then, Peaches put her two front paws in my lap. With her help, I was holding steady.

"Yeah, yeah, sure. I understand." He cleared his throat, his tension matching mine. "The thing is, I was just hoping, now that you've had some time on your own, you know with the house empty and all, well, I was just wondering if you might consider us sort of at least dating again? Just to see if we could make a go of it?" All he heard was silence in response. "Don't hang up on me! I'm thinking sort of casual, you know. Please Lee, this is hard enough as it is—doing it over the phone is torture. Come on, I'll only stay a little while. I think you owe it to us to hear what I have to say."

And then, like the Mount Saint Helens of emotions, I blew. As I shot to my feet, all three dogs tore from the room in self-preservation panic. I spewed the lava of heartbreak.

"I owe it to us? Christ Almighty, Brian—just how much of my blood do you want? I owe it to us? Are you serious? You've had endless chances to get your shit together. I can't help you now. I tried. Oh, how I tried, and bam, just when I'm beginning to get my life back on track, you 'want to make a go of it?' Really, Brian? Where were you all those times when I was trying something new, trying to be different, like keep my mouth shut as you trampled my heart? Where were you when we made agreements that were always broken because you forgot or weren't interested enough to ever follow through on any of them? Ha! Where were you when I was the one desperate to talk? Owe it to us? Well, I don't think so. Nope. All things considered? I don't owe you a fucking thing!" I slammed down the phone.

In the dead silence of the house, the only sound I could hear was my heart pounding against the confines of my ribs. Two more seconds on the phone and it might have actually burst with rage. How dare he say I owe anything to him!

I slowly came back to my senses, aware that my entire body was shaking. I slipped back into the chair and tried to calm my breathing. It was a terrifying feeling, to be so out of control.

The room had just begun to stop spinning when a shocking thought floated into my awareness. Yes, uncontrollable rage was a terrifying feeling, but it was also somehow delicious. I had wanted to say all those things to Brian so many times but I always caught myself. Sure, I had lost my temper during these last few years, but I had never allowed myself to slide down into the mud and sling it back at him with the force of a hurricane. For the first time in my life, I acknowledged how self-righteous indignation lives inside us in a dark but very sweet spot.

The satisfaction of my outburst was fleeting. Guilt swamped me. I had actually said all those terrible things out loud. For what reason? So I could momentarily bask in my own pathetic emotional state, all at the cost of Brian's last remaining shred of dignity? I had to admit that while the logic behind my attack may have been understandable, my delivery certainly wasn't. No one ever deserved to be verbally cremated—it served no purpose other than an ephemeral, self-serving ego boost for the aggressor. I felt like a rat.

I studied my living room. Everything looked as it should, tidy enough and normal. But things were far from normal. I shuddered at the memory of my words. The dogs had not reappeared yet, all three smart enough to know their habitually composed mistress had suffered a cataclysmic meltdown. The phone lay at my feet. How it got there, I didn't know. Leaning over to pick it up, I was aware of my impulse to call Brian back, to turn myself inside out with apologies. I sat up. Still no dogs. The smell of fear must have hung in the air.

I considered what that call would be like, if he would even answer the phone. Me groveling; him giving me the silent treatment. The anger flared again. No, now was not the time to call him. I may be stewing in my own remorse, but I didn't need his two cents thrown in on top of the pile. I'd do it tomorrow, I decided, when the sun was up and I'd had a chance to forgive myself. That way if he blasted me, I'd have time to regenerate another layer of skin.

I started to call Barb but realized the foolishness of that conversation too. Never one known for her compassion, she'd merely laugh and say he had it coming. And then I'd have to agree with her because I knew he did, but still, it wasn't the way I wanted to conduct my life. Barb was all about blasting people out of the water. Me? I'd taken enough blasting from my dad throughout my childhood to know it only left the recipient stung and even more guarded.

Nope, I was flying solo on this one. Well, not exactly.

"Peaches? Nightmare? Jack? Come out, come out, wherever you are!"

I could hear Peaches trotting quickly down the hall, knowing she had been waiting for the all-clear sign. She peeked her head around the corner, her eyes locking with mine, hypervigilant.

"Come on in, mutt, it's okay, your crazy mistress has returned to her body." She was at my side in a flash, leaning into my leg. Nightmare wandered in next, as if she hadn't begun to even understand what had just transpired, but if Peaches said it was safe, then it was safe. I didn't see Jack again until the next morning.

My beer was now warm, and my appetite for alcohol had vanished. Time for some food, a bath, and a different evasion strategy, the flyaway novel I had been reading. Sometimes the best thing to do was escape reality, and this was certainly one of those times.

5

*C*learly I had a problem. Now that I had made my life-altering decision, I had no idea how to proceed. Clueless. It was virgin territory, "and I'm certainly no virgin," I thought to myself one day when I was feeding the animals. It was completely foreign to me, this thing I had done. Yet, in spite of all my misgivings, I knew I had done the right thing. It felt dead-on. But dead-on *what*? Now that was a mystery!

Over the next couple of weeks, my life felt different yet much the same. I went to work, paid the bills, and cleaned the house. But life was also a little odd. I discovered that I was a pretty good housekeeper when there was only one person to clean up after. I stopped cooking vegetables after deciding it was too much of a hassle. Instead, I savored their fresh, crisp, raw taste, even the cauliflower I used to camouflage under layers of cheddar for my family. The television gathered dust from lack of use. My energy suddenly seemed limitless.

And even though these refreshing discoveries felt good, somewhere lurking under this newfound freedom, I had my order in for a couple of helpful epiphanies, something that might direct me to the next phase.

"How does a woman my age re-create herself?" I wrote in my journal. Nothing came. No brilliant answer. Not even a wisp of an idea found its way to the page. I wrote reams. Nothing more than drivel poured onto the paper. I tried getting back to painting, something I anticipated being a real joy. Instead, it was another cosmic joke. Each canvas was a disappointment, the colors flat, without dimension. I turned my frustrations to the garden. Endless weeding produced only perfect rows of vegetables in a garden quickly coming to its end. I had always relied on running for clarity and direction. Not this time. Miles of pounding the pavement didn't produce one insightful thought, just sore knees and a building sense of fear.

One by one, the kids checked in (all except for Sam, who had been checked out since he was twelve). Sean was the first, his email friendly, loving, and full of questions. He probably wondered mostly about my sanity, but he was too polite, and too much like his father, to be so direct.

Dear Mom,

How are you doing? I'm pretty busy with school starting. Looking forward to teaching the calculus this term—they're finally letting the new guy have a crack at it. Good news—Betsy is being considered for a promotion to project lead at the bank. Keep your fingers crossed.

And then came the bullet.

Sorry if I'm out of line, but I've talked to Dad a couple of times. I know he misses you but it sounds like he's trying to be patient. Any chance you could work this out under the same roof? It's killing Dad living in those damned student apartments. Why don't you two just kiss and make up? Sorry. Bad joke. I know it's none of my business. I just don't know what you want. Nuff said.

More than enough, I thought, the little upstart.

Gotta run. Hey, how about we come down over Labor Day—a little catching up would be good. Would that be okay? Love you, S.

His words hit me squarely in the gut. I didn't think it would be okay at *all* to have them visit under these circumstances. Catching up? What's to catch up on? My dear, responsible, problem-solving firstborn determined to talk some sense into his crazy mother? No, I thought, a visit sounded like the last thing I was interested in.

And then I began to cry. Not want my kids to visit? A sacrilege. Had I gone completely round the bend? Perhaps. But at the moment, the thought of having to be Mom for three entire days was fingernails-on-blackboard awful. They wouldn't let me stay in my sweats all day or eat dinner plopped down in the middle of the garden. I couldn't simultaneously watch three different movies on three different channels.

Worst still was imagining being *Bad* Mom—the looks, the questions, the soapbox pleading. The *guilt*!

Nope. The absolute, bottom-line, hard-to-swallow truth was... I didn't want to see them. I cried some more, but it was true. The last thing I needed was my well-meaning but misguided son trying to get his mom to come to her senses. Make up with his father? This wasn't about *making up* at all, which was sadly something I knew my logical, high school–math teaching firstborn might never understand. Could any of my kids understand?

Sophia called at the oddest hours, perhaps hoping she might not actually have to talk about what was happening on the home front. It would be her way.

"Mamacita, whatcha doing?" was always the greeting, so much like Sophia herself, who practiced a seemingly direct but "I don't really want to know" approach to life. A junior at Tulane University, majoring in architecture and setting the world on fire, she was staying in New Orleans for the first time this summer. I was grateful she hadn't been here to go through the final throes with the rest of us. But I knew her absence was no mistake. While Sophia appeared straightforward, when it came to the emotional stuff, my oldest daughter had ultimately landed in the Brian and Sean camp. Thus the family had gone three to three when it came to emotions and what to do with them.

Her tone was friendly, upbeat.

"I've been meaning to call but things are hectic. Sorry."

"Nothing to be sorry about, sweetie. I can't think of anything better at your age than to be busy with life, as long as it's a good busy." If she dared admit it, Sophia was probably the only person in the Western world who thought the carnage of Hurricane Katrina was fraught with opportunity.

"Oh yeah, it's great. I landed that student representative spot with the Design Review Committee for the university. It's really cool; we get to be in on all the building decisions. Heck, I can even veto a plan if it strikes me as majorly ugly." She laughed at the thrill of her power. "Of course, I would never do that as a student—too many important people on the board. I might be begging them for a job next year. Don't want to be burning any bridges now, do I Mom?"

Mother and daughter chatted on aimlessly for a few more minutes. Finally, I helped her find her way into the real topic at hand.

"So I think the MacPhearson grapevine has been working overtime these last few days. Have you heard from your dad?"

"Come on Mom, that wouldn't be like him. Naw, it was Sean. He emailed me, kind of a pain, really. Think he was trying very hard to be the protective big brother and see how I was doing with the separation and all. But mostly, he just painted this awful picture of you not letting Dad move back in, like I should feel sorry for Dad or something." She stopped cold for a moment. "I mean, I do feel bad if he's unhappy, that this isn't what he wants *now,* but I'm not losing any sleep over it. Shouldn't he have thought about all this stuff a long time ago?" Sophia took a breath, quickly continuing before I had a chance to respond.

"Whatever. There's no way to change my big brother. I know my little sister is thrilled with her situation, and it sounds like you're doing just fine, so I'm happy to let it all be for the time being."

I chose my words carefully, making sure I followed my daughter's lead. "Thanks for that, Soph. I'm sorry for all this. Life certainly is weird sometimes. I know it isn't what any of you kids bargained for.

But you're right: I'm content, fine with this phase, actually quite excited about life. So how 'bout we all just keep moving forward, each with our own little lives, with the promise to keep each other posted?"

I could hear Sophia relax on the other end of the phone. Grabbing the opportunity, she dashed on to other, more comfortable topics. I followed along, glad to chat about the details of her young life, well aware there would be other phone calls to help her maneuver through the ruckus her parents had brought down upon her innocent self.

It was Ella who called and emailed on a daily basis, and this night was no different. As soon as I hung up with Sophia, the phone rang. She was full of news—about classes ("Bio sucks"), professors ("kind of like Dad, all serious but you can tell he really loves his students"), and boys ("he's absolutely the cutest guy I have ever seen, except he doesn't even know I'm alive, but I have a plan that is going into effect tomorrow. My goal is a date by the next football game. What do you think Mom, can I pull it off?").

I was confident the poor unsuspecting young man didn't have a chance if Ella had her sights on him. Before I could contemplate the possibilities, she was chattering away in my ear again.

"So, how goes it Mom, without your baby around? You doing okay? I have to hand it to you, you were pretty brave there at the end, a real trouper. And what's up with Dad? He's like all weirded out that he's still living at the Mondo Plastic Apartment. He actually wrote me the most pathetic email. Well, technically, it was a reply to one I sent him about school and everything. Next thing I know, he's telling me all about wanting to move back to the farm and you not letting him. I figure you have some pretty good reasons. He's the one who blew it. Sorry, too harsh, but I have no idea what to say to him. I mean, you've both been really good about keeping us out of the middle. Do you think that's what he was doing, trying to get me to go to bat for him? Well, I won't do it. Not my business, now is it?"

I reassured the MacPhearson baby that she was doing the right thing by allowing her goofy parents to work their way through their separation, and yes, it was just between her father and me, and it might be best just to keep it light with her father. This advice satisfied her, and she brought the conversation to an abrupt end.

"Yikes, we're all going to the midnight showing of *The Sound of Music*. Can you believe it? It's a sing-along! Ha, I know how much you love that movie. I'll belt out a few bars in your honor," she ended, and she was off. Sadly, I knew she'd be calling again the very next day.

Sitting in the now dark house, the phone still in my hand, I thought about my two daughters: lovely, competent, kind, and capable *almost*-women on their paths to adulthood. These sisters, who began their lives in a Guatemalan orphanage, were so alike and yet quite different. Why? Was it their caring but deficient beginnings? Maybe being whisked away from everything the toddler and her little sister had ever known had been too jarring? Of course, growing up under the constant barrage of two big brothers certainly had something to do with how they approached the world.

And now this. What lasting effects would each of my children feel from their parents' marital free fall?

6

I dragged myself down to the kitchen the next morning, my heart wrung out from the previous night. Three out of my four kids now had the latest update. (I wondered what it would be like the next time Sam checked in, if he ever did. Given our history, the only thing that promised to be certain was that it would be painful.) At least the other three knew. No, their parents would not be living happily ever after at the farm. That was that. Having them in the loop didn't seem to make the situation feel particularly better, but I decided it might take a long time for that to happen.

The thing I resented was that each time I heard from one of the kids, there was a dip. No, it wasn't a dip actually; it was more like a momentary drowning in a dark, gooey pool of sludge. They were the only ones able to touch that place I was trying to stay away from. I decided on a course of action for when they'd check in: get through the conversation, allow myself a moment or two of missing them, cry about all the wonderful years we'd had as *The Waltons* impersonators, and then get back to my project, my "very own sweet self," as Barb had dubbed it.

It took a couple of hours to get myself moving. I finally forced myself through some of the blasted chores that were always waiting— hungry animals, dirty dishes, and never-ending bills. But this was not the stuff of jolly making. My attention continued to wane as my spirit slipped even further down into the mud. What could I do to break out of this take-no-prisoners mood?

Fighting the temptation to crawl back under the covers, it came to me. I would indulge in my favorite pastime—roaming the bookstore in search of my next escape. Now I had a purpose. I jumped into the shower, made myself presentable, and headed into town.

I've always found walking into a bookstore soothing. This time was no exception. My heart slowed, my breathing eased, and just as I had hoped, my mood began to brighten as soon as I passed through the doors.

It didn't take me long to discover what I was after. Turning the corner of one of the stacks, I spotted *1,000 Places to See Before You Die*, and I was inspired. But all hope was dashed as I skimmed the pages; I found myself sadly unable to imagine skipping off to Katmandu, the Hardangerfjord in Norway, or Xishuabanna, China. Hell, I couldn't pronounce most of the places I saw listed, let alone even begin to imagine getting myself there.

Then it hit me. Maybe I could come up with a different list. "Ten things I'd like to do before I'm too old to remember my name" might be manageable. Suddenly, my enthusiasm that had been seeping away was back in spades. I got as far as my car, pulled out my trusty journal, and began to write:

#1 – Go to a spa for a week.

#2 – Play my fiddle in a blue grass group.

#3 – Visit NYC for the first time and stay at least two weeks.

#4 – Take a hot air balloon ride.

#5 – Go to a cooking school, preferably in France or Italy (but maybe someplace like the Napa Valley in California would be fine).

#6 – Take two yoga classes per week.

And then I stalled, the engines of my high-flying airplane suddenly deathly silent. I started to panic. Looking at my meager list, I felt incredibly foolish and middle-aged. Old. Nothing more than an empty-headed, self-absorbed woman. I was no better than Brian, full of it, full of myself. An adolescent with saggy boobs, hair in need of a style, and a rebellious streak that was fully thwarted by fear and self-consciousness. The list burned in my hand as I realized there wasn't one mention of world peace or feeding starving children on there anywhere.

My spirited enthusiasm was dashed. It came spiraling down to the earth, nose-diving into terra firma with a thud. The same old chatter roared through my brain. It was the "do, do, do for others. Take care of them, make them happy, be there for them, take a number and line up because that's what women do" chatter. Impatience wound around me like a python, squeezing me to the point of breathlessness. What the hell was I doing with my life? The only thing I was grateful for was my current solitude. My embarrassment was overwhelming, and I gave thanks that there was no one around to witness it.

Eventually I came back into my body. People were walking by the car on their way to something, anything, while I sat there in a self-pitying daze. I heard someone say, "Good God, you're pathetic," only to realize it was my own voice booming in my head.

I threw my journal down on the seat of the car, turned the keys, and very carefully checked my mirrors, just like any self-respecting, mature woman would do. It was time to go home and make Monday night dinner for Barb. As I threw the car into drive, I saw a bumper sticker on a passing car: "Stomp Out Global Whining."

No shit.

7

*B*arb had been having dinner at the MacPhearson house every Monday night for as long as either of us could remember. It started because it was one of her two nights off from the theater, and it stuck because of head-bashing, hog-sweating *Monday Night Football*, which neither of us could stomach. No way. We often wondered why more women didn't seize the opportunity to have a girls' night, since most men were so content to glue themselves to whatever barbaric game happened to be televised that particular week.

In the early years, Monday night dinners for Brian, his buddies, and the kids were simple but good. Then it came to me—why cook at all? The kids wouldn't suffer from one unhealthy meal a week. Throw crappy junk food in their direction, and as long as there was plenty of it, everyone was happy.

While chaos reigned supreme in the family room, Barb and I would spend our time getting lost in all things girlie. Our verbal wanderings would take us everywhere, from politics to shoes... one of Barb's greatest addictions. She'd often fill me in on the latest crisis at the theater, expertly acting out all the parts, and then patiently listen while I recounted the latest MacPhearson drama.

And on the rarest of rare occasions, usually after too many glasses of wine, Barb would actually talk about her inner workings.

Recognizing this precious opportunity, I'd quietly slide right into the conversation. We'd delve into moments of great happiness, our secret dreams, or those profoundly awful moments in life when only a warm bed and dark chocolate would do. Oh, the trust required to share our nitty-gritty selves—this was truly the Divine Girlie part.

It was during one of these Monday Night talkfests that I learned a very important detail about my friend. One of the biggest mistakes people made about Barb was to assume that because she was so short and round she was an easy mark, a pushover, a big but passive target. It was an assumption that got a lot of people into a lot of trouble. Barb explained her "I eat my enemies" attitude like this:

"Being the only child of aged, certifiably crazy Japanese parents was no picnic. There I was, born after years of trying, after both of my parents had survived time in World War II internment camps. Finally, I made my entrance. But near as I can figure, I was a screaming mass of nothing but disappointment from day one—I had all my fingers and toes but was minus the all-important wiener. Pops was a five-foot-three midget monster of bitter anger and resentment, the guy who never, ever forgave the Americans for how they treated him. Can't say that I blame him—not exactly four-star treatment. But if he was that resentful, why didn't he move back to Japan? Good question, and certainly one I never got an answer to. No, instead the man became a whacked-out neighborhood grocer who terrified small children. He kept a loaded shotgun behind the counter and threatened to use it on more than one occasion. Yeah, like I was going to learn how to be a happy camper from him?

"And my poor mother—she was probably equally as angry and bitter, but instead of yelling all the time, she was simply depressed every single stinking day of her life. Still is, although I know her nips of vodka from dawn to dusk keep her moving along. In other words, Role Model Number Two didn't make the charts either. So I rolled along, wondering how to get out and get away from both of them. There were no aunties or uncles to help. My grandparents were long gone. No kindly neighbor down the block to head me in the right direction. I think they were all afraid of my father. Smart people. Nope, you can sum up my childhood this way: seventeen years of three Japanese goofballs bumping into each other in the apartment over my dad's store. I don't ever once remember laughing with them. That's pathetic in my book."

Barb made the break from her folks as soon as humanly possible by graduating early from high school. She took off for the University of Oregon, two states away from her parents, with enough scholarship money to take her all the way through graduate school. I recall her once remarking, after a couple of dirty martinis, "Yep, those Asian kids, plenty smart and very motivated… but has anyone ever stopped and tried to figure out why?"

She studied hard and played even harder, doing and drinking her share of drugs and alcohol along the way. She also maintained she'd never had one "real date." Oh, there had been plenty of drunken trysts, but in her opinion, "Why would anybody in his right mind ask out this tub-o-lard when he could nail Suzi Svelte? Honey, I figured out a long time ago that it ain't brains men are interested in. That's for sure."

I would never, ever say this to her, but she had become her parents, at least in part—bitter, angry, and sometimes pretty depressed about her life. But even though she was as sharp as broken glass, Barb was a charmer. Her humor was Chardonnay dry, clever, and bone-splitting funny. It sent people to their knees. And competent? She wrote the book. After finishing her MFA in theater arts, "a behind-the-scenes genius," she'd say, she was hired by our very own prestigious Oregon Shakespeare Festival, a nationally renowned theater company here in Ashland. Eventually, she worked her way up to artistic director.

In spite of her spit and vinegar, Barb was very well liked by those who came in contact with her, including the creative prima donnas, the psycho producers, and the eager, enthusiastic interns who drove her absolutely nuts each summer. They'd arrive for their two-month placements with stars in their eyes, only to pitch a fit when Barb told them to scrub out the actors' bathrooms. "I've seen at least a hundred twenty-seven variations of 'intern huffy' during my career. Of course, poor neophytes, they can't compete with 'professional theater person-nel huffy,' of which I have witnessed no less than eleven thousand four hundred ninety variations. It's been a long career."

And ours had been a long friendship, which, given our differences, was something of a miracle. In spite of those differences, there was one thing we both always agreed on: our weekly gabfests were far more sat-isfying than anything the NFL could possibly offer. To what degree did we owe our "sisterhood" to this Monday night ritual? Who knew? Who cared? There was no need to analyze our connection. As any woman will tell you, it simply felt right.

8

*I*n spite of how grateful I was to have dinner with Barb to look forward to, it was a twisted drive home from the gallery, and not just because of the winding roads. My mind was cluttered with bits and pieces of thoughts that led me round and round and right back into emotional dirt. It didn't help that *1,000 Places to Visit Before You Die* sat on the seat next to me. Like an uninvited creep who had managed to slide his way into the car, it stared at me. I squirmed and contemplated tossing the thing out into the green oblivion of the countryside.

Finally, I reached the comforting familiarity of my yard. I was greeted by a furry mass of uncomplicated loyalty, as my dogs ambled straight to me, their tails wagging with sheer doggie joy. Patting each of them, I made my way into the kitchen right as a cheery thought popped into my overtaxed brain: this *new* life of mine would make the beloved Monday night dinners with Barb even better. My face and shoulders fell away from the tension that had been holding them hostage. Yes, it would be pure, uninterrupted girl time. Gone were the wild men in the living room, punctuating the silence with war yells. Kids would not hang on my legs, begging me to "pleeeeease" let them stay up. The evening ahead suddenly held great promise.

I had already made Barb's favorite pickled beets the day before. (Pregnancy had elevated her desire for this spicy concoction to an all-time high.) But I suddenly realized that I hadn't given the rest of our meal much thought—something historically unusual but currently quite common. Maybe it was because I was having too many thoughts about other things, like my entire life. But whatever my excuse, I knew it wouldn't do. Dear Barb needed bulk these days, the spicier the better, and hold the lectures, please.

I surveyed the cupboard. Okay, what else could I pull together? I knew I could do a quick stir-fry with veggies from the garden. There was tofu in the fridge. But that wouldn't do. Barb would scoff at such a meal, saying, "You're more Japanese than I am!" No, Barb demanded fat to satisfy her hormonal urges.

I suddenly remembered the Mexican casserole I had in the freezer. Martha Stewart would drop dead on the spot if she saw this combo, I thought, as I put it into the microwave to defrost. I stared at my reflection in the door as it closed. It worried me a little that I wasn't bothered more by Barb's lousy diet, that somehow I was aiding and abetting a criminal operation, a less-than-healthy baby factory. It was that responsibility thing again. I had been telling myself for the last few weeks that I couldn't be responsible for anyone but myself. I didn't believe it, of course, but I figured it was worth a try. So I'd feed my friend and her unborn child a meal that would send them both into gastronomical spasms and hope for the best.

An hour later, Barb burst through the kitchen door singing, "Roll me over in the clover, do it again," a favorite sailor song she had picked up somewhere in her travels. She stopped mid-lyric. "Well, a girl can dream, can't she? What's for dinner?" She made an awkward landing on a kitchen stool. "So, I was contemplating some trivia on the way over. How much do you think a pregnant orca weighs? Why do I ask? Because I'm pretty sure I could give one a run for the money. In other words, I don't care what you or my doctor says. I have never been this hungry in my entire life. Forget the eating for two crap—I figure I'm packing it away for at least six or seven, so bring it on."

Which, of course she wasn't—packing it away for a litter, that is.

I put a bowl of almonds down in front of her. "Nope. As I recall from your ultrasound last week, I saw one, and only one, baby girl blob floating around on the screen." I teared up, remembering my own precious baby blobs.

"How can you cry over a blob?" Barb rolled her eyes like a teenager.

"Because blobs turn into babies and babies turn into people and the next thing you know, they're all gone, and what the hell am I doing to them with my craziness?" I was bawling by this time.

"Here we go again. What's with you? Just so you understand. That's the last time I'm taking you to any ultrasounds. That tech looked pretty weirded out by your storm surge."

"Well, it didn't help that you started telling me to shut up or leave. Who says that to her friend?"

"I do, of course."

Simultaneously, we both erupted with peals of laughter. We were off, my tears for days gone by now replaced with an unexplainable yet exquisite case of the giggles.

Barb seized the moment.

"And who in the hell was the genius who decided that booze was bad for growing baby blobs? I'd kill for a cool, crisp lemon drop right now."

"I can make you up a virgin drop," I offered between gasps. Barb threatened me with a skillet.

"That's a cruel, cruel thing to say to someone who has been stone-cold sober for months now. And let me get this straight. I have to continue on this holy path for as long as I'm a nursing sow?"

"You got it. In fact, you might as well get used to the idea that your wild ways are pretty much curtailed for the next eighteen years. Tonic?"

Barb moaned as she nodded.

"My life has been reduced to *tonic*. Well, considering booze got me into this current mess, eighteen years of boredom may not be such a bad idea." She popped an almond into her mouth. Her voice dropped. "I sure hope I haven't entirely fucked up this poor kid, what with her less-than-perfect conception."

I thought back to the night six months before when Barb had sat, wide-eyed, in my kitchen, revealing her pregnancy to me. She had seemed so bewildered. "You know me, Lee. I was just after a great quickie with that handsome guest director I'd been secretly drooling over for the entire run. Tall, dark, handsome, and, best of all, scheduled to leave the very next day. Just the way I like 'em. Those damned cast parties. Oh, we theater people do know how to let down our hair. It was late; everyone else had left the theater. We surveyed each other through our drunken eyes and suddenly found ourselves in a major lip-lock. Next thing you know, we stumbled to my office and made a truly ugly splashdown on my rickety couch. Then it all gets pretty damn blurry. No surprise there. I mean, who in the hell ever remembers anything from one of those nights? And I sure wasn't thinking about the possibilities of making a life-altering, forever kind of turn."

"Maybe not, but I, for one, am quite happy you decided to keep the baby," I had added, once she had revealed that she would.

"Yeah, that's easy for you to say," she retorted darkly.

Tonight I reassured her for the hundredth time. "This is going to be one amazing little girl. I can just feel it. Don't forget, all the tests have come back with one hundred percent perfection."

"Christ—your optimism can be so annoying. But as much as I hate to admit it, I have my fingers crossed that you're actually right this time." Barb's face flushed red. She did not wear vulnerability well. In a flash, her eyes began to dart around the kitchen. She sniffed the air like a wolf on the hunt. "What smells so good? Mexican? Did you whip us up a little something hot and chilified? Please say yes. Mexican would be the best part of my day."

I confirmed her question with a nod in return. She smiled as I began to make the salad, telling her, "And it gets even better. Look on the second shelf in the fridge. Just for you."

Barb squealed when she saw the bowl of shiny pickled beets floating in the sweet-and-sour brine.

"You are an angel. But you know that you're the only one eating any of that salad, right? Between the beets and the casserole, I'm set." Pulling a fork out of the drawer, she started in on the beets.

I put the salad on the table and turned to face my friend. The words came out of nowhere.

"Please, eat something leafy and green for me." As soon as it was out, I realized I had broken the promise I had made to myself—I would not mother the mother-to-be.

"Sorry. Forget I said that."

"It's already forgotten," Barb snapped back. It was impossible to miss the edge in her voice. She quickly moved on.

"What have you been up to this week? Is your mid-life crisis progressing nicely? You look great. Confusion becomes you." She lowered herself into one of the kitchen chairs. It groaned under the weight of mother and child.

I put my unfinished list of "Ten things I'd like to do" on the table for Barb to read. "How's this for a laugh? It's all I could come up with. Pretty pathetic, don't you agree?"

Barb started picking away at the salad, which I figured she would, because Barb grazed like some people crack their knuckles or twirl their hair, and she read the list.

"A cooking school? That's stupid, you already know how to cook."

I interrupted. "Look, I'm trying not to critique your pregnancy. Can't you do the same for my mid-life crisis?"

"Ouch, one point for the cook." She looked back at the list. "Oh, this one. It's too, too rich. Come on, just one more and then I'll be good, I promise. Number four, hot-air ballooning? You're too tall. Your hair would catch on fire if you stood up straight in the little basket thingy."

I glared at her.

"Sorry. I couldn't resist. Okay, time to be serious. I'd better behave myself or all I'll get is this rabbit food for dinner."

She quickly scanned my list. "Let me see. Is this a secret ballot, or can I just tell you which ones I think you should do?"

She didn't wait for an answer. "By all means, join a bluegrass group.

I think it's shameful that you haven't played your violin in months, and fiddle music would be fun for you. A real change. Ah, but first, number three, yeah, that's the one! I think you should go to New York, you know, do some research about this new musical direction."

"Yeah, New York, home of the country's finest bluegrass fiddlers. Don't you think Nashville would be a little better for that?"

Barb feigned a scowl.

"If you end up in Nashville, I'm having you committed. Seriously, why not New York, just for the hell of it?" She took a huge breath, savoring the smells floating around the kitchen. "Do you have any real sour cream? I don't want to ruin my Mexican num-num with that watery, fat-free crap you usually have around."

"Sorry, you know me." I plopped the container of fat-free sour cream down in front of her as I contemplated her suggestion that I actually travel across the entire country.

"What in the world would I do in New York? I'd probably get mugged the first day."

"Probably. Naw, the city is actually quite safe, and even you have enough brain cells to be out of Central Park before dark, right? I think you're on to something. Yeah, yeah, yeah… a trip to a place you've always wanted to visit. Think of the art! I can see them throwing you out of the Metropolitan at closing time, you on your knees, pleading for them to let you stay just a few more hours. And all the galleries in SoHo. You'll go nuts. It's a done deal. I know the perfect little hotel, the Excelsior. It's right on the park, so you could do your stupid running thing each morning, and I can get you a ticket at the Delacorte, a delicious outdoor theater right inside the park. Maybe it's too late in the season. That would be a disappointment. They do some mean Shakespeare there. No matter. Tell me what you want to see on Broadway and I'll call in some favors. You're going. Queen of the Wonder Belly has decided."

I carefully considered everything Barb had described. For the first time since being on my own, I felt excited. Or was it fear? Mostly fear, I decided, but it was a thrilling, shivering fear that actually appealed.

And then I imagined Brian's face when he found out my plan. I went flat.

"Bri will think I've gone loony on him. Well, even loonier. Okay, that was one big fat reality check. Besides, how in the world can I afford to do something like that?" I sounded like I had been run over by a tank. "Set the table, would you?"

"Screw Brian. This is about you, right? I have millions, zillions of frequent flyer miles you can use. Probably can even get you an upgrade to first class so you won't have to curl up like a six-foot pretzel in coach. I know we can get you a corporate rate at the hotel, since you'll be there on gallery business, right? This is a business trip, isn't it? And since you don't seem to require food, the nuts on the flight should carry you the first week, and a loaf of bread will get you through the second."

"Two weeks? I can't be gone for two weeks. Who's going to feed the animals? Tom can't run everything for that long. He needs his days off." I spun back to the oven and checked the casserole's progress.

"Did I tell you I had coffee with Brian last week?" I said to the open oven.

I knew I hadn't mentioned it because the last thing I wanted was Barb's opinion on that part of my life.

"Did he order up yet another serving of crow?" Barb wanted to know.

"See, that's why I didn't tell you last week. Forget it." I went silent.

Barb shifted her tremendous girth in the chair. "Sorry, you know how I am. It's the hormones—everything is looser, even my tongue, if that's humanly possible. Really, I want to know, how was it?"

I put the olives on the table, taking a moment to think about how the time with him had felt.

"Well, actually, it was kind of nice. We had made a deal not to do any of what he calls 'heavy' talking, to just be friendly and respectful of our two different lives. There was some chatting about the kids, of course, but he didn't pry, and there was a distinct lack of ass kissing. He didn't throw himself at my feet and beg for forgiveness. Even once. I liked it, almost too much. He is my best friend, after all, and I've missed that about him."

"Great—so I'm right in there with Hertz, best friend number two trying harder. Or was it Avis who runs second? You know, that campaign just went into the toilet after OJ moved on to his other pursuits, the crazy bastard."

Putting the casserole on the table, I sat down across from her.

"You know what I mean, Barb. It was reminiscent of the old days, when we laughed and really seemed to listen to each other. I felt like I had his complete attention, and I liked it. I liked it a lot. Made me wonder just how long ago it was that we started sliding into that auto-pilot mode that eventually led us to crash and burn. I don't know. There are a lot of things I like about that sweet guy. I hate it when I start questioning myself. It was a nice lunch. What makes me think it would be like that enough of the time?"

"I think it's way too early for you to be worried about that part of your future. I can't even get you to commit to a trip to the Big Apple. Why don't you just take it for what it was, a good lunch with a friend, and not analyze it to death?" She stared at me. "Good God, you think too much." She shifted her attention back to what she considered more pressing matters. "Are we just going to stare at that casserole or do we get to eat it? Baby cakes and I are pretty damn hungry." She got up for the utensils I had forgotten.

I took my cue and started dishing up the dinner while Barb finished setting the table. It was comical. This woman, who looked like she hadn't combed her hair in a week and didn't even know there was such a thing as an iron, laid out the utensils with a precision that appeared in only a few limited parts of my character. Placing the knives and forks exactly one inch from the edge of the table, Barb spoke over my shoulder.

"Look, you've been telling me for as long as I can remember to trust my instincts. That's about the only reason I'm having this baby. Somewhere underneath all this blubber, I have a feeling that this little girl is going to be the most amazing thing to come along in my entire lifetime. You've always told me to believe in my sixth sense, which I admit might as well be voodoo talk as far as I'm concerned. But this is about you. Now it's your turn. You are all of one month into this solo flight. Seems like you should just hang tight and try that trust—the very thing you are always cramming down my throat."

She sat down at the table and we began our odd little dinner. I looked her straight in the eyes and asked, "So, do you think I can get a famous New York cheesecake through security? That could be our entire meal the first night I get back!"

Barb let out a huge belly laugh.

"Well honey, let's start plotting. And just so you know, one cheesecake won't be nearly enough."

9

*T*wo weeks later, Barb showed up for Monday night dinner hauling two huge suitcases. While I stirred the apple curry on the stove, she dropped them on the floor, clicked them open, and started pulling out clothes.

"I rummaged through the wardrobe department and picked out some things you would look great in, because you can't show up in the big city in your jeans and sweatshirt. Now, it's not like I could get you pants or anything. You have those giraffe legs—nothing long enough for you except the leggings from the last run of *Hamlet*, and they were all smelly. Pretty darned crusty. Think someone forgot to run them through the dry-cleaners. But here, look at this cashmere sweater from *Some Like It Hot* a couple of years ago. All soft, just a little retro, and the perfect fall color." She threw it at me, and I barely managed to save it from a curry bath.

"And this, I could just see you in this. Try it on."

I turned down the heat and slipped into a form-fitting black leather jacket.

"Ha, I knew it would fit you. Soft, isn't it? And lightweight, perfect for fall. Lamb I think, poor beast. What a fate. Better to get eaten or worn to Manhattan? Remind me to never complain again about where I am on the food chain."

She plopped herself down on the floor, a little breathless from her rummaging, and looked me over with a critical eye.

"Remember when we did that one-act, *Life in the Print Lab*? Terrible, terrible play, and the lead was the most obnoxious little queen to travel in these parts since Lewis and Clark. We had to special-order that jacket for him. I remember the fight well. He wanted it fitted, to 'accent' his shoulders. A pair of three-dollar shoulder pads would have been fine. Well, two pair, one per shoulder. The guy sloped like the bunny hill at Mount Hood."

She motioned for me to turn around and then gave me an approving nod.

"It looks perfect on you. No one will ever know you hail from the land of potbellied pigs and Walmart. Now, what are we going to do about the hair?"

"All right, enough is enough," I snapped as I reached up to pull a few wayward strands back behind my ear, suddenly a little too self-conscious. Doubt began to make its entrance. "What's wrong with my hair?"

"Well, nothing is all that wrong with it when you let it down, but you always keep it pulled back in that miserable stub of a ponytail. It looks like a cat that got caught in the barn door. Maybe a trim, refresh the color a bit, and wear it down. They say long hair is the new in look for older women. Promise me you'll wear it down? It's New York, for Christ's sake. Listen, when all you have for a lifetime is straight, black, won't-hold-a-curl-to-save-your-soul hair, you want to see others celebrate their good fortunes. It's the Japanese way. So I've made you an appointment with my stylist. Next Tuesday at ten o'clock. Tom's working. I already checked."

Barb had a point. The ponytail was not hip and cool and *SNL*, but then neither was I. What I had lived with for so long was utilitarian hair. Cleaning house? Who needs hair in the way? Chasing kids, dogs, pigs? Pull back that mass of hair and get to it. Unloading canvases? The ponytail fit the bill.

On the appointed Tuesday, I entered the salon with more than a touch of trepidation. Stylists could be so damned territorial, the gods of hair, which was why I tried to avoid them. I puffed up, ready to explain exactly what I wanted. But Bruce—"I swear to God, that's my real name," he'd said—was funny and gentle and actually cared about what some middle-aged woman wanted done to her hair.

"Honey, you have to live with it, not me. What will it be?" I walked out of there feeling lighter and all-over happy. A simple trim. A bit of color. I felt bouncy and grateful to have a blunt and generous friend.

I had predicted everyone's reaction to the trip with dead-on accuracy. Sean's email came back in a flat, accusatory kind of way. He found it "hard to believe" that his dad would be happy to stay in the house and take care of things while I was gone. "I guess you have to get this out of your system" was how he signed off.

"Yep, still a little shit," I had said out loud, glad to be alone when his judgmental words arrived on my screen.

Sophia asked me if I wouldn't mind "checking out the progress they're making at Ground Zero" for her.

"Exactly what will I be checking out?" I wanted to know.

"Oh, I don't know, Mom, just how it looks and feels. Tell me if you see any famous dignitaries standing there in hard hats looking important." That was Sophia. Forget the rock star du jour. She was a New York dignitary groupie.

Ella thought the trip was "cool" and wondered if I might find my way into Bloomingdale's. "Christmas is coming, you know." And then, anxious to get to her full report on the cute guy living upstairs in the dorm, she added good-naturedly, "Have a blast, Mom."

Sam didn't even know I was going anywhere because he didn't know where he was, let alone where his mother was.

Telling Brian had, of course, been the kicker, which really pissed me off. I resented even thinking twice about how I would present it to him, let alone the fact that I found myself staring into the darkness in the middle of the night, practicing well-chosen words. Out loud, no less. I'd had too many years of that. No matter, those feelings still bubbled right up to the top. Finally, the day came when I had to tell him. I could put it off no longer. I tried to keep it light, matter-of-fact, sort of like I was going to Eugene to pick up a crate of packing materials. But we quickly found ourselves falling headlong into old patterns.

"New York? Don't they have good enough art in Seattle or San Francisco? Guess you're doing pretty well to afford a trip like that, huh?" he wondered.

I countered with my usual defensive and pathetic justifications.

"Barb has given me her frequent flyer miles and she even brought me clothes from the theater. Guess she doesn't want Ashland embarrassed. She even got me complimentary tickets for a Broadway show." I felt my chest tighten, the anger beginning to rise up in my throat. Brian felt it too.

"Sorry, Lee," he quickly apologized. "You'll hardly be a poor representative of our humble burg. You already stand out among the Ashland locals. Always been a smart dresser. I doubt anyone who ever comes into the gallery thinks you're an honorary local."

His voice dropped into that caring, serious place I knew well.

"But it's not like you've never been out of here. Are you wishing I had done more traveling with you? More than the annual Portland, 'Let's listen to Brian grumble about the traffic a little more' trip? Did I ever go there with you in a good mood?" He was poised and ready to take off into doo-doo land. My jaw tightened, determined not take his bait. How dare he try to make this trip somehow about him? I wanted nothing of it and opted for the high road.

"I'll be fine. Anyhow, I was wondering if it would be strange for you to look after the animals? Maybe that's too weird. Tell me if that's too much to ask. Obviously, you could stay here and everything." (Were we really having this conversation? I felt self-conscious. It was as awkward as talking about sex right after we'd had it for the first time.)

But Brian surprised me by making a 180-degree turn. He jumped at the offer.

"I'd be happy to be there. No problem. The idea of being back in my house for a couple of weeks… when do you want me to start?"

I tried to ignore the "my house" part. No luck. I found myself feeling very prickly. The next words out of my mouth came as a surprise, but I was glad I had the nerve to say them.

"You know, this isn't the first step to you moving back in or anything. I don't want to give you the wrong idea."

Brian locked eyes with me. When he finally spoke, I realized he was trying for more friendliness than his look had communicated.

"Oh yeah, I know that. Believe me, I got that one down. Nope. I'm trying my damnedest to just go along and see where we end up. I meant it about being your friend. We're too old to throw that part away." He looked out the window of the bakery where we were having coffee.

"Besides, Pissant Man says I need to understand why I threw everything away. For what? A couple of guilt-free fishing trips, a few worthless dates, and a whole lot of stupid sexual fantasies? He says if I don't get it straight, I'll just make the same mistakes all over again. I told him I added up my learning curve, and if I did the math correctly, that would make me about ninety-five years old and a two-time loser. He didn't laugh. He never does."

I didn't know which was more shocking—that Brian had actually continued seeing the counselor on his own, or that he was delving into his inner workings.

He couldn't miss the look on my face.

"You look surprised. Yeah, I go see the hairy little fart every couple of weeks. It's weird. I really hate it in some ways, but I think it's working. He thinks it has to do with my mother. Not too original. I told him that was crap but that it was probably true."

We sat in silence. Then, without warning, I reached across the table and took his hand, a gesture so familiar to both of us that it took a second to realize I had even made the connection.

He pulled away.

"Hey, I'm not going for the sympathy vote here. Sorry. I honestly didn't mean to tell you any of that. You go to New York, and I'll be happy to have a two-week vacation from the Plastic Palace. And when you get back, maybe you can tell me all about it over dinner. That's what friends do, you know."

I nodded my agreement. For whatever reason, neither of us let go of the other's hand.

10

While we were waiting for the plane, Barb looked me up one side and down the other, like I was a kid off to summer camp.

"Not bad, not bad at all. Casual chic becomes you. And no one need ever know that you will turn into a pumpkin if you don't have your entire wardrobe returned by the stroke of midnight... two weeks from now. It's really a shame most of it has to go back to the bowels of the theater."

"You know I couldn't have pulled any of this off without you, right?" I dared not gush with appreciation. "The clothes, the hair, well, just the vote of confidence."

"Yeah, yeah, but admit it, that bag is the gold medal of accessories, right?"

Barb was absolutely right. I closed my arm over the elegant leather shoulder tote she had given me the night before. (I'd had trouble accepting such an expensive gift—clearly not something she'd borrowed from wardrobe.)

She craned her neck, insisting I give her a look inside at all the contents.

"Ha! Talk about right. Look at all that crap. You're always dragging around that God-awful backpack, crammed full with your books and journals, bottled water, nuts and berries to munch on. I knew this would come in handy." Straightening herself up, she repeated what she'd said the night before. "Remember, it's a little treat, one friend to another, because in another couple of months, it'll be payback time." And she patted her belly.

And now here I was, a mile high in first class, even more grateful to Barb for upgrading my ticket. I stretched out my legs, sliding my oversized seat into a reclining position without any worry about the comfort of the passenger behind me. Sipping my complimentary mimosa, I relished in the softness of the cashmere sweater, though the sleeves were pushed up a tad, in what Barb called a "jaunty look," to camouflage the fact that they were at least two inches too short for my long arms. The flight attendant, a flawless morsel of youth, arrived with my appetizer on a white china plate, spring rolls far better than the ones served in my favorite Chinese restaurant at home. How could that be possible at forty thousand feet in the air? The cocktail was working. I smiled at the thought of people who knew me, wondering what they would think if they could see me now.

But as the plane finally touched down at JFK, I thought I might puke right there in the aisle. What in the world was I doing? I had decided that whenever the fear grabbed me, I would do something, anything, to make it go away. Imagine my surprise when the moment my stomach started churning, I began silently humming "Whenever I feel afraid."

With that, I decided there was no question. I was certifiably nuts. No matter. The nausea passed as the plane came to a stop. I smiled at the thought of the Julie Andrews song, one I had always hated. Looking around, I realized no one was the wiser, so I gathered up my belongings and wondered just how sick I would be of that idiotic tune by the end of two weeks.

Having flown United countless times to New York, Barb had repeatedly walked me through the next phase:

"Follow the Baggage signs to the left, but first pee here, because you won't find another bathroom until you get to your hotel. Go down the ramp and give praise to Allah and the rest of the crew if your bag appears on the carousel. Go outside and get into a cab—not a car—a cab. The drivers will swarm you. Don't be intimidated. Stand tall. Think cab. Get in, tell him the address, then sit back and resume praying—Allah, Buddha, Jesus Christ himself—because a cab ride into Manhattan during rush-hour traffic can be a near-death experience, the long, slow, painful kind. You might want to close your eyes. I'm not kidding."

But I couldn't possibly close my eyes as we sped along one highway after another. There were more than a couple white-knuckle moments, but my driver, Middle Eastern and extraordinarily friendly, managed to make his way through the traffic. By the time I spotted the Empire State Building, I had heard his entire life history and figured he loved America more than I did. In no time at all he was making a U-turn in front of my hotel, stopping two lanes of traffic so I would be deposited directly in front of the entrance. I gasped at the maneuver, and instinctively my eyes slammed shut. When I opened them, a pasty-white, slump-shouldered young doorman with crooked teeth and a huge smile was welcoming me to the Excelsior Hotel.

From my seventh-floor room, I looked down onto the scene below, dark and nearly still by now. People scurried to wherever it was they were going. I wondered what kind of huge trees were across the street, realizing how I took my trees at home for granted. Their half-naked branches made shadows under the streetlights, the same way the line of maples behind our house danced in the light of the moon. Thanks to Barb, I knew these trees stood sentinel for the Natural History Museum.

"I don't know if you'll actually want to go in there," Barb had warned. "Lots of creepy insects and whale bones and screaming kids. But hey, it's your trip."

I stared at the silent structure, its mammoth walls pushing out against the surrounding lawns. My mind was suddenly flooded with memories of the kids and the countless bugs they had collected. I began to cry. Then, leaning against the window, I sobbed, glad there was no one there to see my distorted face, knowing better than to look at my reflection in the glass. My sense of loss gave way to fear. Was this how I was going to live my life from here on out? Discovering that all the dreams I'd harbored for years would only sadden me or, worse yet, terrify me? What was the use of being here if I had no one to share it with? Was I simply a herd animal at heart, not the lone wolf I had tried to imagine?

Sitting on the edge of the bed, I cried. Forget the dripping faucet; this was Niagara. I cried so hard that my head took on that deep underwater-pressure sensation. Why had I ever imagined scuba diving would be an enjoyable experience? I made a feeble attempt to breathe out of my snotty nose, only to discover that something I'd always taken for granted was not currently an option. I looked at the balls of tissue scattered on the floor, surrounding me like a wild hailstorm that the Weather Channel would feature with great fanfare.

All I really wanted was to talk to someone I knew, but that would spell defeat. They'd hear it in my voice as soon as I said hello. Barb would probably laugh, since overt, in-your-face vulnerability was not an emotion she dealt with well. Brian would be supportive but secretly, deeply satisfied. Tom would stay cool and try for the "buck up" coaching speech I had heard him deliver a thousand times to every kid in town. And I'd never, ever, not in a hundred million years, call one of the kids. Sliding to the floor in utter defeat, I stared out the window at all the glowing buildings behind the museum, feeling like a pathetic rumple of midlife foolishness.

Were there any other options? Check myself into Bellevue? Tempting. Head out on the street to blend in with other crazies? Perhaps. Order up a bottle of gin and drown myself? Warmer. I stared at the lights again, counting the rows and rows of humanity living out their own personal dramas behind their glow.

Finally, it hit me that there was only one thing to do. And it was so thoroughly embarrassing that I actually looked about the empty hotel room to make sure no one was watching. It was feeble at first, but gradually I gained momentum. "Whenever I feel afraid... " By the second verse I was laughing, sitting up straighter. The sound of my voice warbling through my congested nasal cavities was good enough for a late-night television comedy sketch. Good God, perhaps I did belong out on the street. I started to come back to my senses. Here I was, and there was the Big Apple.

Like it or not, Julie and I were going to see New York together, after enjoying at least a glass of gin in my room and good night's sleep.

Sunlight manages to take the fear out of most situations. I stared out of my window the next morning. Of course it was the same street, the same trees, but by light of day, the view was far less desolate and lonely. Dressed in my running shoes, I contemplated an actual run. Could I really take myself out into the teeming masses? Far below me, I spotted not one but two New Yorkers similarly attired. From around the corner came a woman sporting a ponytail with her Nikes. Ha! For this part of my day, I might almost fit in.

"Out the door and to the left. You can't miss it" were Barb's instructions for finding Central Park. "And if you do, return home immediately. You have no business traveling alone."

I didn't miss it, and the moment I entered the park, everything felt better. I'd already stretched in my room, too self-conscious to do that in public. Adjusting my ponytail, I wondered if other people could tell I was stalling. I could put it off no longer. Like a baby learning to walk, I put one foot in front of the other, hoping I wouldn't trip, and gradually eased into my regular pace. The rhythm was reassuring, the sound of my breathing familiar. I settled in. Running was something I knew, and other runners, even those in Central Park, were, as Barb would say, my people.

With my pace established, I dropped into a comfortable distance behind two men who were running side by side but not saying a word, eyes straight ahead, ears plugged with their iPod ear buds. (Why did that term creep me out? I always thought of aliens growing out of people's ears when I heard the words "ear buds." Bad marketing. I smiled. Yeah, terrible, to the tune of billions.) The first sound that registered was the crunching of autumn leaves under my feet. Stretched out in front of me was a path covered with red, gold, and brown leaves. It was a promising, familiar sight. For the first time, I was finally able to take in my surroundings.

The landscape was unlike anything I had ever seen. Stunning, towering trees—sycamores, pines, maples—lined the path, then gradually wandered up and away from the asphalt in thick patches. Rounding a corner, I discovered a pond. No, not a pond. We had a pond. This was a lake, a calm, gray lake full of contented mallards and a few random swans, each as satisfied with his capacious surroundings as the birds who called our pond home. It struck me as funny, these urban-dwelling waterfowl.

But when I looked up from the wildlife, I realized something important had happened. Not only had I not tripped or been run over by those joggers giving the rest of us a bad name (it's called jogging, people, not sprinting), but I was also finally confident enough to allow my gaze to truly wander. My eyes followed the terrain up and over the heads of people walking their dogs, others hurrying to somewhere they knew they had to be, the old couples slowly walking hand in hand, and up into the trees and then beyond. This view, this magnificent skyline, was like nothing I had ever seen. In Oregon, the only thing behind the forest is more forest. But this New York forest had plenty behind it, an entire city that seemed determined to be as close to nature as possible. Huge, elegant, seasoned apartment buildings, packed as thickly as the trees themselves, sat just on the other side of the park. They jetted up toward the sky, their mass dignified and genteel. It was like running in a snow globe, as if we could all turn topsy-turvy and lovely snowflakes would gently fall down on the scene, our perimeter making us safe and secure.

The runner's drug, those blessed endorphins, had fully kicked in. The run had worked its magic, my very own little victory lap completed.

I found myself smiling at unsuspecting New Yorkers as I made my way back through the park, unfazed that some of them responded with a look that said, "Lady, you are one loopy broad." Waiting for the light to change, it occurred to me that I might not actually perish in this intriguing but strange land. With horns honking at who knows what, I crossed the intersection wondering if I might actually enjoy this adventure.

After a good long shower and coffee and a scone at the corner bakery, I felt ready to take on Manhattan, or at least the easiest part of the city, the Metropolitan Museum of Art. Barb said it was the other thing I couldn't possibly miss: "Just walk all the way through the park until you come to Fifth Avenue. Look to your left, and there she is. Don't know if the street vendors will be out, but they usually have some interesting stuff to look at, and they're a friendly group."

◆

Four days into my urban expedition, I stood on the bustling sidewalk, breathing in the air around me. Though mixed with exhaust and other city smells I didn't particularly want to identify, the air had an underlying quality that was unmistakably autumn. Was it the temperature, the essence of it rather than the smell itself? That was it, the similarity. The air didn't smell like home, but it certainly felt like home.

It had been the perfect day, and I hadn't even been here a week. The secret had been the morning runs. Why didn't I realize that the very thing that calmed me, that focused and sustained me in Oregon would do the same in this intriguing, stimulating foreign land called Manhattan? With my now-daily routine of run, shower, and coffee with the locals at Out of the World Espresso, each day had unfolded with enthusiastic energy. I hadn't heard from Julie Andrews once.

Here I was, standing outside a Chelsea gallery like a New Yorker, I thought, taking my share of this city. I reviewed the Kara Walker exhibit I had pored over for the last few hours in the Sikkema Gallery, absorbing the vivacious color, the airy feeling achieved with tiny brush-strokes. My discussion with the gallery's owner was lively, spirited. Did I expose my utter shock when he actually knew of my tiny little enter-prise in the "Wild, Wild West," as he had referred to it?

I couldn't help but ask. "You've heard of my gallery?"

His smile was patient, with just a hint of attitude. "Well, dear, I do try to keep up. It's my responsibility to keep tabs on all aspects of the art world, even those a continent away." He then leaned into me, his expression softer, friendlier. "To be perfectly honest with you, a friend of mine was in Ashland to attend your Shakespeare festival, which he said was surprisingly good. We New Yorkers are a bit spoiled, you know. But it was he who happened upon your gallery. You need to understand that my friend has an excellent eye for art. So naturally, I was curious. I looked up your website and found it rather fascinating that such an isolated gallery would carry such quality pieces. Kudos to you. Now tell me, what brings you to our little corner of the world?"

I found that I had relaxed into his manner. We continued to chat for a few minutes. He referred me to his favorite "must-see" galleries and exhibits. Little did he know how much I secretly appreciated our conversation. I was taking New York, maybe just one tiny little piece at a time, but it still felt awfully good.

Fortified by the memory of this simple interaction, I started toward the curb to hail a taxi, something that, like everything else, just days before had been far too intimidating. Those first couple of days, I'd leave the hotel in a cab (figuring a buck was well worth having the doorman flag down a ride) but would then spend the rest of the day on foot, afraid to try the cab grab by myself. Yet somewhere around that odd little still life in the MOMA, I decided that dodging cabs had to go, especially since I had a vague thought that if I kept avoiding them, I ran the risk of meeting up with Julie and that obnoxious tune again. "Just fake it," I could hear Barb saying to me the last night before I left. "In the bedroom or on the sidewalks of New York, it will get you what you want, out from under being stranded!"

So, like an accomplished actor in one of Barb's plays, I had taken a moment to study the art of hailing a taxi, the position of the arm, the flick of the wrist. And then, before any suicide-promoting melodies could lodge in my brain, I threw out my arm. Success was mine in a matter of seconds. Riding back to the hotel, I savored the sweet victory.

Forty-eight hours later, I now approached the task like a seasoned veteran. One step off the curb—careful to watch for other cars, as I'd nearly been creamed the day before from failing to include that little detail—shoulders back, arm fully extended, act as if you've done this a million times before, and be patient.

But today was taking longer. A lot longer, and I momentarily questioned my technique. "Perhaps they do it differently here in Chelsea," I thought, having realized there were differences, some subtle, some glaring, in neighborhoods of this vast island population. I stared at the traffic again, yellow ribbons of cabs squeezing through the narrow streets when it hit me: it was rush hour, and taxi demand was at its peak. It was reassuring to discover it wasn't my faulty technique. I waved my hand and settled in for a longer wait.

Within minutes, a cab coming through the intersection saw me and sharply changed direction to pull over to the curb. (I realized later that I had actually squealed over my success and hoped no one had heard me.) I collected my bag of souvenirs, readying myself for the quick entry. But when I looked up again, the taxi had stopped short. I had been duped—he was stopping for a man who had taken up the taxi-hailing position fifteen feet ahead of me.

"No fair," I thought, but then I immediately realized I had said it out loud and in an obviously frustrated voice. About to get in the taxi, the man turned abruptly to look at me. Another Barbism entered my consciousness: "Prepare yourself. People will yell at you for no apparent reason; it's sort of a civic sport. Just yell back. It feels pretty good."

But he wasn't yelling. In fact, his tone was warm, even amicable.

"Oh, I'm sorry. I didn't see you there. You're right, very bad form. Here, it's yours." He made a gallant gesture with his arm, a knight ushering in the damsel. I wanted to crawl down the nearest manhole, suddenly feeling very much out of my league.

"Oh no, you go ahead. There'll be another one along." I'm dying, right here, right now, twelve years old if a day. Was my face red? I looked back into the mass of cars and pretended to concentrate on the task at hand.

"Are you going uptown?" he called. "We can share. Come on, get in or we'll both be out of luck."

I started for the taxi like the good little girl I had been trained to be. The quite proper man stood back and held the door. Maneuvering my bags and purse, I crawled into the cab, my entrance ungainly and amateurish. I collapsed onto the weathered seat with an audible thud. What would Barb think? Would she approve or think I had just made a huge tactical error? What if this guy was a leech? What if this was some well-orchestrated scam? I could see the headline: "Con Artist and Cab Driver Team Up to Rip Off Naive Middle-Aged Tourist." Barb's going to kill me if he doesn't first. My palms started sweating. I'd say nothing, pretend I didn't speak English. No, I'd already blown that. Maybe go with ticked off, give him the cold shoulder and get out as soon as I could.

The door slammed shut. He gave the driver his address and then turned to me.

"Where are you going?" A simple question, really nothing too threatening there.

I sputtered out the hotel address, and it actually sounded a little foreign, all garbled up in a Garbo sort of way. Funny what adrenaline could do. I stared out of the window, feigning disinterest, a Manhattan ice queen, only to quickly discover that a lifetime of good manners could outvote my survival instincts in a heartbeat. How could I not acknowledge the man sitting twenty inches away from me?

I slowly looked over at him. My first realization? He barely fit inside the back of the cab, his long legs nearly resting under his chin, like an NBA player courtside, perched on those tiny little folding chairs.

He looked quite uncomfortable and very comical, like one of the sur-realistic prints I'd seen earlier in the day. He caught my expression.

"Yeah, I know. You should see what I used to do on planes in the early days of my career. A regular contortionist. I seriously considered life in the circus, but those carnie types scared me." He paused, read-justing his lean frame in the cramped space. Sticking out his hand, he introduced himself.

"Hi, I'm Stephen Brunswick."

His friendliness took me by surprise. Though rattled, I managed to shake his hand.

"Oh, I'm Lee MacPhearson. Thanks for the ride."

"No problem. Sorry I 'took cuts' on you. My mother must be roll-ing over in her grave. She was determined to raise a gentleman, and instead she got me. I always forget how tough it is to get a cab in this town during rush hour. You'd think I'd learn, but I got so wrapped up in what I was doing, time got away from me. It usually does." He was as comfortable with himself as he was uncomfortable in the inadequate space. He continued. "So, you live on the West Side by Columbus? Nice neighborhood."

I was pleased, as though I had aced a test, passing as a local. But, as always, it was the truth that came spilling out of my mouth.

"Oh no, I live in Oregon. I'm just here on business." I stumbled over the last word, feeling a fraud. When I actually did business, it was in those relaxed West Coast cities of Portland, maybe Seattle or San Francisco. And, to be honest, even when I was traveling throughout the West, I never thought of myself as "on business." And now, to throw that phrase out, in this arena? Barb would be doubled over laughing by this point in the story.

"Really? I assumed you were a native. What sort of business are you in?"

Horns blared around us, and I realized we were at a standstill. Our driver was cursing under his breath, and I struggled to recognize the language. I caught my backseat companion staring at me.

"Sorry," I offered, "every time I get in a cab, I'm curious about what particular nationality I'm going to experience. I like that about New York."

Liquid awkward was again running through my veins. We weren't going anywhere fast; no one seemed to be. I surveyed my situation. If he made one false move, I could make a run for it, safe in the middle of four gridlocked lanes of traffic. My hand was poised on the door handle, like a gunslinger in the Old West with an itchy trigger finger; I was ready for the bad guy to make his move.

"To answer to your question, I own a small gallery in Ashland, Oregon, which, by New York standards, is an itsy-bitsy town in the middle of nowhere. I'm sure it's smaller than Central Park."

"Ashland, really? Not possible." His surprise filled the crowded backseat. "I've been to Ashland. It was years ago, but the plays were exceptional. I remember being struck by how beautiful the sets were. Good acting too. And nice people, friendly. A great town. You're lucky to live there. What's your gallery?"

"Mad Dog, a couple of blocks over from the theater. Tiny little place… "

He interrupted me. "Sorry, but is it in a renovated storefront, across from the best bakery in the world?" I nodded yes.

"That's yours? I can't believe this. I bought a small watercolor from you, by René Masterson. Do you remember that show? An exquisite landscape. It hangs in my office and often makes me wonder why I don't get out of city life. I'm up in Boston—an attorney who has somehow made a living representing artists. Well, it's probably no surprise to you. They typically don't have much business sense. Creative, yes; contract oriented, no way. Huh, small world, isn't it?"

It was all a little surreal—me, the cab, a handsome man who had actually bought something from my gallery an entire solar system away. The current circumstances had my head spinning. I could hardly wait to tell Barb. Finally, I found my voice.

"Indeed, small world. Feels about the size of a stamp at the moment."

I concentrated on maintaining a cool and casual demeanor, hoping that he wouldn't be able to see my heart pounding out of my chest. I pushed on.

"Yes, René is a fine artist. Her use of color surpasses most landscape artists." Oh my God, what crap! Worse yet, the drivel kept coming. "She paints right up to the edge of reality, using color as Mother Nature would on a perfect day." Please, God, make me disappear right now. I decided on a quick change of course: trying to relax and be myself.

"You might be interested to know that she's also a very nice old lady and makes the best apple cobbler in the county."

He laughed. "Ha! I recall being very pleased with the information the man in your gallery gave me when I purchased the painting, but he didn't mention her culinary skills."

So that's why I didn't remember him—I didn't sell him the painting. For some reason, that realization made me feel better. It was awful to think that I couldn't recall someone so engaging… and tall and, good God, handsome. Mysteriously fortified, I made an attempt to carry my end of the conversation.

"Well, I'm not surprised. You met Tom, a fine artist himself. At work, he's all business, but off the job, he's enjoyed his share of René's cobblers." The driver cursed out loud, and we both laughed.

It was then that his utterly cramped position truly registered.

"Here, turn your legs this way," I offered, moving my bags under my legs so there would be more room. "I have some experience with trying to fit into small spaces."

His face seemed to relax.

"Thanks, I was starting to seize up." He repositioned himself and settled into the corner of the cab. "Yeah, when I turned and saw you on the street, it struck me that I wasn't looking very far down at you. Not my usual experience."

It was at that exact moment that I realized I was having a rather different conversation with this stranger. Somewhere in the back of my mind it felt vaguely familiar, this kind of easygoing chatter. It was certainly friendly and comfortable. That was it—this lanky Bostonian seemed intent on making the most out of the traffic jam by getting to know me. And while not openly flirtatious, some kind of juicy energy was darting around the backseat with us. It was fascinating, incredible, even a little schoolgirl-crazy making. I actually felt it through my pores. Barb would love it, a true romance novel moment.

Then, wham, zing, and reality hit me upside the head. Was I actually thinking these thoughts? Time to regroup. I silently grabbed hold of my senses, put them in a headlock. Butt squarely on seat? Check. Dress pulled over knees? Check. All buttons fastened? Check. Was this ride merely more fodder for Barb? Check! She'd howl over this one. Silly me.

But the gods were with me that day. What should have been a fifteen-minute ride took nearly an hour. By the time we reached my hotel, I knew quite a bit about my Boston cab companion: divorced ("since the beginning of time" was how he put it); father of two grown children, a daughter in medical school, his son a lieutenant in the navy.

"I don't begin to understand that decision," he volunteered. "I'm a Vietnam veteran who thought I'd taught my children every possible lesson about the perils of a military career, but I guess only one of them was listening."

Having grown up in the Midwest, he fled the confines of "cornfields and hog-calling contests" as soon as he graduated from high school. Settling in Boston after law school, he had become interested in representing artists because he was "a closet artist, you know the type, the ones who paint but don't have the talent or the guts to show anyone." He admired and appreciated the world of art, and he felt drawn to representing "the poor souls who could create beauty and then get ripped off because the business of art is very different from the business of creating art." His career had been long and satisfying.

And then we were at my hotel. As my pimple-faced doorman opened the cab door, Stephen unfolded himself and stepped out onto the curb. He turned back toward the cab and offered me his hand. The gesture caught me completely off guard. I reacted like he had unzipped his fly and whipped out his Johnson. I was a deer in the headlights, frozen, waiting for the impact. Finally, Barb's voice screeched in my head: "It's just a hand, offered in a thoughtful gesture. Take it, stupid. Move." And I did.

Once on the curb, I was in back in full awkward overload. It was a scene in a bad movie, one in which a starlet is cast in a role far beyond her range. I stumbled for money to pay my share of the ride, realizing that this was the worst possible time for me to admit I was mathematically challenged.

"Just round up," I thought, rather than try and figure out my share plus tip. I couldn't do this without a calculator let alone under fire. Why didn't I pay better attention in the fourth grade? It all comes back to haunt you. Nonsense numbers raced through my brain. Perhaps I'd be saved. Spontaneous combustion, where are you when I need you? Suddenly, I realized Stephen was talking, interrupting my private panic attack.

"Please, put that away. It's my treat. I enjoyed having the company."

"Oh, thank you," said the twelve-year-old girl masquerading as a middle-aged woman of the world. Keep the small talk going for just a few more minutes.

"It's been a pleasure getting to know you," I said.

How dorky was that? I put out my hand for a cordial handshake. Stephen took my hand firmly in his. "I'm sorry there wasn't more traffic. I'll look you up next time I'm in Ashland."

I tried to extricate myself from his grasp, but it was taking some effort. He didn't seem to want to let go. "Maybe he really is a wacko," I wondered to myself, but the moment called for confidence. I managed a quick, "Yes, you do that," and headed straight for the revolving door, hoping my timing was right, that I'd sail into position, magically meld with the revolutions of the glass and steel.

I didn't dare look back, choosing instead to count all thirty-seven steps to the elevators. When the doors finally opened, I lurched forward and nearly knocked over an elderly couple on their way out. Glowering at me, they mumbled their displeasure in thick German.

"Lo siento," I offered.

The doors shut, and I burst out laughing. Why had I apologized in Spanish? That made no sense at all. Well, at least they wouldn't think I was a rude American.

The elevator raced to the seventh floor, but my belly stayed a floor or two behind. When I was finally deposited on number seven, I stumbled into the hall. Realizing I was actually a little disoriented, I quickly straightened up and made sure no one was there to witness my bizarre behavior. "Get a grip, woman, it was only a taxi ride," I thought to myself.

But as I opened the door to my room, I thought about what a ride it had been. A ride with a *GQ* magazine, knockout-handsome stranger who (I finally entertained the possibility) thought I was interesting and perhaps even a little attractive. It was a ride with an intelligent man who could talk art. Better yet, he seemed to be able to talk emotions, a rarity in my experience. It was a ride that allowed me a freedom I hadn't felt in nearly thirty years. I flopped down on the bed and savored the moment, the lights from the surrounding buildings shining in the clear night.

Just then, the phone rang, jerking me back to reality. I hated the ringing. Couldn't I hold on to my fantasies for just a little while longer? What was worse was that it was probably Brian or the kids. I didn't want to speak to any of them at the moment, especially Brian. Maybe I should let it ring. I considered that option for a split second but no longer because the thought delivered a tsunami of guilt. I dove for the phone, hoping I'd answered in time.

"Hello?"

"Hi. I was beginning to wonder if you had gotten lost between the curb and your room," Stephen joked.

I was speechless.

"Hello, Lee? This is Stephen, are you there?"

I was there all right, but not there at all.

"Yes. Hi, I'm here. I was just caught off guard a little. Where are you?"

"I'm in the lobby. Don't worry. I'm not some weird stalker or anything. I just got a couple of blocks up Columbus Street, and it seemed foolish that we both needed dinner and we were both going to be eating alone. I thought we might as well have some great food and continue our conversation." He stopped, then quickly continued when I didn't respond.

"Sorry. Perhaps I'm being too bold. It wouldn't be the first time someone has accused me of pit bull behavior."

I caught my smiling reflection in the mirror. But before I could think of what to say, Stephen was speaking again.

"I've put you on the spot; forgive me. I wasn't any better at this at sixteen." His discomfort brought me out of mine.

"No, no apologies necessary," I finally said. "The silence you hear is me shifting gears, from dinner alone to dinner with a friend. Give me a minute to freshen up, and I'll be right down." I'd done it again. Something entirely moronic had found its way from my brain out of my mouth, and now it hung in the air like the smell of bad cheese. Freshen up? What the hell did that mean?

But the next thing that happened completely floored me. He bought it.

"Great." He sounded pleased. "I'll be sitting in one of those chairs that looks like it's waiting for Louis the Fourteenth to arrive."

Was I really going to do this? Head out into the night with a complete stranger in the middle of Manhattan? Was I nuts? Apparently so. I stared at the woman in the mirror, not entirely sure who she was at the moment. This was no time for heavy thinking or I'd chicken out. Quickly running a brush through my hair, I added a fresh layer of lipstick, popped in a breath mint, and headed off to the lobby, hoping I wouldn't encounter the grumpy Germans on my way down. My ability to maintain the current mood was limited. See them, and anything might happen.

Stephen stood as I approached him. The short walk from elevator to Louis the Fourteenth gave me a socially acceptable way to finally have a good look at him. He had perfect posture; his clothes were impeccable. I wondered how much his haircut cost, knowing the razor cut must have taken place in a well-appointed salon. And my, how his shoes glistened from a recent polishing. Not the kind of man seen wandering around Ashland. Ever. This was fun already!

He stuck out his hand to me, as if we were meeting for the first time. This time I didn't panic. I took his hand, enjoying his strong grip, relieved it wasn't one of those namby-pamby handshakes most men offer women. When I looked up from our hands, I realized he was speaking.

"… since it is still early, I wonder if we could stop by The Plaza so I can drop off my briefcase, maybe have a drink at the Oyster Bar. Do you like that lounge? I've been accused of being a creature of habit. Maybe that's true. I liked The Plaza twenty years ago, and I like it now. But after a long day in this city, the Oyster Bar is relaxing. It's pretty civilized there, calm." He laughed and continued, "I'd bet my daughter would translate that into 'boring.' She's right. No hip, loud, swinging hot spot for her old dad. But I don't need to call the shots; it's just convenient. Maybe you have a favorite; is there another place you'd prefer? I'm all about flexibility." He waited for my response.

I was still trying to take in the scene, watching myself from a place somewhere up around the ceiling, an out-of-body moment. He was trying to read what must have been an odd expression plastered on my face, and he unfortunately read it all wrong.

"Trust me, I'm not trying to get you to my hotel! I was thinking I could order us a couple of drinks and ask your indulgence while I ran my briefcase up to my room. Hell, I'll just get a bellman to run it up so you won't have to wait alone. A major gaffe. Here I am stepping all over your toes, and we haven't even made it out of the lobby." He stared directly into my eyes, waiting for me to say something.

I quickly reassured him.

"You didn't step on my toes at all. If you are a wild crazy man, I think you're running a little low on sinister. No, I was just thinking that I like the way my evening is unfolding."

I couldn't believe I'd said that out loud. But it was true. I was happily settling into an adventure and all it offered. My old farmhouse on the hill was a full continent away. What would I be doing right now if I were home? Eating a peanut butter and jelly sandwich and reading the newspaper? Maybe channel surfing or listening to Barb bellyache about some aspect of her overburdened life? Deleting the latest email lecture from Sean about how I was screwing up everyone's lives? No, drinks at the Oyster Bar sounded like an excellent plan.

"Shall we?" I asked.

Over the best dirty martini I ever tasted, Stephen wondered if I was in the mood for Spanish "cuisine," a word he used naturally, without a hint of pomposity. I admitted that such fare was completely foreign to me, and he lit up.

"You'll love it. I promise. There's a wonderful little Midtown place. I don't know if a martini and sangria would clash—I hope not. They make the best sangria in town. And wait until you taste their tapas."

Everything about Solera's—the staff, the food, even the color of paint on the walls—was rich, warm, and inviting. My first tentative sip of the sangria was surprisingly smooth. The combination of red wine, brandy, citrus fruits, sugar, and sparkling soda warmed my tongue and went down far too easily. A few sips later, I recognized that nearly imperceptible shift in my physiology. I had always been a cheap drunk—one glass would be enough; another would put me at risk of behaving outlandishly. Trouble was, I was dying for the experience another layer of alcohol would permit, but I was terrified of the fallout. I nursed my glass.

The appetizers were a parade of exotic flavors—patatas bravas, espuma, piquillo peppers, goat cheese, and ham. I completely filled my belly with the tapas and had to pass on an entrée, too full to even think about more food. I leaned back in the chair, happy to watch Stephen savor his paella, rich with lobster, scallops, muscles, and shrimp. He insisted I have at least one bite and brought a forkful of the delectable morsels to my mouth. It was an intimacy that threw me off.

"Maybe martinis and sangria really do clash," I thought as the paella worked its way over my taste buds. I was having too much fun.

We stayed long after dinner, a Kahlúa and coffee my dessert. Conversation never lagged for a moment. It was easy, full of intellectually stimulating topics and delightfully simple observations that each of us had about the crazy world. The banter was also quite silly. We laughed at the same things.

"It's not often that I meet someone with the same warped sense of humor," Stephen offered as we made our way back to my hotel in a cab. He looked out of his window and then turned directly toward me.

"Listen, tomorrow's Saturday—I'm not working and neither are you. I think we should go over to the botanical gardens in Brooklyn—not a whole lot happening this time of year, but the leaves will be beautiful, and there's always something in the conservatory. How about it? What time are you done with your run? We can have some breakfast and make a day of it."

I couldn't decide which was more surprising, his invitation or the hopeful look on his face. I knew I needed to say something; leaving the air empty for too long would lead him to another erroneous assumption. This man seemed to appreciate quick, honest answers. As I started to answer him, it struck me how lovely it was to find myself speaking my mind so easily.

"Really? That sounds great." I paused and took a breath. "But I have to admit that I'm a little thrown off by the invitation."

"Don't be," he said. "I've just had a very satisfying evening. More than that, it's been downright great. Look, we're both here, let's enjoy ourselves. Deal?"

"Deal," I agreed.

We had reached the hotel. He exited first, offering his hand to me as he had earlier in the evening. This time, I didn't panic. Instead I took his steady hand and enjoyed its strength. But by the time I was actually standing next to him on the sidewalk, panic returned, and my mind went wild. "Holy crap, what if he tries to kiss me?" I thought.

Words finally stumbled out of my mouth.

"I've had a wonderful evening. Thanks, and I'll meet you at ten, in the lobby." I tried to sound casual and confident, though I felt neither. "Look for me in the Louis the Fourteenth chair. Okay?"

I used my long legs to start for the door, knowing that in two strides I would be out of range.

"I'll be there," he called after me. "And, for the record, that was one fast getaway."

I heard him laugh, but I knew better than to look back while trying to maneuver the revolving door. The chance of taking the door in the face or stumbling onto the marble floor upon exit was too great. I concentrated on matching my steps to the revolutions, grateful I'd limited my alcohol intake. When safely inside, I finally turned to wave. His taxi was gone. The adrenaline rush gave way to disappointment.

I lay in bed that night thinking about my evening. "So, am I married even though I haven't lived with my husband for two years? Technically, yes. Well, really, yes, since we still have a marriage license to prove it, even if I haven't been able to find it for nearly thirty years. Wonder if that was an omen? But Brian was the one who wanted his freedom, the women, the sex." I was working myself up to a pretty solid case of self-righteous justification for how I had spent my evening.

In the dark, I spoke to the ceiling. "A taxi ride, a dinner. Tomorrow the botanical gardens. It doesn't get any more benign that that."

Suddenly, I realized I had wandered into some very nasty memories, like the night Brian admitted he had actually had a date with someone, the instant rage I had felt, the desperate sorrow that had ridden its heels. Or the time our cars passed on the road, he with a young woman in his truck who looked about the same age as his daughter-in-law. For a flash, I had considered turning around and slamming into both of them at about a hundred miles per hour.

But this time, instead of sliding into a black hole as I had done so many times before, the images seemed to fortify me.

"Screw it," I announced to the chandelier. "If Brian can have his wanderings, so can I."

Saturday was the botanical gardens. Sunday was a drive to Long Island. Monday night, music at a little club on the West Side and dinner. Our time was easy and relaxed, yet lively. I found it alarming at times. More than once, I told myself to stop analyzing and just enjoy myself.

But that was the problem: I was enjoying myself far too much.

Alone at night in my hotel room, I was filled with doubt, desperate to call Barb. I resisted, fearing a bona fide conversation with my best friend would make everything all too real. The magic would be squashed. I would be sent back to the safety of my former self.

No. It was better to just take each encounter as my private little escape. I was dancing through another world, another life, which proved to be much of the enjoyment. It felt like a huge game of dress up. I was living someone else's life, and it was great fun. The places we explored fascinated me. My brain was fully engaged, and I found our conversations exhilarating. The time together was rich.

I savored the way Stephen attended to me. He had the most endearing way of waiting for me to catch up to him in a museum, anxious to share a painting with me, eager to hear my reactions. He was always holding the door open or pulling out my chair. I was so accustomed to slogging my way through life, and I wondered why I had always equated being independent with opening a door for myself.

One night, in the dark privacy of my hotel room, I finally admitted that I loved the way he looked at me when he thought I wouldn't notice. Once this was out in the open, I finally allowed myself to realize that Stephen seemed to actually like me, that he found me attractive, interesting, funny. The realization sent my endorphins flying. Sleep didn't come for hours.

But every night at the curb in front of my hotel, I was reduced to adolescent panic, fearing a kiss yet curious about what a brand-new pair of lips would feel like on mine. My confusion had not been lost on Stephen. He'd been wise to me since our second dinner together. Hugging me, he had said, "I realize you're more than a little gun-shy, so I'll be a gentleman and not pressure you for anything more." He gave me another gentle squeeze and whispered in my ear, "Just know that it'll take effort."

I had lingered, aware of his cashmere sports coat against my cheek, appreciating the feel of my head under his chin, something I hadn't felt since I was a teenager. It was oddly comforting. I finally looked up to him. "Thanks. Sorry, but it seems to be the way it is."

We continued to meet each day, at out-of-the way galleries I never would have known about and for superb lunches and delicious dinners at perfect little restaurants. One day, at Stephen's insistence, we even went to the New York Public Library. He explained, "Anyone who reads like you do needs to just go sit there and absorb. The wood oozes literature. Millions of thoughts seem to float in the air. You can feel the place through every pore."

His passion was appealing. I smiled at his enthusiasm.

"You think I'm joking? Ha, I'll show you." And he did. Months later, I could still feel the weathered leather on my back, hear the murmurs around me, sense the words hanging in the air. It had been one of my favorite experiences of the entire trip.

It was on our last night together, over a delightful Turkish dinner, that Stephen finally asked me about my marriage. I looked at him, wishing he had never brought up the topic.

"You really want to know?"

He nodded his head.

"Well, most of it was pretty darned good. Not as good as this goat cheese, however." I took a bite. "And in the end, it was awful." I looked down at my food. "The marriage, not the cheese."

Stephen encouraged me to continue. "It seems like you've told me pretty much everything about your life—your kids, your profession, even the ducks on your pond, but you haven't said a word about your husband. Bad topic?"

"Not one I would put up against my pistachio-stuffed quail here. Are you sure you don't just want to talk about this delectable dinner we're having?" He was not to be dissuaded. I caved.

"I don't know what to say about Brian. I guess it's because this trip was supposed to be about me and what I wanted and who I thought I might be as a single woman. I've purposely tried not to think about him. He's not a bad man, don't get me wrong. He's actually a wonderful man—very smart, great father, so devoted to his students, and for all those years, a truly wonderful husband."

"But in spite of all that, he still wanted his freedom?" Stephen asked, recalling the implication I had made a few days before.

"Well, yes, and I gave it to him. Actually, that's not entirely true. I dragged him to a marriage counselor and looked for every opportunity to make him feel guilty." I looked at the poor little skeleton of the bird on my plate. My appetite was slipping away.

"And then, just when he was ready to come back and make a go of it, I realized that freedom had tremendous appeal for me. Funny, he broke my heart and then I broke his." I aimed for the last few bites of garlic mashed potatoes, determined to not have the evening ruined.

Right at that moment, the busboy arrived at the table to refill our water glasses. I was grateful for the distraction and tried another bite of the quail. It tasted good again. Nodding my thanks to the attentive young man, I looked at Stephen.

"It was odd. One day, truly for no apparent reason, it occurred to me that maybe I should step outside my comfort zone and define myself and my life in a different way. I briefly considered the possibility that I was having a breakdown because the idea was so completely alien to me. I'd spent so many years doing things by the book, rarely risking. Oh, I guess I ventured out with my business, the building and all, but that's been the sum total of life on the edge for me. The years with the kids, the responsibilities of a dedicated community member, the joys of a faculty wife—I got sick and tired of doing the right thing, the expected thing."

I thought another moment. "But old habits die hard, I suppose. Look at how I've been with you every night at the curb—by the book, scurrying to the safety of my room! Miss Manners would be proud." I laughed at myself and Stephen joined me, which made his next question a complete surprise.

"When do I get to come to Ashland for a visit?"

Ashland. In one word I was dragged back into a reality that I had been trying to fight off for the last ten days.

"Frankly, Stephen, I can't even fathom that. You, in my neck of the woods? As out of place as finding my old one-eyed pug tied up to a lamppost outside this restaurant."

He was dumbfounded.

"You have a one-eyed pug?"

"Had one. Miss Piggy. It's a long story." Stephen settled back in his chair and nodded for me to go on. I put down my fork.

"I'll give you the short version. It was quite a few years ago when, from out of nowhere, this mangy canine wandered up to the back door. Immediately, the four young members of the MacPhearson Rescue Squad got her food and water. When I came home an hour later, Sean ran out to meet me and said we had to 'get the new dog to the vet right away because her eyeball popped out.' Just then, Sammy carried the pathetic beast out from the kitchen. Sean wasn't lying. To put it bluntly, she was the ugliest son of a bitch dog I'd ever seen—even the good eye was awful. Think Marty Feldman with crooked teeth and a massive head. But the kids were adamant. How could I say no? So I piled all of them into my SUV, threw the one-eyed wonder into the back, and headed off to town. The vet diagnosed her as having proptosis, apparently a not-so-uncommon condition in pug land. Their eyes really can pop out of their sockets. Kind of disgusting, actually. After surgery, a variety of shots, and a thorough disinfecting, she was back among us. Cost us a fortune. Miss Piggy lived for years; she was ugly as ever, snored like a sailor, and was the most loyal critter of the entire menagerie."

Stephen was having difficulty containing his laughter. "The image—Miss Piggy, the one-eyed pug! What a great life you have given your kids. Didn't miss a beat, huh? Everybody in the car and off we go."

"I imagine the Bostonian children under your roof fared pretty well?"

His mood shifted with my question.

"I'd like to think they did, but I have major regrets. Too much work, the traveling, not enough family time. They were such tender souls when we divorced. I think it could have been a whole lot better for them. Being a weekend dad was certainly not in my plan, but we all tried to make the best of it." He took a bite of his dinner and turned the conversation back on me. "However, I believe we were talking about you, remember?"

"What's to say?" I paused, then inhaled deeply. "Bottom line? I don't know what I'm doing in my life. I can't imagine you in Ashland. I don't even know how I'd walk down the street with you. It's a tiny town, and people know me, my situation. You can't imagine how many necks would be craning to get a better look at the tall handsome stranger in town."

"But do you want me to come out?" he asked. "That's what I want to know. What do you want to do next?" There was that direct approach that I had come to enjoy so much.

We sat in silence as I tried to honestly consider my answer. It didn't get any riskier than this. Finally, I spoke.

"What do I want to do next? I want to stay in this world of museums and international delicacies and strong hands that help me from cabs. I want these movie moments to never end, me with the handsome stranger, swept off my feet. Cue the orchestra! You ask me what do I want to do next? Honestly? Talk about the movies—what I really want to do next is go back to the hotel and make mad, passionate love. Little old me between six hundred–count Egyptian cotton, lost in luscious, forbidden sex, rolling around like a couple of kids. Just light the bed on fire." I took a deep breath. Stephen's face was full of hope. I needed to get to the point.

"The reality is, I can't do that and we won't do that any more than I'll invite you to come to Ashland."

11

*B*arb and I had once visited an old, crusty psychic. Heavy on the eyeliner and rouge and light on accuracy, the woman had predicted, among other things, that I would enter local politics. Wrong. But the slightly cross-eyed soothsayer had also warned me, "No matter what, my dear, be careful what you ask for."

Apparently, the old broad had some talent, because in at least one situation, she was right on the money. I had told Stephen not to call, and he hadn't.

It had been four weeks since my return from New York, and here I was, alone on this churning gray morning. I stood in my cold kitchen sipping coffee. Through the window I could see the last of the robins scurry around for unsuspecting worms. No Stephen. Was this really what I wanted?

Reentry into my Ashland life had been difficult, beginning with the flight home. I cried most of the way. The nice little old lady sitting in the next seat offered me her hand-embroidered hankie.

"I've met some very unhappy people on planes," she mused. "Odd, isn't it, that happy people take trains, but the sad ones take to the air. Don't try to talk, honey. Let's just get a couple of cocktails down you, and you'll feel much better."

Barb was there to pick me up at the airport.

"What the hell is the matter with you?" she asked as soon as she saw me.

I filled her in on how astonishingly good I had felt in New York: the liberation, my boundless energy. And how it was a colossal shame that I had to leave it all behind and come home to my boring, tedious, dumb, sorry-ass life in the middle of nowhere. What I never mentioned was word one about Stephen, having decided that he was the last thing I would tell another living soul about. Was it guilt or bone-chilling embarrassment? Both.

"Great, just great. We send you off for a little adventure, and you come home a bigger mess than you were when you left." Barb pointed to my bag on the luggage carousel and stared at her red-eyed friend.

"Like I'm going to pick it up? Come on, let's get going before I have this baby right here." She turned and started for the door. "Nice scarf, by the way. Bloomie's?"

Later that night, she beamed when she opened the tiny rose jammies I had bought for the baby. She even tried on the Lilliputian knit hat covered with blossoms in all shades of pink. It sat like a miniature rosebush planted at a goofy angle atop her shiny black hair.

"This must have come from the Village?" she asked.

"Right. I thought of you two immediately." I reached into my bag. "And here's one for the mommy-to-be."

Barb ripped open the paper like a kid on her birthday. Out fell a cocoa-brown cashmere shawl. It cascaded over her swollen curves like chocolate syrup. She wrapped it around her shoulders and beamed. "It's so soft, velvet soft."

"These next few months, you just might find yourself up in the middle of the night a little, and I thought something luxurious to keep you warm would be good. Lesson number one of motherhood: Limit personal discomfort whenever you can because one thing's for sure, there will always be more. And here, one last thing." I pulled out the cheesecake I had hand-carried all the way home. "I'll get two forks."

Barb took one look at the offering, stretched her awkward frame to give me a hug, and burst into tears. Taking as much of her into my arms as I could, I returned the squeeze.

"Suck it up, Mommy. You're about to blow your tough-girl image," I warned her.

Each night, I wrote copious amounts in my journal. Each morning, I ran just as many miles. During both of these solitary pursuits, my obsession was the same: How do I hold onto the woman I had been in New York? Was I so locked into my life, my definition, my responsibilities that I couldn't shake things up just a little here at home? But how? What would that mean; what did I want to be different? The answers eluded me.

I waited a few days before calling Brian and suggesting we meet for dinner. He sounded thrilled to hear from me.

"I knew you were back and wondered when you'd finally call."

I felt the zinger right away but chose to let it pass. He also seemed a little disappointed that I suggested we meet at a restaurant.

"I'd be happy to bring over some Chinese," he had offered. But I didn't want him at the house—that was clear to me. After settling on the time and place, I hung up the phone feeling flat. Had I called out of guilt and nothing more? Could I sit across from him and not spend the entire time thinking about Stephen?

The night of the dinner, I looked at myself in the mirror—hair pulled back, slacks, and a nondescript sweater. "My Ashland look," I muttered. Suddenly, I found myself stripping down to my underwear and starting over with some of the clothes I had bought in New York— Gap jeans, red Anthropologie sweater, the Bloomie's scarf.

If it worked there, it can work here, I tried to convince myself. Out came the ponytail and on went some lipstick. I raced out the door before I could chicken out and revert to my old self.

The last-minute clothing crisis had made me late. Brian was already waiting when I arrived. As I walked over to the table, his face lit up. Rising to his feet, he surprised me by extending both hands in a warm greeting. But what really caught my attention was what his eyes were doing—checking me out from head to toe and all points in between. I quickly tried to recall the last time this had happened and came up empty. I couldn't help but smile.

"It looks like New York agreed with you. Pardon me if I'm out of line, but you look downright, well… ravishing."

Ravishing? Did the engineer just call me ravishing? I didn't even think he knew what that word meant, let alone how to use it. I took his hands and we shared a light hug that actually felt good.

Dinner was comfortable. More than that, it was fun. I volunteered to order the wine, "something I had in New York—a smooth Merlot I think you'll like." And he did. Conversation was surprisingly easy. The stories bubbled out of me. Brian seemed content to just listen. We lingered over coffee. Only then did the children come up.

"Sophie called in a panic over some paper, but we managed to solve the problem. She insisted I call you. I hope it was okay that I didn't. I know how much I've enjoyed some of my fishing trips and thought you should have the same time off."

I thanked him for his consideration. "Exactly the right move," I think I said, and, though difficult to admit, I told him I was a little glad she hadn't called.

"Does that make me a bad mom?" I wondered.

"Not at all," Brian reassured me. "I think what we're both trying to figure out is how to take care of them and ourselves at the same time."

Did he really just say that? It was mind-boggling.

As if by some unspoken agreement, we quickly moved on to other non-kid topics—work for Brian, his latest community recycling event, the weekend backpacking trip he had taken his students on, how Nightmare had managed to get locked out of the house one night and had howled "like a wolf in deep grief," according to Brian. The conversation was easy and comfortable, familiar as favorite socks yet somehow new. I was thoroughly enjoying myself.

Driving home that night, I allowed myself to feel good.

"I can choose to overanalyze this, choose to grumble about my life in Ashland or, as I did in New York, I can simply take the moments for what they are and go to sleep with a smile on my face." I wrote nothing in my journal that night, and I fell asleep more quickly than I had in months.

The ringing of the phone cut through my dreams. I shot up like someone desperately trying to escape from the dead.

"Hello?" I feared what was on the other end, my heart pounding in the stillness of the chilly night. The voice shot into my ears. It wasn't one of the kids. I relaxed a notch, only to ratchet back up in an instant. It was Barb.

"I... I... I think something is wrong. My water just broke. Well, I think it did, or I just peed the bed. It can't be my water, it's too soon. Shit, what do I do?"

I was suddenly very much awake.

"Are you having any pains? Is it rosy-colored?"

"Oh yeah, like I'm going to look at it. Gross. Pain? My belly feels heavy, but I think that may be from the package of Oreos I munched my way through while watching a really bad movie on the Oxygen Channel." The line went quiet. Then a barely audible, "Lee, I'm scared."

I was already out of bed and pulling on the clothes I had worn to dinner.

"Okay, either you call 911 or I do, but we're not taking any chances. On second thought, you call 911. I don't think I can get to your house before they do, so I'll meet you at the hospital... "

Barb interrupted me.

"No way, I'm not doing this without you. You promised to be with me. First thing, and now my birth coach is crapping out on me? I'll give you a seven-minute head start and then you'll all arrive in time to see who can get through my front door first. Seven minutes. GO!"

I was out the door and on the backcountry road before Barb had hung up the phone. I drove far too fast, but as a local who had traversed these back roads for a lifetime, I could practically take every dark corner with my eyes closed. I wondered if I could make it in seven minutes but then realized that knowing Barb, there wouldn't be a 911 call until my headlights were shining in the driveway of my friend's windows.

Barb was waiting for me in the front doorway. I quickly ushered her into the living room, nearly forcing her to lie down on the couch. Fortunately, the ambulance crew was right on my heels. They sprang into action, shouting questions, unloading equipment, and wheeling Barb into the ambulance. Before I knew it, they were whisking Barb off to an exam room in the hospital. As I raced in behind her, I suddenly appreciated the beauty of rural living—no gunshot wounds or gangland slashings to get in line behind.

The ER doctor looked about twelve years old, but she seemed to know her stuff.

"You're four centimeters dilated. Looks like you're going to have a baby tonight. Who's your obstetrician?"

For the first time in years, Barb was actually speechless. I jumped in.

"But she's only at thirty-five weeks. Her OB is Dr. Simpson. How fast do you think she can get here?"

With this news, the young woman clicked into high gear.

"Well, it would be best if we could get this baby to hang tight for a few more weeks. Excuse me." And she disappeared behind the curtain.

In the end, the baby didn't wait. Barb gave birth just before dawn. Her delivery was fast, hard, and deafening. But what was even more shocking was what happened when the slippery bundle made her entrance: there was no spontaneous baby bray. With doctor and nurses huddled between Barb's legs, the handoff was instant. A nurse whisked the tiny, limp infant over to a bassinet, placing her under the warming lights. Two nurses and their four hands began rubbing the baby far too vigorously, I thought. It was difficult to see what was going on. Adults surrounded Barb's daughter in a protective ring as the on-call pediatrician began the exam. Barb craned her neck to see what was happening.

"Is she all right? Is she breathing?" The only sound in the room was whisper-soft squeaks finding their way out of the scrawny, fifteen-second-old baby. It was too much for Barb.

"Goddamn it, somebody tell me, is she going to die?" Barb's questions filled the silent room and the minds of everyone present. Already in love, she called out to her struggling daughter, "I'm here, Lily. Oka-san is right here."

One week after that terrifying night, Lily was getting sprung from the NICU. As the pediatrician signed the baby's discharge papers, she offered reassuring praise to the new mother: "I think you have yourself one tough little cookie." Barb, with precious Lily secure in her arms, nodded in agreement and put out her hand to the physician.

"Thanks. I'm not sure how you did it, but you managed to take care of both of us this last week. Kind of amazing and very much appreciated."

With that, we walked out into the fresh air. Barb wrangled her sleeping daughter into the car seat, grumbling the entire time about "baby torture," and off we went. The new mother, wearing her brand-new suit of maternal worry, looked over the backseat every thirty seconds to make sure her daughter was okay. (Admittedly, I found myself driving with great caution, so aware was I of my tiny, beloved passenger.) Finally realizing Lily was very sound asleep, Barb whispered, "Hallelujah, we're going home!"

"Home" meant my farmhouse. Though not the original plan, sharing my place with Barb after her disastrous introduction to motherhood was the logical choice. Barb accepted the offer with gracious enthusiasm, but not for a moment did she forget my newfound independence.

"We'll stay long enough for me to learn the front from the back of a diaper," she insisted, going on to admit that she had once again put Lily's diaper on backward. "The nurses think it's hysterical. I think it's pathetic. Tell me this will get easier?"

But I knew it would only get harder once Lily left the hospital, so I was glad to offer a roof to mother and child during this life-altering transition. Besides, Christmas was just a few weeks away, and the sentiment of the holiday seemed to call out for people in the house.

When we all arrived at the farm, the first thing Barb did was to stop on the porch and show Lily the view.

"See, sweetie, there's the pond, just like I told you. Yeah, it looks a little bleak now, but wait until next spring. You can come out here to visit Auntie Lee-Lee, and she's just crazy enough to pack you around and show you all the wildflowers. Maybe the ducks will be back by then. Wait until you hear about the ducks. They're mystics! Consider this your home away from home!" With that, mother and child disappeared inside for a very long nap.

We three females settled into a fairly comfortable routine. Barb, the natural night owl, was happy to take night feedings. Though I would wake when Lily cried in the night, I'd stay put, rolling over to listen to the sweet sounds of Barb's comforting murmurs to her hungry daughter. Then, with years of morning routines embedded into my brain, I'd be wide awake and raring to go when the sun came up and Lily started howling for her breakfast. It was a good fit for all three of us. By the end of the first week, Barb pointed out that she hadn't "screwed up on the diaper thing even once" since leaving the hospital. "Maybe I'll get the hang of this yet."

Plenty of people had been by to meet the baby—mostly a steady stream of theater friends, each bearing a wildly creative and imaginative gift. There was a framed poster of Elizabeth Taylor as a child actor, tie-dyed cloth diapers, and a porcelain rabbit reminiscent of the Mad Hatter. "Oh, the life this girl is going to have," I thought.

Brian had made a brief visit to see Lily in the hospital, having always had a real thing for babies. Years ago, with our first newborn, I figured it was the scientist in him. He had quickly corrected me: "No, it's the miracle of life itself."

When he finally stopped by the house, he came in with a huge stuffed giraffe, Barb's favorite animal, and a tiny gold locket.

"I thought Lily needed something precious to commemorate her birth," he told us. Then, without waiting for an invitation, he gingerly scooped the baby out of her mother's arms and took her to the rocking chair by the woodstove. There the two of them rocked for what seemed like hours. I watched him from the doorway.

"Here," said Barb, handing me a tissue, "now you're the one who's leaking."

I had been unaware of the tears in my eyes, tears for that most tender part of Brian, his gentleness, his genuine regard for life.

Barb threw her arm around me.

"Blow your nose and let's go make lunch. Did I mention my appetite is still the biggest thing about me?"

After that first visit, Brian came by nearly every afternoon, saying we women needed a break and he had to get to know Lily a little better. Nobody objected, least of all Lily, who seemed to listen to his rich deep voice with an interest she didn't show either her mother or her auntie. It was as if he belonged here. Barb commented on it one night after he had left.

"Like it or not, he really is part of the clan, isn't he?"

I thought she was on to something, but exactly what, I wasn't sure.

12

*I*t was four days before Christmas, and the Farmhouse Three, as we had taken to calling ourselves, were in deep preparation for the big day. I found myself moving around the house humming, even singing. Forget Julie Andrews; it was all-out Aretha. The prospect of a house full of family was exhilarating. I was in my element. New York seemed like a lifetime ago, and best of all, I didn't even care.

But part of my enthusiasm was also due to the very different way I was approaching Christmas. As much as I had always loved this holiday in particular, I was determined to savor it this year, to appreciate what it was truly supposed to be about. And if I was going to accomplish this, I knew things would have to change.

"Damn the guilt," I had announced to Barb. "Maybe this old dog can learn some new tricks." Not only would I have to ask for some help, a bone-chilling first, but I would also have to let go of some of the control. We had always enjoyed *my* decorating, *my* choice of color for the table's candles, *my* apple cobbler, which was inhaled by happy revelers. In spite of the pleasure I felt from this, in the end it added up to a whole lot of work. Not this year. No, this year all I wanted was to look forward to the mass of much-loved souls who would descend upon my house.

The decision had not come easily. Years of practiced martyrdom stood between me and the joy I imagined such a holiday could bring.

Finally, after a fitful night with Lily, I composed an email to all the family and friends who would be in attendance. Briefly explaining our current circumstances, I announced the new game plan, asking each of them to volunteer for one task. I tried not to think about how my request would be received. Would there be any tsk-tsking over the impropriety of a woman not handling every stinking detail herself? Any "Poor Lee, she can't do it without Brian" speculation? Would the kids revolt and believe I had surely gone round the bend? I hit the send button and went on about my day, determined to not look back on such a wildly out-of-character decision.

But, to the letter, each one of them emailed back with enthusiasm, happy to be so involved in the celebration we all shared every year. They neither questioned the new plan nor passed judgment on it. It was going to be grand.

With this much of the holiday preparations spread out among dear family and friends, I was gloriously unburdened. Copious amounts of precious time seemed to greet me at every turn. I actually had every present wrapped, a task that I typically left for the last minute on Christmas Eve. I even managed to finish up the last batches of cookies I made every year as gifts. The house was clean from top to bottom, bed linens changed, fresh towels in the two extra bathrooms.

Barb, never the domestic diva, pitched in here and there. Given her circumstances, I wasn't bothered. (In fact, it concerned me a little that the new mother didn't seem to be getting her strength back—she seemed way too tired for too long. But I shrugged off the thought, chiding myself for not being able to recall the killer fatigue babies brought with them.) She did manage to polish the family silver in between naps, snacking, and tending Lily—sweet Lily, who made the most valuable contribution of all by sleeping at least five hours straight each night.

Both Ella and Sophia were due home the next evening. Sean and his fiancée would arrive the day after. I could hardly contain my excitement. Lily and Barb napped while I organized the cloth napkins and tried to decide which combination of rings I would use for the eighteen people due to celebrate with us. Lost in such trivial thoughts, the knock at the door surprised me, since I hadn't heard anyone drive up and none of the dogs had barked. Perhaps a very clever evangelist had managed to make it to my door, though that would be a first.

The second knock was stronger and louder. I stepped up my pace, concerned and a little irritated that the sound would wake Barb, who had had a very rough morning with the baby. After the third knock, I threw open the door, ready to scold whomever it was who had the nerve to disturb the silence. But when I saw who stood on my porch, I caught my breath.

"Hi, Mom." Sam stood tall and healthy. Though he was still very thin, his color was good, his hair was clean, and his eyes were clear. After his handsome face registered, I immediately tried to remember the last time I had seen his eyes so perfectly clear and focused.

I rushed toward him, gathering up my son for a long hug. As I began to pull away, Sam continued to hold on to me by the shoulders.

"You feel thinner, Mom."

"Well, I guess I am," I acknowledged. "It must be the yoga. And you feel stronger."

He laughed, "I hope I am."

I gestured and said, "Come in, come in."

Sam beamed. It was the same smile he'd had when, as a toddler, he found a ripe strawberry in the garden to eat or, as a first-grader, he had gotten a second, unexpected cookie for dessert. It was a charming look of sheer joy. I started to cry.

He quickly wrapped his arms around me again.

"I'm sorry, Mom, I didn't come here to make you cry. I just wanted to see everyone and try to make amends. You know, step nine, Alcoholics Anonymous?" His voice faltered. "No, you probably don't know. Sorry. I should've called. I was just afraid of what I might hear. God, this isn't how I imagined things at all. I'll leave if you want me to."

I stood back to take in my all-grown-up Sammy. How long had it been since his father and I had told him to get out and not come back until he had his life together? Four years, maybe five? And now, here he was, standing in the living room of my house, healthy, clear-eyed, and very much alive.

"Leave? That's the absolute *last* thing I want."

Taking him by the arm, I ushered him into the kitchen. As he had done so many times while he was growing up, he settled in on *his* chair at the old oak table. I went straight to the fridge and began pulling out food. Surveying the wild array of tidbits I had put before him, he eagerly filled up his plate. Suddenly, I found myself a little self-conscious about what sat on the table. The regular items from the USDA food pyramid that I'd always offered my children were nowhere in sight. I hurried through an explanation.

"Tastes have run in some wild directions of late, with one ravenous new mother, one old mother who seems to have worn-out taste buds— or maybe it's a matter of worn-out cooking buds—and a newborn who seems to be sensitive to curry, much to her mother's disappointment."

Sam's eyes opened wide with confusion. Trying to make sense of what I was telling him, he quickly finished a mouthful.

"New mother? Newborn? Mom, slow down. What are you talking about? God, my little sisters aren't old enough to be reproducing, are they?"

I tried to collect my thoughts. There was only one way to do this. Out tumbled a quick summary of the last few months. Sam honed in on every word.

"Barbie has a daughter? Unbelievable, Barbie as a mother. Whoa! I guess I'm not the only miracle currently in your house." He stopped. "Oh man, that was arrogant. Sorry." Sam dropped his eyes. The familiar flush on his cheeks and his nervous little laugh followed. He resumed munching away on my latest batch of pickled beets, he being the only kid who had ever given Barb any competition for the flavorful root vegetable.

"Are you a miracle?" I wanted to know. "I mean, right now, you look like one to me. Here's something that might blow the socks right off your size twelves. I've been praying for this moment ever since you left. Believe that, if you can. Me, the mom who always admitted she didn't have a clue if God existed but who insisted that we would all live as though he or she did, just to be on the safe side."

Sam wiped his mouth and gave me that tremendous smile. "I think you're one of the most spiritual people I know, Mom."

His comment caught me off guard. "Me, spiritual? That's a new one. You know my track record with church."

Sam swallowed a mouthful of pasta salad. "But you went to church nearly every Sunday that I can remember, weather permitting." His eyes played with mine.

I was flabbergasted by the comment. "What in the world are you talking about?"

"You and your hallowed pond. Didn't you ever know that on Sundays, when Dad would be fixing pancakes, he'd tell us, 'Your mother is still at church. She'll be back in a few minutes,' and we'd beg him to let us go down to the pond to be with you? We'd see you sitting there, staring at the water. Dad said that bench we made you that time for Mother's Day was your pew, your latte a blessed sacrament, and the old crocheted blanket your vestments. For the longest time, we never knew what all those words meant, but all along, we knew that we weren't allowed to bug you. Dad was very clear about that."

Though a bit startled by this piece of family history, I was also pleasantly surprised.

"Well, I suppose there's some truth to that. I sort of grounded myself down there; pardon the cliché. It has always held me somehow—one with nature and all that."

Sam reached for another platter of leftovers.

"Face it, Mom, you're more of a Buddhist than I am."

He took a bite of a phyllo chicken roll I had heated up in the microwave.

I considered his statement, as it had thrown me back into the front seat of this roller coaster we found ourselves on. Forget for the moment how he apparently had come to view his mother. Did my son just refer to himself as a Buddhist? It was all too weird. I sipped my coffee, fearing too many questions would send him shooting out the door, never to be seen again.

He continued, "That's part of why I came home. I wanted to tell you what I've figured out, what I've come to believe, where I see myself headed. Maybe it sounds corny, but it felt like the only honorable thing to do, considering everything I put you guys through." He took a sip of milk and paused. His next question jerked me back to the table. "When will Dad be home? Do you think he'll let me stay for a couple of days? Just so you know, I've been clean and sober for twenty-three months."

"When will your dad be home? Now there's a good question." My mind raced through the last few years. It was as if Sam had been in a coma or had just recovered from a major bout of amnesia. There was so much he didn't know.

"Cup of tea? We have some catching up to do, bud." I squeezed his arm on my way to the stove to put the kettle on. Man muscles, I noted.

Determined to give Sam the quick version first and fill in the blanks later, I had made it all the way up to my New York trip when Lily began to cry. I ran to get her just as Barb was rolling out of bed. "Never in a million years will you guess who's down in the kitchen!"

Barb started to change Lily's diaper, looking completely frazzled and dead-dog tired. She had dark circles under her eyes, and I wondered if she could actually be thinner despite all the eating she was doing. "Lee, I just got up. This is not the time for a guessing game. How about I wake up first?"

I couldn't wait a second longer. "It's Sam, our Sammy—I swear to God. Wait until you see him. You won't believe how, geez, how healthy he looks."

Without a word, Barb handed me the diaper and charged out of the room.

"Sammy? Sammy my boy—where aaaaarrre you?"

I finished diapering Lily, who had begun to cry again at the first whoop out of her mother's mouth.

"It's okay, sweet cheeks," I said to Lily. "One thing's for sure: You'll never have any trouble reading your mother's moods." I started toward the stairs with the baby on my shoulder, gently patting away her tears.

When we reached the kitchen, Sam and Barb were doing their happy dance around the room, jumping up and down, swirling in sheer joy, gripped in the best of bear hugs. Barb was squealing with delight. It was loud enough to get Lily going again, at which point the happy revelers stopped cold and stared at her. Sam's mouth dropped open. He rushed to us and carefully took Lily from me. Cradling the baby in his long arms, he began to walk the room, speaking to her in low, soothing tones. Lily stopped her crying, thoroughly enchanted by the handsome young stranger.

Barb collapsed on a stool, breathless but with a huge smile on her face as she watched the two of them move around the room.

"Oh shit, she's only seven weeks old and already she's falling in love."

"Wow Barbie, she's a real beauty," Sam offered. "I mean, really—not like one of those babies that pops out all mushed and weird like a Conehead from *SNL* reruns. Good job." Barb and I burst into tears.

Sam was shocked by our outburst and immediately started to backpedal.

"Guys, guys, that was a compliment, really it was. I'm sorry if you thought I was being a smart ass. I wasn't at all." He looked down at the smitten infant and smiled. "I think she's absolutely beautiful."

We walked over to our children, wrapping our arms all the way around both son and daughter to complete what for years had been known as the Famous MacPhearson Pickle in the Middle Sandwich, our blessings lovingly sandwiched between two weeping mothers.

What a reunion it was. Sam and Barb fell right back into their affectionate, sparring selves. Stories were told, people accounted for, old jokes repeated, new jokes delivered. Gap after gap was filled in as the kitchen perked with laughter.

Well past midnight, Barb called it a night. Gathering her sleeping daughter from Sam's arms, she stood on her tiptoes to plant a quick kiss on Sam's cheek. "I can't believe it. Me, the first one to leave a party. What's the world coming to?" Making her way to the door, she added, "Get used to it kid. I'm sorry to say, it's the new me." With a cockeyed nod to me, one mom to another, she disappeared down the hall.

Mother and son talked well into the night. Sam was utterly dumb-founded by Brian's and my separation. ("You and Dad? Never, I mean *never* in a million years.") And I was equally astounded when Sam explained that his chance meeting with a Zen monk seemed to have offered him the lifeline he so badly needed. Our conversation was honest and direct, warm and affectionate. And very teary. But even the long silences that peppered the reunion were comfortable. I felt that I finally had my son back.

But when Sam took his dirty dishes to the sink, he broached a subject both of us had been avoiding. Staring out into the black night, his voice was low. "So, will you call Dad or should I? I mean, will he even want to see me? He was a little pissed off the last time I saw him." We both laughed nervously at his understatement.

"Why don't you let me tell him," I said gently. "I'll go over there first thing in the morning, and I bet a million that he races over here. You are the best Christmas present either of us could have ever hoped for."

"I hope you're right."

I made my way to his side, giving him a playful punch in the arm.

"Come on, none of that. This has been one of the best nights I've had in ages. We're going to end it on a high note." I walked to the cupboard and pulled out the last of an applesauce cake I'd made a few days before. "I hope this is still one of your favorites?"

"Mom, tell me you have some vanilla ice cream to go along with that. Because if you do, things are definitely looking up!"

13

When I finally crawled into bed that night, content knowing my son was just down the hall, I listened to the sleeping house, grateful for the people it held. But as I lay in the darkness, I couldn't help but wander back over the years that had been Sam's childhood.

He had always been such a bright boy, so smart and quick, off the charts in math and science. The trouble was, he couldn't sit still long enough to finish any assignment. I had once tried to explain him to one of his many baffled teachers by saying that Sam had arrived on the planet wired differently than everybody in the family. And that was true. There had been years of turmoil with him, his defiance, his anger—but what had it all been about? No one, least of all Sam, had ever come close to figuring out the answer to that question. His angst began long before it ever should have, and our reactions to it weren't very polished. Our frustration and fear surely added a variable to the equation that compounded his struggles. There were years of trips to the principal's office, after-school detentions, groundings that seemed to last for eternity. In middle school, a counselor proposed that he be put on an antidepressant, explaining, "We've run through every diagnostic test we can come up with. Sam doesn't have any learning disabilities; there's no ADHD. He's so bright, but he refuses to perform academically in school. Perhaps he's just depressed. The medication would at least give us an opportunity to see if it makes a difference."

I was out of my chair, furious not at Sammy but at all the so-called professionals who had let us down. My voice filled the tiny windowless room.

"Perhaps he's just depressed? About what? We've all talked to him until we're blue in the face. There's no history of depression in either of our families. Peeing in a cup week after week proves he's drug free. What's making him so sad? Wouldn't it be better to know that before we drug him?"

Brian was fed up, and so was I. But drug him? That seemed drastic. I fought the suggestion because Sam was so much more than the problems everyone focused on. I continued to plead for him.

"He's an artist, a painter who once brought the view from his upstairs bedroom to life with his simple set of watercolors. He sees the world in living color. But more than that, there is a tender spot deep in his heart, his soul." I turned to Brian, frantic about what was happening.

"Remember that time he went after Sean for torturing that beetle he had found under that rotten board in the barn?" I faced the counselor. "Sam's the one who will bring home the birds with the broken wings and nurse them back to health. Sam has hand-fed every runt of every litter we've ever had. Whether it was a kitten or a piglet, he'd set his alarm and get out to the barn to feed them, usually beating me out there." These had been some of the best moments for the two of us, sharing the stillness of the barn, Sam determined to save a tiny animal, me appreciating my boy's gentleness and compassion.

But by day, Sam's terror would return, and I would be left wondering where that sweet boy of the darkness had gone.

"No, I don't want him on medication," I had protested, "because of the goodness that is Sam, his creativity, his empathy for the other guy—all that would be flatlined, dead. I don't want him to try and face the world as a zombie boy."

At that, Brian jumped in. "Well, I don't want a serial killer for a son. All the love in the world isn't going to make Sam better. When are you going to get that through your head?" He stared straight ahead, his breathing and my sobs the only sounds in the room.

I slept on the couch for a week after that. I knew Sam had never been violent, but in the silent darkness, I forced myself to consider that I couldn't trust that to be true forever. It was then that I did my homework on depression and treatment. I was reassured by what I learned, recognizing that I had bought into so many of the myths about depression that permeate our culture. There didn't have to be one clear-cut answer to why he was depressed—it had to do with brain function and biochemistry. For the first time in years, I felt some optimism.

Sam reluctantly agreed to try the medication, but he only took it for a few months. He hated the way it made him feel—sluggish and out of it, he would say. More importantly, it didn't help his behavior in the least. All the medication seemed to do was add to his frustration, and therefore the intensity of the explosions. Sam barely made it through three years of high school. The only reason he did was because of Tom's TLC and "don't mess with me" approach to teenagers.

But during the fall of his senior year, without any notice, Sam disappeared for a week. He came home looking like a strung-out junkie and sporting a tattoo of a pissed-off angel. After that, our fights were endless, Sam becoming less and less content to just walk off in a huff, choosing instead to taunt us until one of us would finally take his bait, and then a battle would commence. The girls would hide out in their rooms; Sean had finally escaped to college. In the fallout of the fights, Brian and I would turn on each other. It was an ugly, dark time.

The final blow came when Sam took off in my car after defiantly grabbing a bottle of vodka from the cupboard. I'd been unable to stop him, having to call the police in desperation. Brian was enraged when they brought him home two days later. Sam had left my car on the side of the road sixty-three miles away when he had run out of vodka and gas.

His father blew.

"That's it, Sam. You're eighteen now. You're out of here. We won't be in a situation where we're liable if you hurt someone. Obviously, we can't control what you do to yourself, but we have the girls to think of and ourselves. You've proven that you don't want to live by the rules we have in this house. If you can find a place that is better for you, go ahead and try. You're welcome back here when you get your shit together. And, if for some unimaginable reason you don't know what that means by now, it means clean, sober, and ready and willing to be part of this family. Get your things together. I'll give you a bus ticket for anywhere you want and take you into town." He turned away from his son.

Sam grabbed a few belongings and cleared out of the house in a matter of minutes. He left the bus fare sitting on the table in the hall. I watched him wander off down the road into the night. I was absolutely numb at first and then became enraged at my husband's behavior. But I also found myself somehow relieved by his departure. With that realization came heavy, sickening guilt. I hated that night more than any other in my lifetime.

The house was dead. Brian had taken himself up to bed early. The girls had scattered hours before with the first sound of the fight. Eventually I tried sleeping on the couch, but I could not sleep any more than I could stop thinking about my son. Sitting curled up in an afghan, I was unable to close my eyes and face the dark reality of what had happened to my family. It was the stuff of Jerry Springer—and it was my life. There I sat, staring into the darkness, motionless and terrified, unable to decide what I should do next.

Sometime just before sunrise, a strange light slid slowly across the wall opposite the couch. Its sudden presence startled me. I followed the light as it passed silently over the painting my grandmother had done, rippled down the floral wallpaper, and eventually came to rest on a vase of flowers. Then, as suddenly as it appeared, it was gone. I contemplated its meaning. There was no logical way to explain the light here in the rolling hills in the middle of nowhere. Our isolation had always been something I treasured. Now it just felt spooky, empty. All I could think about was Sam, and I wondered where he was out there, angry, sad, alone.

And then I thought about myself, his mother, and his father and sisters, realizing that each one of us had felt every bit as much as he had that night. In that moment, the epiphany was complete—there was an entire family at stake here. Sam would have to find his own light, his own way. As heartbreaking as this realization was, I knew it was time for me to let go of Sam and allow him to either succeed or fail. Tears, bargaining, fighting, and pleading had done no good, would do no good. I tightened the afghan around me. By letting him truly go, I knew I was trading one kind of maternal terror for another, but the thought brought a kind of acceptance with it, and I felt calm for the first time in months.

With that, the light reappeared on the wall. Only this time, there were two, and they were accompanied by the faint sound of tires rolling slowly over gravel. I smiled in the darkness at my own foolishness, suddenly remembering the work crews who had been repairing the lines on the other side of the valley.

"They must be coming in early to beat the heat," I reasoned, still grateful that the Mysterious Light Epiphany had delivered much-needed emotional clarity.

And so, in these last few years, Sam had been the dead son who wasn't dead—at least that's what I prayed for every night. After Lily was born, I had confided to Barb.

"How hypocritical is it that I don't know if God exists but I pray that my son is safe and will someday return to me?"

Barb was thoughtful. She rubbed her cheek against Lily's peach-fuzz head.

"I'm beginning to get the idea that, when it comes to their children, mothers will try just about anything, including praying to a God they don't even know exists," she said softly.

And now, my Sammy was home. While I couldn't go so far as to believe my prayers had been answered, I couldn't entirely deny that Sam was something of miracle. The last person I ever expected to see, the one I most hoped to see, had simply arrived on my doorstep. Really, what else could it be than a miracle? I smiled, aware that thoughts of what the morning might bring lurked in the darkness. Selfishly refusing them access, I burrowed down into the blankets. Closing my eyes, the sweetness of the moment wrapped me in its arms. I was about to enjoy a very good night's sleep.

14

As I waited outside Brian's door the next morning, I wondered if perhaps I should have chosen a more decent hour to spring the news of Sam's return on him. When he finally opened the door, I had my answer. What hair Brian still had on his head was rumpled, his face full of sleep. But as he registered who was standing in front of him, his eyes quickly filled with concern.

"What's wrong?" he asked.

"Nothing. Good morning. How about a cup of coffee?" I walked into the room, hoping I wouldn't find some woman's bra on the couch and its owner languishing in Brian's bed. I was trying for normal in a situation that was anything but.

"Sam's back," I said, rushing on before Brian could say anything. "Really, I'm not just being 'blinded by motherly love' like you used to say—he's different, truly different. The things he says, how he looks, what he's learned. He is full of remorse, too much if you ask me. He's not looking for a handout, Bri. He showed me his checkbook and he actually has a healthy balance. He's been working. Sam has money in the bank, Brian, can you believe it?"

To my astonishment, Brian's eyes filled with tears, which he self-consciously brushed away. It was the last thing I had expected. We gathered each other up and sat on his dilapidated sofa for a long time.

Without looking at me, Brian asked, "So you think he's legit? I mean—and I'm trying to be careful here, remember how Pissant Man used to tell me to be careful about what comes out of my mouth? That's what I'm going for here, okay? But you're sure you're not just seeing what you want to see? We can't go down that road again, Lee."

"I completely agree with you, Brian. None of us can afford to do that again. But I was awake most of the night, going over and over every single thing he said and did. Honestly, I think he's truly back."

Brian pulled away, dragging his handkerchief from his back pocket. "I really want to believe you." After wiping his face and blowing his nose, he looked me straight in the eye.

"Sorry. I don't know where that came from." He blew his nose again. "Naw, that's bullshit, I know exactly where that blubbering came from. Listen, there's something else I want to say, and it's not about Sam. It's about me. Maybe this isn't the time, but I've been wanting to tell you for a while."

I felt my heart thud, and I waited. Here it comes—he's met someone else. I knew it. But what I hated most was realizing that I cared.

"Brian, maybe now isn't the time to talk about us. I mean, one bombshell a day is about my quota."

He took my hand and relaxed. The wrinkles at the corners of his eyes cradled smiling eyes. "This isn't exactly about us. It's about all of us, really. Can I explain?"

I nodded, and I vowed to myself not to cry.

"I've been doing a lot of reading this last year, books I never would have opened before." He surveyed his apartment. "Believe me, I've had plenty of time. But there was this one, I can't even remember the name of it, but it was poetry. Can you believe it? Me reading poetry? But wait, it gets better." He tried for a little laugh, failed miserably, and continued.

"Anyhow, there was this sixteenth-century Spanish mystic, Saint John of the Cross. He wrote about the dark night of the soul. I can't do it justice, but he had a sort of spiritual depression. Everything that made him feel good, made him feel worthwhile, just dried up. Happiness disappeared."

He looked out of the window and then directly into my eyes.

"That was my world for a few years there, the one I dragged all of you down into. I know you always wanted answers about what was wrong with me, why I wasn't happy. Those were legitimate questions. I felt like crap that I could never explain exactly what was wrong. Now, I'm not saying I've turned all religious on you, but this Saint John guy, I think he was on to something. He wrote about knowing one's self and that the only way to do that is to know one's misery. He talked about not being able to find the light until you survive the darkness." Brian waited for me to take in what he was saying.

I nodded.

"Sort of a shocker coming from your engineering jerk, right? Trust me, Lee, I don't think this emotional mumbo jumbo will ever be second nature to me, but I've come to believe a little dose of introspection may actually have some merit. Just now, as I've been listening to you describe Sam, I think I finally understand that Sam's been navigating his own dark night of the soul for years." The tears returned to his eyes. Brian stopped to collect himself, then finished his thought.

"I wish I had known myself better all along. I might have been better equipped to help my son. Guess we'll never know. But this isn't about looking backward. Sam has made it through! Good God, is there anything better than that?"

I sat very still, feeling relief in every cell in my body. Brian hadn't fallen in love with someone else. Not only that, he had even managed to figure out some things. I was a little dizzy from all of it.

He pulled me to him for a wonderfully familiar hug and whispered in my ear, "Give me five minutes. Then we're outta here."

When we arrived at the kitchen door, Sam was at the counter having a cup of coffee, his head bent over the latest *New Yorker*. He stood quickly when he saw his father.

"Hi, Dad."

Brian stared at Sam for the longest time—long enough for me to wonder if I had misjudged his reaction, long enough for me to feel as though I was once again right in the middle of the two of them. But just as I was about to break the awkward silence with some lame remark, Brian rushed past me and grabbed Sam in the biggest hug imaginable, lifting his son off the ground and bouncing him like he used to do when Sam was a four-year-old kid and had just brushed his teeth without being reminded. Their laughter filled the kitchen.

"Geez Dad, you're pretty strong for such a scrawny old dude! You can put me down now."

Brian lowered his son to the floor, then quickly pulled up his shirt sleeve to expose a flexed arm.

"Ha! Who you calling scrawny? Take a look at that, you pup. I could still beat you at arm wrestling." Sam let out a laugh of sheer disbelief and fell back into his father's shoulder. "Oh yeah, I'm shaking in my boots."

And then, like the men they were, they both tensed up ever so slightly, aware of what had just passed between them. Taking a step back, they each looked down and away from the emotion that had slammed them together. Brian broke the heavy silence.

"Good to see you kid, really great." He turned to me, "Do you have anything to eat around here or has Wonder Boy already scarfed it down?"

It was one of the best Christmas celebrations in the history of the MacPhearson clan. The children were amazed and delighted to have their brother back among them, their jokes full of endearments and jabs that only siblings can get away with. Eventually, even Sean had kind words and physical affection for his little brother, a fact that was not lost on Brian or me. The girls followed Sam around like puppies, tumbling over each other to tell him one story after another. Friends greeted the once-lost boy with open arms and few questions. Tom simply threw his arm around Sam and didn't let go for a long time.

We put three tables together, end to end, stretching from the dining room out into the living room. The collaboration on food was a huge success, as specialties from each different family, each person's expertise, were passed from hand to hand. Someone would groan at the sight of giblet dressing, just as the next person's jaw would drop at the sight of his favorite Jell-O and fruit salad. Still another hungry reveler announced, "Forget the bird, just give me the stuffing. How can you not love this?" Laughter greeted Ella's contribution of baked tofu. "It's damned near un-American," Tom chided her as he wolfed down a huge bite.

Lily was passed around to all the welcoming arms, everyone happy to have a turn holding the newest member of our loyal and lively coalition.

Brian and I sat together at the end of one of the tables. Before dinner, he had asked me where I wanted him to sit. Once again, I appreciated that he hadn't made any assumptions about anything for months.

"How about next to me?" I had answered. And now the two of us surveyed the scene, the abundance of laughter and affection, the chatter of friends. Good fortune filled the room. I reached under the table and rested my hand on Brian's knee. He took it and, as he had done so many times before, gave it a gentle squeeze.

15

*C*hristmas came and went. As quickly as the house had filled with happy chaos, it had emptied. Barb, Lily, and I slipped easily back into our routine. Sam fell into step seamlessly with the rest of us. In the post-holiday lull, there had been much discussion about continuing the current living situation. Barb had been the first to bring it up.

"You know, we've been hanging out here for over two months. I don't believe that was in our original contract, was it? Oh, that's right, we didn't have a contract. And, if I can remember my former self, I was the one who insisted that living on my own was the only way to go. But I get no sense that your well-aimed boot is about to land squarely on my fat ass. I bet it's my cute kid you can't part with."

I was sitting in the rocking chair with Lily, who strained to maintain her focus on the bright crystals hanging in the living room window and their colorful interpretation of the winter sunbeams. I took my eyes off the content infant and looked at Barb laid out on the couch, snuggled down in her mommy wrap. The words were out of my mouth before I realized it.

"Mama friend, you don't look so good to me. How are you really doing?"

Barb shifted her weight, which seemed to be less than ever before, and for once she actually considered her reply.

"How the hell should I know? I mean, shouldn't I feel better by now? I'm getting sleep. Between you and Sam, I have all the help I could possibly need. You told me yourself that Lily is the best baby imaginable, sleeping through the night. I know I never was one for marathons before, but am I always going to feel this way? My gut aches twenty-four-seven, my back is sore, I'm still leaking. I really think my uterus was too old for this. Or maybe it's because I was a total slug during my pregnancy that I'm paying for it now. Maybe it's because I've been a total slug my entire life." She paused, pulling the cashmere around herself.

"Lee, to be honest, I can't imagine being back at my house right now. And then there's the day care issue—the thought of that curls even *my* hair. I have to go back to work in a month, which sounds like a nightmare just waiting to happen. There, I've said it. Okay, cue the boot. Time for whiny mom to face the music and get on with her life."

I didn't pause a second. "There's no boot in your future, Barb. How can you even ask? I think it's absolutely wonderful that we've all settled in like this. I love having you two here, haven't given it a second thought." I paused and took a breath. "No, the truth is, I'm a whole lot more concerned about your complete lack of energy, those dark circles under your eyes that don't go away. Your lack of appetite—come on now, a nursing mother should be ravenous."

"Great, at my six-week checkup, my doctor told me I'm dandy, and now Dr. Quinn, Medicine Woman, tells me there's something wrong with me. Seriously, who would you listen to?"

Lily, who had drifted off to sleep, stretched and murmured one of those sweet, tender baby sounds. I patted her gently.

"Right now, I'd listen to Dr. Quinn—because she's known you for years and she sees you every single day. Did Dr. Birchard check you for anemia at that last visit?"

"Ye gads, now you're diagnosing! I find discussing my health to be a real bore, and you know how well I tolerate boredom. Now, weren't we talking about being housemates?" Barb had spoken. Like it or not,

I knew we were moving on. "Listen, the theater called me wondering that since I was living with you, would I consider renting out my house to them so they could put up a couple of prima donnas scheduled for the next two runs. They pay top dollar. It would easily cover my mortgage, taxes, all that crap, and I could pay you rent. That's only fair, but it's not something you, oh wise businesswoman, have ever considered, have you?" She paused, a bit breathless.

"What I mean is that I need to figure out where Lily and I are living, and from my standpoint, this is the best thing going. I'm not trying to get out of anything. It just seems like the best for Lily. Okay, the best for me too. There. I said it." With that, Barb struggled to get off the couch.

"Think about it," she added. "Shit, right now I'm feeling like a charity case. I'm going to take a nap."

But before she could reach the stairs, I called out, "There's nothing to think about. It works for me. You're right; it works for all of us. And I'll take your damned money for rent if you insist."

Barb stopped, turned slowly, and walked back down the hall to me, a grin on her face.

"Well, it didn't take you long to come to your senses," she gloated. And then, in what was for her a real show of affection, she put up her closed hand for a fist bump. I happily met her gesture midair. With that, Barb headed back toward the stairs.

"Okay, now I'm on to more important business—my nap."

The next day, Barb greeted me with, "I told the company they can have my house for six months. They didn't blink at the rate. Maybe I should ask for a raise?" She looked up at me. "Am I shrinking? Lordy, maybe you're growing? And one more thing. Just to get you off my back, I made an appointment with Dr. Birchard. There, are you happy?" We shared smiles.

Discussions with Sam about his living arrangements had gone about the same. I found it bit surprising, and satisfying, that he was as proud and determined as Barb to make it on his own.

When I laid out my plan, Sam was slow to accept the offer.

"I'm not looking for a handout, Mom. Besides, Dad won't like it. He'll think I'm taking advantage of you."

"Well, I'm not giving you a handout, and besides, this is between you and me." I realized that the tone of my voice didn't match my words.

"What I meant was, both Dad and I are convinced that what you've managed to pull off is amazing. More importantly, we're behind you 100 percent. I see you going to your AA meetings; I know you've been putting in applications around town. You pick up after yourself, even clean the house. Holy cow, I can't tell you how good it feels to come home after work to find dinner cooked—"

He interrupted me. "Mom, nobody says Holy cow. Holy cow? I mean, what exactly does that mean? Is it a reference to the Hindus? I doubt they'd be pleased that something so sacred to them is completely bastardized by the Americans."

Now it was my turn to cut him off. "Don't interrupt your mother, and, more importantly, don't try to throw me off my game with a bovine mini-lecture. I'm wise to your tricks, mister. The point I'm making is this: What you are doing with your life is amazing, Sam—the changes, the consistency, the adult feel it has. And with regards to the temporary arrangement I'm offering: I'm very aware of all the contributions you make to the household and to each of us living here."

My handsome son stood quietly for a moment, his head down. Then he looked me straight in the eye.

"It means a lot to have you say all that, Mom."

Keeping my tears in check, I continued. "Sam, my boy, if I'm reading you right, you seem to want to stay here for a while. Trust me, I like that. Live here and keep doing what you're doing. It helps all of us to have an extra set of hands for Lily. That girl has such a mad crush on you. Leave now and she'll be brokenhearted." I reached out to pat his arm. "This is a tough time of year to get a job in this town. What I've been thinking, and I've even run this by your father, Mr. Smarty Pants, is that I could use your help down at the store."

"No, that's too much, I—"

"There you go interrupting again!" I smiled. "Hear me out. Has it occurred to you that Tom is in his seventies? That dear man has been picking up a lot of slack since your Dad and I began our mid-life fandango, and then Lily joined the clan. Tom's been a workhorse. I would love for you to learn enough of the business so we could let him have a shorter week, at least for the rest of winter and into the beginning of spring. When the theater opens up, well, you know how busy it gets. And then there will be more job opportunities for you." I watched for his reaction, then added, "Tom will insist on a full week, making us believe we can't do it without him." I waited while Sam considered the plan. "Admit it, Sam, your mother is brilliant!"

He smiled, and I knew he was in.

Barb now referred to the four of us as the Farmhouse Three plus One, and it was an arrangement that was working well. She left most of her furniture in her house, having written in a healthy penalty "in case the divas burn a hole in my antique gold brocade ottoman." Some of her eccentric belongings found shelter in the barn, since the farmhouse wasn't really big enough for her Roman pillars or the larger-than-life-size Mardi Gras masks. But with creativity befitting Martha Stewart—okay, Martha Stewart on drugs—most of her personal belongings settled into the two bedrooms and bath she and Lily had been using. "Our countrified condo," she called it.

Sam suggested to Barb that "come summer, we use some of your weird crap to build us a place down by the pond. It'll be cool." Barb, insisting it wasn't crap, fully supported the idea of a "summer place at the lakeshore."

Sam threw himself into learning everything he could about the shop and the gallery. Working again with Tom was natural and easy for both of them. I would often hear them laughing from the other room, and I wondered who was benefiting most from their current arrangement. Tom eventually reduced his days to three a week, but it wasn't unusual for him to drop by on a day off for a cup of tea in the afternoon. He'd insist, "I'm not here to work, but I have to keep an eye on you two."

Lily was thriving under the arrangement, full of happy gurgles and coos. I thought she was one of the easiest babies to ever land on the planet, but I realized, seeing so many adults fawning over her, that maybe each of us could benefit from that much love and attention.

Brian continued to come by on a regular basis, often staying for dinner. He and Sam had resumed their nightly game of chess, a tradition that had begun when Sam was a little boy. One night after dinner, Barb surveyed the scene: Sam and his dad bent over the chessboard, me rocking Lily to sleep by the fire, some Chopin playing in the background. She broke the mood. "Geez, people, it looks like the return of the freakin' Waltons in here. I can't believe this is my life."

16

I dumped the grocery bags on the counter just as one of them tore open. Reacting quickly but awkwardly, like a Barnum and Bailey reject, I scrambled to catch the apples rolling across the counter. Two managed to make it past my fingers, falling to the floor and landing with a thud. There they sat on the hardwood floor, red against amber, shiny and pristine on the outside, bruised on the inside. Their condition struck a chord, and I was glad to be moving beyond my own bruising from these last few years.

As I bent down to scoop them up, the phone rang. I started for the receiver but immediately realized it wasn't in its cradle. Drat these modern cordless phones, so convenient except when you can't find them. I carefully followed the ring, a modern tracker in a kitchen landscape, hoping I could get to it before either Barb or Lily woke up. Ring number two: not under the dish towel. Ring number three: not behind the laundry basket on the counter. Ring number four: my goose was nearly cooked and the damned phone was nowhere to be found. Then the beep and silence. I kept searching as Tom's gruff voice floated in the air.

"Hi. This is Tom." (As if he needed to identify himself, but he always did.) "Sorry to bother you. Believe me, it's going against my grain, but I know you, Miss Follow Through Even If Someone Ticks You Off.

Anyhow, there was a guy in here just now, some fancy-dancy artists' rep from New York, wait a minute, let me get his card, uh, his name is… "

I heard Tom rummaging through papers, but he needn't have bothered. I only knew one person from New York, and it so happened he represented artists. Finally finding the receiver under a stack of Lily's doll clothes, I picked up.

"Hi Tom, sorry about that. I couldn't find the phone. Let me guess. Was his name Stephen Brunswick?" It seemed to take forever for Tom to answer.

"Yeah. You know him? He said you met on your last trip to New York. Don't worry, I didn't blow your cover and tell him it was your only trip to the Big Apple. He was sort of irritating, but he looked like he had money, and he sure did know art, so I thought I'd better play along. He said he's representing an artist he knew you liked and wanted to see if he could place a couple of paintings with you. I told him I was the gallery manager and could make that decision."

"What did he say?" I waited.

Tom made a little grunting noise, and I knew he was miffed.

"He said you had spoken highly of me but that he really did need to show you these slides himself, that you had admired them, and that he was hoping to catch up, whatever that means. Then he said, 'Why don't you just call her and we'll let the lady decide what she wants to do.' That was the last straw. He acted like he was Gregory Peck or something."

I smiled at Tom's reference: Gregory Peck, the film icon of his generation. And then I imagined Stephen standing in the gallery, calmly, confidently talking to Tom, politely refusing to take no for an answer. Gregory Peck was a pretty good match.

I didn't know what to do.

"So then what happened?"

"Well, I told him I doubted you'd have the time right now, since you'd already left for the day and all. And you know what? That S.O.B. stood right there, smooth as ice, and asked me to call you anyhow. That was too much. You know how that kind of thing goes over with me.

Sorry, Lee, but I have no patience for pushy New Yorkers. Well, pushy anybodies, I suppose. I sent him on his way but promised I'd call you." I thought I could actually hear Tom's blood pressure rising.

"It's all right, Tom," I reassured him. "You did the right thing calling me. What's his number?"

Tom snorted with satisfaction. "Ha, at least he didn't get that one right—he said you had his cell number."

But Stephen did get that one right. His number was written down in my journal. I had looked at it perhaps a few hundred times during these last couple of months, in the darkness of the quiet nights, playing and replaying what could have happened, always a little curious about what might have been.

"So, you really want it? I mean, it's no sweat off my back to call him and tell him you were happy to have me make the decision." The line was quiet for a moment. "You know how old dogs like to give the pups a hearty nip on the butt now and then."

"Sorry to deny you such a juicy opportunity, Tom. No, what's the number? I'll call him."

Tom recited the ten digits as I scribbled them down on the back of the power bill.

"Thanks, and Tom? He's not a New Yorker. Nope, he's a Bostonian. And you're right on the money, he really knows his stuff." As Tom mumbled good-bye, I could tell he was still irritated by the whole thing. But that was part of his value to me: his ability to run interference, not to mention his loyalty and protective nature.

Hanging up the phone, I leaned against the counter and stared at the number. The apples, still on the floor, caught my eye, and suddenly I felt equally bruised. Stephen in Ashland. Why would he not call all these months and then suddenly show up unannounced? It was no coincidence. I slid onto a kitchen stool. Stephen in Ashland. I struggled with what I was feeling, finally admitting to myself that I was tickled. More than tickled, I was downright dumbstruck. Moonstruck. Awestruck. No. Mac Truck struck! The adolescent thrill I'd known in New York washed over my entire body at the mere thought of his standing in my gallery.

But reality came crashing down with similar speed. Stephen in Ashland! What the hell did that mean? I had kept him in the most secret part of my heart, cataloged the days with him as a once-in-a-lifetime escapade, and now he was here. There was no one to talk this over with because no one knew about him. I looked around the kitchen. Panic sat poised on the edge of my brain, waiting for the chance to burrow in, making me completely useless.

I began putting away the groceries with the speed of a pro, as if I could work away the adrenaline by stacking cans into gravity-defying towers, controlling their height when I couldn't control my thoughts. What was I going to do?

Barb's voice broke through my hyper-speed merry-go-round of thoughts.

"So, you gonna call him?"

Spinning around, I was surprised to see her standing not even four feet away from me, eating grapes I hadn't washed yet. I knew that she knew, but I didn't know how she knew, and that was the first thing I wanted to know.

"You have a pretty satisfied look on your face, like a cat that just swallowed a mouse. Whole, no less. Just what do you mean, am I gonna call him?" I returned to the groceries.

Barb laughed a big, hearty laugh, something I hadn't heard in a while. It made me smile, and it forced me to stop my useless activity. I turned back to her as she continued.

"Oh Lee-Lee. I've been waiting for this moment ever since you came back from New York. I watched you walk toward me at the terminal, and I could tell that you weren't ready to tell me everything that had happened in New York. Pissed me off, but I knew I'd have to wait you out. Took you long enough! Ha, look at your face! I knew it would be priceless, and it sure is. I can count on one hand the number of times in the last twenty years that I've seen you squirm, and this has to be the very best one of them all." She plucked a grape from its stem, popped it into her mouth, and lowered herself onto a stool.

"You finally ready to tell me who this Stephen Brunswick is? Because you can't imagine how hard it's been waiting to find out. Come on, out with it." Her eyes glistened with excitement and anticipation.

"Not so fast," I began. "First you have to tell me what you know."

"Well, I'm sad to report, I don't know much at all except that one day while you were back there, a day when I was really, I mean *really* bored, I called your hotel a couple of times and you never picked up. I decided against leaving you a voice mail on your cell. I mean, you're still a little technologically challenged, and I didn't want to tax your tiny brain. Finally my curiosity got the best of me. I haven't spent my life in the theater for nothing. I called the desk and said I was your gallery manager and I needed to speak with you immediately about an important show you were in New York to arrange, that you weren't picking up your cell, and did they happen to know where you had been all day? There's a little desk clerk at the Excelsior who should be fired because she spilled just enough beans to blow her job security. She even apologized, saying that all she could tell me was she had seen you going out that night with a really tall man and that you two had been talking about art in the lobby the night before. But if I wanted her to take a message, she would be happy to make sure you got it when you returned later that night.

"So I asked her why she thought you'd be back later, not sooner, and she said, 'Well, Ms. MacPhearson was obviously dressed for a night out, and I assumed the night staff would be seeing her later on.' Bingo. Damned if a big ol' smile came over me, imagining you heading out into the night, hopefully dressed to kill in that amazing black skirt I made you pack. You wore that, right?"

I had to laugh.

"Okay, you win," I conceded. "You and your incessant sleuthing. I can't get anything by you even when I'm three thousand miles away. You must have been really bored to go to that much trouble. Why couldn't you think of anything—"

She cut me off. "Enough about me. Back to the topic at hand. Who is this guy? Man, that must have been a blast—a handsome New Yorker, and a giant no less. I want all the juicy details." She moved over to the table, sat down, and started in on a bowl of pistachios. "Come on, out with it."

I joined her, knowing defeat had landed squarely in my lap.

"One thing—you have to promise not to laugh."

She crossed her eyes and cracked open another nut.

Knowing it was pointless to get her to agree, I told my story. Giving her a somewhat condensed and carefully edited version, I went through each day Stephen and I had spent together. Every time I came to the end of the day, she'd interrupt. "Okay, so now you're back at the hotel. Get to the good part. How was the sex?"

And every time I told her there hadn't been any sex, she moaned like a wounded buffalo and cursed my timidity. I ended by telling her I had asked him not to call and that now, here he was.

"Shit, I can't believe you—a tall, well-off, intelligent man, who wined and dined you for days on end, in New York for God's sake, and you chicken out. Not once but each and every time? Are you crazy, as nutty as these pistachios? What a waste. It's a sad state of affairs when two obviously horny people can't indulge in some crazy wild sex. Oh Lee," she sighed dramatically, "I'm so disappointed."

In hindsight, I had to admit it had been a waste. I had often wondered what it would have been like to allow myself that final adventure, those intriguing moments of luxurious sensation.

Barb's words broke through my thoughts.

"But, lucky you. Apparently he hasn't taken no for an answer. Yippee, you get a second chance. There may be a God after all. Call him. Stephen, not God, although that would be a nice trick if you could pull that off. I have a few things to say to him—God not Stephen. Anyhow, I want to listen. This should be rich!" She passed me the phone.

"Yeah, right, like I'm going to call him. I've made it this far. It was just a little blip on the screen, nothing more. It was great for my ego, but to pick it up now, after I've managed to settle back into my life? Brian and I have finally made it to a place that's comfortable. No way. Not going to happen."

Barb chewed a few more pistachios.

"Chicken," she taunted, as she began trying to make clucking noises with a mouthful of nuts.

Barb was dead right. I was a chicken. A confused chicken. We sat there, Barb slowly munching away, all the while staring at me as if she could somehow *will* me to pick up the phone.

I broke first.

"You piss me off, sitting there all calm and cool, chewing away. This is big, this is huge—"

She cut me off. "Oh crap, Lee, it's only as big as you decide to make it." She cracked a shell between her teeth. "And frankly? This is damned fun, watching you squirm. So, what are you going to say?"

Barb asked the very question that had been bouncing around my brain. What in the world would I say? A jolly, casual, "Hi, how are you?" as if it were the most normal thing in the world? Hardly. No. I didn't know what to say because I didn't know what I was feeling. Was I angry that he had taken things into his own hands, disregarding what I had insisted on? Or was I actually happy that he had decided to take the lead by ignoring what I said I wanted? It seemed to make so much sense at the time. Now it made no sense at all.

"Barb, I don't know what to say." Truly, I was stumped.

"Well," Barb continued, "I have a brilliant suggestion. Pick up the phone, dial, and when he answers, say hello. I imagine he can take it from there. You know, you've always had a tendency to think too much. Knock it off. Trust me, it's like riding a bike. The social chitchat will kick right in, and pretty soon you'll be rolling right along."

"Okay, okay, but you sure as hell can't listen! Outta here. Now! No, wait a minute. You can't be trusted—you'll get to the other side of the door and throw your back out straining to hear every word. I'm going down to the pond. Given your complete dislike of nature, I'll be adequately protected." Before Barb could land another shot, I grabbed the phone and made for the back door.

———————————————◆———————————————

Sitting on my faithful bench by the pond, I considered my options. I could: 1) be polite but very busy, too busy to get together; 2) meet for coffee in the morning, preferably somewhere on the edge of town, like on the other side of the Oregon/California border; or 3) agree to a casual, broad-daylight lunch and see who this man was on my own turf. But none of these felt right. I stared out at the pond as I had done a million times before when I had to make a decision. The soothing waters usually helped me identify exactly what I was feeling or what I wanted to do. But this time, all I saw was my own confusion lapping quietly against the muddy edges of the pond. How could the water be so calm when inside I felt like a sea of whitecaps?

I revisited the whirlwind of the last couple months: the arrival of both Lily and Sam, taking on Barb as a roommate. My household was once again brimming with life, and happily, miraculously, I only felt partially responsible for any of them. This was different, very different, and it felt healthy and right. Everything was moving along so smoothly that the ease of it continued to surprise me.

Then, without warning, I thought of Brian—dear, loyal, determined-to-make-it-better Brian. How had we managed to arrive at this satisfying place? Had we actually learned something from our time apart, or were we simply falling back into old patterns out of habit? Most of the time I didn't think so. I made a mental list of everything that was different: I didn't hesitate to tell him when I wasn't available; I never did anything for him that I didn't want to do, as I felt no obligation toward him; we frequently had long, emotionally rich discussions about everything from global warming to his attachment to Lily, and he seemed comfortable, competent in speaking what was a new language for him. I stopped and considered this last thought.

Really, how could a man actually be so different? It floored me, his newly developed capacity for insightful, emotional expression. That didn't exist in male DNA, did it? Trying to read between his lines was gone, making our communication nearly effortless. If he was angry, he simply presented his case. He didn't lose himself out in the barn or disappear in his office on campus. He didn't curse at the innocent dog that happened to be sleeping on the porch as he left the house in a huff, or snap his book shut, slam it down on the table, and sit in stone-cold silence. Perhaps most importantly, he never pushed me in any direction, as if he now respected my independence and was not threatened by it. I had to admit it—Brian was a very different fellow these days.

Of course, I also had to admit that I was different too. Not only had I figured out how to stop being responsible for the entire planet, but I had also managed to cut myself loose from the need to control every possible thing in my personal universe. I was finally free from the burden of trying to be the perfect faculty wife, the perfect mother of four, the perfect business owner. Hell, even my gardens used to be perfect. I thought back to all those years of impeccable flower gardens, green beans befitting the cover of *Home and Garden* magazine, row after row of pristine, weed-free corn. I laughed at myself, grateful for the turmoil that had been the last few years of my life.

No, we hadn't just stumbled into this place by default; we had both worked hard to get here. And yes, it felt very comfortable because of our history and, more importantly, because we had put each other through the wringer and come out the other side stronger than ever before. The reality was, our time together truly felt like a well-thought-out choice we were both making.

Then, like some special effect from a black-and-white movie of yesteryear, Stephen's face floated into my consciousness. Tall, handsome, charming, bright Stephen, who for whatever reason had called me. Honestly? I was thrilled beyond belief, bathed in a moment of pure, self-satisfying joy. But where did he fit into all this? Might the grass be greener on the other side? Was I actually considering exploring what he might have to offer? Was the risk worth it? Wait a minute, exactly what was the risk? And why couldn't I begin to answer any of these questions?

Of course, it all came back to Brian. For months I had avoided looking at exactly what it was the two of us were doing. Pulling my legs up under me, I stared at the pond, realizing I was stumped.

And then I saw the turtle. I strained to see his markings, then smiled. It *was* Captain Salsa, the same turtle the kids had discovered years before, observing that his moves weren't anything like the hot, gyrating dance we'd seen at a recent Cinco de Mayo festival. They'd all been disgusted, their father so utterly disinterested he walked away in search of a taco. Ignoring them all, I had lost myself in the pulse of the music, wondering if I could get my hips to move in that incredibly sexual, passionate way and knowing I never would be able to.

And now, here was Captain Salsa, making his way up onto the log that had always been his place to sun himself. I smiled at the gift he brought with him, remembering my Captain Salsa Epiphany. Ever since that Cinco de Mayo celebration, I had wanted to take a salsa class. But did I? Never, not once would I allow myself a dance class, fearing the embarrassing laughter of my children and the disinterest of my husband. What a waste! Why had I been so afraid to do something so simple?

I picked up the phone and dialed Stephen's cell phone number. One ring: nothing. Oh, here we go again. Two rings: my resolve began to fade. Three rings: I cursed Alexander Bell for his invention. On the fourth ring, I prayed for a bolt of lightning to my temple. I couldn't stand it and started to hang up.

"Hello," his rich voice answered.

"Hi Stephen, it's Lee." I hoped Barb was right, that a lifetime of talking would magically bubble right back into place and I wouldn't sound like a tongue-tied neophyte.

"Ah, hello. How nice to hear your voice. I wasn't sure you'd call me after your very clear and direct decision in New York. But, really, I'm not stalking you—I was making the rounds for some clients, scouting some new galleries. I mean, since I was in the neighborhood, how could I pass up Ashland? Wouldn't be good business, now, would it?"

"In the neighborhood? Come on, the only other art market of any substance is in San Francisco or Portland—Ashland isn't exactly a direct route!" I was relieved he laughed. "So, you really do have some paintings you want me to see? I figured you were trying to pull a fast one over on Tom. I guess my ego got in the way of that one." I couldn't believe I had said that out loud. The phone was quiet. Finally he spoke.

"Okay, busted. But did you really think I was going to settle for what we had in New York? I waited for you to call, but it didn't take long to realize you weren't going to. It didn't surprise me. But it wasn't what I wanted so, sorry, here I am. How about an innocent little dinner at The Peerless Restaurant, over in… wait… let me check my notes," I could hear him rummaging through papers, "in the Railroad District. The desk clerk said they have fantastic food, and I want to see what this neighborhood is all about."

I stared at Captain Salsa as Stephen's words flew around inside my head like crazed birds, aware that I was starting to slide into something gloomy and restrictive. What would Brian say if he knew I was having this conversation? Why did I suddenly feel like I was cheating on him? Good God, what if he drove up right at this very moment? I'd explode in a mass of guilt. But why… why?

Fortunately, like bullets from a Gatling gun, Barb's words sprayed into the middle of my flock—she was right, I did think too much. I opened my mouth, hoping that whatever came out would make sense.

"Okay, you win. You'll like The Peerless. It's one of Ashland's little gems. What night works best for you?" I was trying very hard to sound friendly but cool. It wasn't working. I broke. "Oh Stephen, this is just too weird. I kept wondering why you didn't call, knowing all along that it's what I had asked for but wishing you would and now that you have, I feel completely goofed up!"

"Goofed up? Now there's a little phrase I don't often hear on the eastern seaboard. Is that Oregonian-speak?" We shared an awkward laugh. He was the first to break the silence that followed.

"Listen Lee, I thought about picking up the phone a dozen times, more than that. But you were so adamant that night, and truth be told, I felt pretty burned. Every day we spent together in New York, well… it seemed like something quite special was happening, and then you calmly drew a very big line in the sand. It threw me, big-time. It's taken a while to lick my wounds. But then, one day when I was back in New York on business, it hit me, sort of, 'Screw it, call her, you stupid bastard. The worse that can happen is that you get kicked in the gut again.'"

I was stunned.

"Stephen, I'm so sorry. I never dreamed I hurt you. Honestly, you struck me as such a dashing man-about-town, sophisticated, well traveled. I figured your curiosity about this hick from the sticks was interesting but nothing more. As clichéd as it may sound, it seemed like you could have any woman you wanted. So when you brought up coming out here, I was it completely knocked off my pins. It was like hearing a language I didn't speak. I remember staring at the naked skeleton of that poor quail on my plate, wishing I knew what to say next. The only thing I did know was that I was too recently separated and still trying on my new life. It seemed too dangerous to toss another man into the mix. Please, accept my apology. Now I feel like goofed-up scum."

I noticed that Captain Salsa had slipped back into the pond. My mood was slipping right in behind his bony tail. Stephen's laugh surprised me.

"Buy me a Peerless martini, and all is forgiven. What time shall I pick you up tonight?"

In an instant, he had moved on. I shook my head from side to side, like some cartoon character trying to come to her senses after a one-two knockout punch. Pick me up? Tonight? Come out here and see my life? I don't think so. I was relieved I rebounded so quickly.

"How about I meet you at the gallery? I can give you a real tour before dinner and look at your slides. You do have some to show me, right? That wasn't a complete scam, was it? How about seven? You can park in the back. The door will be open."

"Seven it is. I look forward to it, Lee. Bye." And the phone went silent.

Stephen in the gallery. Stephen and me at The Peerless. How could this be happening? What would I wear? What would John, the maître d' and my friend of many years, say? And then the worst question of all arose: What would Brian say if he found out?

Captain Salsa was nowhere to be seen.

It was Barb's voice that finally interrupted my contemplation. I turned to see her yelling at me from the porch.

"Come on. You're not going to make me come all the way down there, are you? Trot your skinny ass up here and fill me in on all the juicy stuff because, though I hate to admit it, eavesdropping from this distance is downright impossible!"

———◆———

After years of working late in the gallery, I knew each and every alley sound by heart—feral cats that would appear after dark to root through the garbage cans, the occasional homeless soul in search of a place to sleep, a random dog free to chase the moonlight. So the approach of Stephen's car was easy to identify. I heard the wheels come to a slow stop on the gravel, the sound of the door opening and gently closing, his steps to the door, and then the quiet knock.

I looked in the mosaic-framed mirror that hung above my desk, checking my hair for the tenth time. Giving myself one last pep talk, I quickly walked over to the back door and opened it. He stood back a few feet and to the left, his face hidden in the shadows. But it was the man I remembered: tall, impeccably dressed, smiling in the evening light, and holding a bouquet of roses. With just one step, he was on the porch.

"Nice to see you again," he said as he handed me the flowers. "Yep, you're still as beautiful as I remember."

I reached speechlessly for the flowers.

Stephen took a step toward me, and as we met, he opened his long arms and gathered me up. The kiss was long and delicious, the fragrance of the flowers like frosting on a sweet, ambrosial cake. Without hesitation, I relaxed into his arms and savored the moment.

"Oh my." I caught my breath and took a small step back. "Nice to see you too."

He laughed. "Yes, I'd have to agree."

I grabbed Stephen by the arm and ushered him into the gallery, nervous that someone would see us. I motioned him into the main room.

"These roses are absolutely beautiful. Thank you. Why don't you look around while I get them into a vase." I disappeared into my office, grateful to have the opportunity to collect myself, but his voice followed me.

"You have some really interesting pieces here. This pastel and ink by Addy Desmone—I like it. Do you have anything else by her?"

I stared at the flowers, my finger navigating their soft, gentle curves as my brain tried to process what was happening around me. Suddenly Barb's voice blared inside of my head, "Stop thinking!"

"Uh yes, there are a couple of her sculptures near the front door—I especially like her *Dark Horse*. See it? The one with the copper base and ceramic body that's embellished with stones and apparently anything else she could find."

I brought the vase out into the gallery and set it on my desk. Stephen stood in front of the sculpture, taking in every detail. He turned when he heard me return.

"I like her work, really like it. It caught my eye when I was in earlier today. I think I know of a little gallery in the Village that would like it too. Mind if I have her number?" At that moment, I realized he was all work. We were in a professional exchange that I found familiar, comforting. I knew how to behave within such parameters. I began to look through my files, found her number, and wrote it down and handed it to Stephen.

"She's in eastern Washington. I happen to have these pieces because she wandered in here last theater season and we hit it off. Nice woman. She shows mainly throughout the western states, so New York would be an incredible opportunity for her."

This was easy. I could talk business, even with Stephen. I relaxed and began to enjoy myself as we moved from piece to piece, painting to painting, sharing our view of each work in an easy, casual way. Mostly we agreed, but on some things we didn't. I enjoyed the lively feel of our disagreements, each of us willing to defend our beliefs without attacking the perspective of the other. I felt happy to be in his company.

Stephen looked at his watch.

"I made our reservations for eight thirty—looks like we might have time for a drink before we eat. What do you think? It's your call." We stood close, his hand gently resting on the small of my back. From out of nowhere, I suddenly imagined Tom showing up unexpectedly, and I flinched at the thought.

"What?" Stephen asked.

"Oh, this is just too weird. You in my gallery, us sharing this physical space. Bear with me, I seem to be having a moment—exactly what kind of moment, I'm not sure I can explain. I think I'm a little panic-stricken at the thought of being seen with you in public. How would you feel about ordering a pizza and having a picnic right here?"

He looked at me hard, a frown on his face.

"Are you ashamed of me, or is there something I should know?" He waited for my response. When there wasn't one forthcoming, he continued. "Are you back with your husband? Is that it? Is that why you're so jumpy?" I was aware that his hand had fallen from my waist. I missed it already.

I sat down on the carpet. Stephen looked around for a chair, and when he couldn't spot one, he settled in next to me on the floor.

"You could use a bench or something in here." His voice was sullen; his mood had shifted. I hadn't seen this side of him before. He stared straight ahead and waited.

"No, I am not back with Brian, but that's not to say we haven't been seeing each other." I paused. "That's part of why I was so shocked to hear from you. I had come to accept my time with you in New York as something I thoroughly enjoyed, which, if you must know, is a real understatement. Those two weeks felt like a possibility that could have turned out quite differently if only we had met at a later time in my life. I took so much away with me from our time together. I liked who I was with you, and I've kept those parts around."

Stephen inched closer to me. "I imagine your husband likes those parts too. He'd be a fool not to." He tugged at the edge of my sweater. "Okay, so I guess I'm still in the game?" His good mood returned, and he rested his hand on my knee. I was glad I had decided not to wear nylons. The touch of his fingers exploded on my skin. It was hard to concentrate, even harder to know what to say. But I didn't need to worry. Stephen leaned over and kissed me again, then whispered in my ear.

"Enough talking. Let's go get that drink and just see what happens."

I had to agree with his wisdom.

———————————◆———————————

As a longtime resident of Ashland, I knew The Peerless would make me proud. It was always one of the restaurants I recommended to travelers, and I knew Stephen would be pleased. We ordered our drinks and settled into a cozy table by the windows overlooking the garden. He perused the menu.

"I'm starving. What do you recommend?"

"You know how it is: Locals don't often eat in the places visitors frequent. To tell you the truth, the last time I was inside this restaurant is when I delivered that little watercolor hanging just inside the front door. But I recall waiting for the owner to come out from the kitchen, and when the door swung open, the smells alone filled my stomach."

The waiter arrived at our table, and Stephen led the way.

"Well, I can only tell you what I think looks good. We're not in any hurry, so let's take our time with this menu. How about a little food sharing? I'll start with the Dungeness crab parfait. You?" He turned to me.

The menu was a blur. I realized I was waging a small war with reality and that I was losing. Somehow I managed to ask for the cheese sampler with Rogue Blue and Fog Light assorted grilled vegetables— whatever that meant.

"Great!" Stephen seemed pleased with my choice. "I'll trade you a bite of my parfait for a taste of your Rogue Blue. The Rogue—that's a river around here, isn't it?"

The entire time Stephen was ordering, I had been fighting to keep my butt in the chair. It felt like I might float right up to the ceiling, like some weightless astronaut bouncing around above the planet. What if someone saw me? What if the owner came out to talk about the painting? Oh my God, what if Brian showed up at the next table? That thought stopped me cold—the realization that Brian's reaction to this cozy little scene would matter so much to me. I dropped back into my body. Somehow my voice found its way out of my throat in spite of the cognitive logjam going on between my ears.

"Yep, the Rogue is a beautiful river. Plenty of rapids to run and some fantastic swimming holes." I stared at the magnolia white linens, desperate to relax, determined to find the right words.

Stephen reached over and took my hand.

"This isn't working, is it?"

I looked across the table at Stephen. In the privacy of my own thoughts, he had jumped right out of the pages of a romance novel. Perhaps Stephen offered me a real page-turner, but what I knew in my heart was that Brian offered me a classic sequel of exceptional worth.

"No, Stephen, this isn't working." We sat in silence.

He was the first to speak.

"Can't say I'm not surprised. I knew I was taking a huge chance coming all the way out here." He finished his wine in one swallow as he pushed his chair away from the table. "Mind if we call it an evening? I have to drive to Portland tomorrow, and I'd like to get an early start."

And right before my eyes, Prince Charming disappeared. It was a side of him I hadn't seen. Polite but cool—very cool. For a moment, I wondered how much of this I would have seen over the course of a relationship with him. And then, a tiny wisp of vindication for having made the right choice filtered down through my bones. Stephen had his warts too.

There would be nothing more from this handsome man. My heart began to dip, but I caught it before it hit the floor. For in that precise moment, I finally realized the most important thing of all: that even without Brian or Stephen in my life, I treasured what I had in this beautiful little town, who I had become, what my life meant in all its stunning simplicity. I finally had myself, and that was priceless.

We drove back to the gallery in silence. After an awkward good-bye, I locked myself inside, grateful for the warm, forgiving surroundings. Too bad the decision I had just made was staring me in the face.

Sure, New York had felt good, and parts of this night had been quite appealing. But all I could think of was the energy it would take to start all over with someone new, even if he did make my heart flutter like full-blown atrial defibrillation. Was that a pathetic reflection of my fear? My age? Wait a minute—perhaps it was a realistic reaction to my marriage and the irreplaceable value of a relationship that had proven itself to be satisfying, resilient, and comforting. Stephen offered mystery, an excitement I hadn't felt in years, but I realized that the familiarity of knowing another human being so completely was far more exciting to me. The effort Brian had made these last few months to understand himself and to understand me... Who needs Dr. Phil? We had Pissant Man, as well as Brian's relentless determination to be different in this world.

Which was not to say that he had achieved perfection. Hardly. His need to organize the entire pantry, labels out, irritated me beyond belief. I still resented the way he could get so completely lost in thoughts about work or a difficult student. And more than once, I had thrown something on the floor just to see how long he could stand having it there before he quickly and quietly picked it up and put it in its proper place.

But the reality was that I, too, was walking imperfection. I still didn't balance my checkbook every month like a normal adult. Yes, at times I had a blind eye when it came to animals and children, and even worse I'd come to acknowledge how I'd used my maternal responsibilities to hide from the intimacy Brian needed and we both deserved. And, try as I might, I was still quick to burn and slow to recover. For years I had labored against these imperfections, working overtime on many fronts to compensate for my shortcomings. Now I acknowledged them, worked on them, and accepted the fact that neither one of us came close to perfection.

The bottom line? Brian and I continued to love each other, warts and all. It had always been that way, and that was the strength of the relationship. We had survived the worst of the worst, the tears, the arguments and disappointments, and through it all, we managed to keep moving forward.

Barb was rocking Lily in the sunroom when I returned home. The house was shadowed and still, except for the smooth, rhythmic sound of wood on hardwood floor. I sat down across from her and slipped off my shoes.

"Looks like you dumped him again?" Her voice was soft. This woman knew me well.

"Yep. It would have been a great fling, but I'm not in the market for flings."

The sound of gentle pats on baby flannel floated throughout the small room. Barb stared out into the night, took a slow, deep breath, and continued.

"Well, can't say I'm not disappointed. Personally, I was in the market for a vicarious fling. It would have done me some good. But that's it, isn't it? My Moll Flanders to your Elizabeth Bennet?"

It was easy to see Moll Flanders, but Elizabeth of *Pride and Prejudice*? Me, a nineteenth-century character? She saw the look on my face.

"Don't freak out on me. Think about it—you're pretty quick witted, smart, loyal, a real looker when you let your hair down, and, most importantly, not about to settle for the second-best Mr. Collins—who always struck me as a real wiener, probably quite unlike your Mr. Brunswick in that respect. Don't you remember when Elizabeth rebukes him?" Barb slid into a perfect British accent. "Do not consider me now as an elegant female but as a rational female speaking the truth from her heart." She caught her breath and stopped rocking. "Am I right or what? Yeah, I wanted you to have the fling. Any woman in my situation would agree. But truly, when it comes to this relationship crap, hell, life in general, you've always been twenty steps ahead of me. I'm glad you managed to listen to yourself and not me. Then again, you usually have, which probably explains why each of us finds herself where she is today. Three cheers for you, Elizabeth!"

17

*F*ollowing my evening with Stephen, I was... how can I describe it? Ho-hum? Perhaps. Lackluster? Indeed. Blah, bland, beige? No, not beige. Blue. I moved through my life as though stuck in one of Picasso's paintings during his Blue Period. Full of melancholy and resignation, like the Master himself, I seemed to be in the throes of silent mourning. But Picasso's grief was justifiable grief, the suicide of a young friend having triggered this profound phase of his creativity. Me? Come on, no one had died! I felt silly, embarrassed by my mood. They made no sense, these feelings that weighed me down. That night at The Peerless, my decision not to proceed with Stephen had arrived with such clarity. It was the right thing to do, and here's the weird part: I trusted that it still was. My confidence had not wavered. So why did I feel flatter than an armadillo on Route 66?

Imagine my surprise when Brian was the one to finally drag me back from mucking around in the blue mud. Through his platonic helping hand, I was restored to rosy pinks and cheery yellows.

He happened by the gallery late one afternoon, something he had rarely done over the years; he'd once said he felt "out of place among all the fine art." I had resented the comment. It smacked of something I didn't quite understand, yet I knew it represented some of our deepest troubles. But on this day, he came in quietly through the back door to find me stuck talking with a demanding tourist, a woman from Georgia who had obviously missed the requisite "Southern Charm" course. She seemed to find great satisfaction in haggling over the price of a painting, as if we were standing in the middle of my driveway during a Saturday yard sale bickering over a chipped Blue Willow saucer. But I refused to give an inch. My loyalty to this particular artist was strong, as she had been exceptionally kind to me years before, when my mother died. There was no way on God's green earth that I would ever broker a deal on one of Pam's paintings with this rotten Georgia peach.

Brian in the back of the gallery broke the spell this beastly woman seemed to cast upon me. I found my true voice.

"No," I said, "I won't take a penny less than the listed price." The glare from my eyes matched my disingenuous smile. My delivery was strong. "I don't believe we have anything more to discuss."

With that, the polyester-clad, diamond-dripping matron waddled out of the gallery in a huff. I couldn't have cared less.

Brian grinned as he walked up to me.

"Nice work! I can't imagine how you managed to keep your cool."

I laughed. "It was easy. She was trying to steal one of Pam's paintings. Need I say more?"

Brian nodded his head in agreement, knowing my history with Pam. Then he looked around the gallery.

"Are we alone?" he wondered.

His question surprised me.

"Yes. Quite. I always work Wednesday afternoons. Tom's at his blessed boccie ball league, and Sam's—"

He interrupted me, "Sorry, I forgot. I mean, I know that. I just didn't remember it when I should have. I… " he stopped cold. He was flustered.

I put my hand on his arm.

"Bri, what's the matter? You're a little antsy. Has something happened?"

"No, nothing's wrong. I just had it on my mind to thank you for something, and now that I'm standing here, it seems a little silly and I hope you take it the right way." He looked at the floor. "Do you know what day it is?" he asked.

"Well, yes, it's April 7." I waited.

"Do you remember what happened on April 7, 1982?"

I mulled the date over in my mind, but before I could answer, he pulled a small gold package from his coat and put it in my hands.

"It's the day I was hired by the university. Remember? Sean was almost a year old, and we were living in that crummy little house over on Third Street."

I remembered it as if it were yesterday. We'd had a tender celebration that night. In the pouring-down rain, Brian barbecued steaks on the back porch and we shared a bad bottle of champagne. We knew a huge piece of our life puzzle had finally fallen into place.

Taking my hands, Brian continued.

"I've been thinking about it lately, and I don't think I ever properly thanked you for your part in my getting that job. The hours you worked, the sacrifices you made. It was no picnic." Suddenly, he seemed self-conscious.

"Well, thank you, Lee. One friend to another, I wouldn't have had my professional success without you." He nodded to me to open the package.

Untying the gold satin ribbon and carefully peeling away the exquisite brocade paper, I discovered a book bound in rich Moroccan green leather and worn with age. *The Wind in the Willows* was my favorite book from childhood, and I had read it to our children countless times. Brian's excitement broke through my thoughts.

"Open it up; look at the illustrations," he prompted.

I gently thumbed the pages until I came to a fetching, dreamy color plate. I knew the style immediately, recognizing it as the work of Arthur Rackman, a leading illustrator of the Edwardian period. Quickly flipping to the front, I noted the publication date.

"Good Lord, Brian, I can't believe you found an original of this edition. You've always known my love of Rackman's illustrations. This is a treasure, a gem. I think this may have actually been the last book he illustrated, published posthumously. Amazing. Where in the world did you ever find it?"

Brian's face lit up.

"Oh, I've been doing a little sleuthing on the Internet. It was actually easier than I thought." He looked into my eyes.

"Lee, I don't think I ever appreciated so many different things about you like I should have—our incredible kids, the way you always stuck beside each and every one of us, even the way you saved our stupid one-eyed pug. I'm afraid I took you for granted, and I regret that." His eyes filled with tears.

I hugged him, relaxing into his arms and a delicious moment of familiarity.

When I finally pulled away, Brian broke the silence.

"Won't it be great when Lily is old enough for you to read it to her?"

Driving home that evening, I realized I felt lighter than I had in days. Gone was the molasses mood that had been my second skin. I contemplated the shift. What was it about Brian and his thoughtful gift that brought me back to where I wanted to be—clear, positive, and moving forward? There was the genuine simplicity of the moment: his gift was pure, without expectation. Certainly, it was the book itself, the selection a lovely reflection of our history and his intimate knowledge of me. But his ability to acknowledge something so significant about himself, about us, to finally articulate his appreciation of me—that was the real gift.

Coming around the final curve in the road, my beautiful farmhouse came into sight just as another painful truth floated into my mind. Perhaps we were both guilty of taking the other for granted. Why did married people do that to each other? I'd faithfully thank the gas station attendant for a clean windshield but fail to properly appreciate Brian for washing the entire car. Such an act was simply bad manners, practiced on the people we cared most about in the world. Ridiculous. A waste. Turning into the driveway, I vowed to express my appreciation more.

Pulling my jeep into the backyard, I wondered if we might have an early spring after all. The ornamental cherry trees that lined the south edge of the pond were in full bloom, and daffodils filled the pastures. That was one good thing about getting rid of the sheep last fall—the return of the daffodils. I watched as the bright green stems with the happy yellow blossoms swayed in the evening breeze, understanding why even a dumb sheep would find them appetizing.

I was surprised to see Barb's car parked under the old oak tree. Wasn't it Sam's turn to look after Lily? He hadn't been at work, so where was he? I hoped he hadn't blown it. Balancing dinner groceries on one hip and my overflowing bag on the other, I pushed my way into the warm kitchen.

"I'm home," I called out.

"We're out here, soaking up some rays," Barb answered from the sunporch.

Putting everything on the table, I hung my bag on the back of the chair and made my way to the front of the house. Kicking off my shoes in the hall, I turned the corner and walked into the warmest room in the house. I found Barb curled up in the wicker rocking chair, looking out over the pond. Lily lay at her feet, plump and happy, trying hard to grab the elusive shadow the wind chimes made on her flannel quilt. I smiled at the tableau.

"Well, isn't this a grand scene to come home to?"

"Yeah, the Madonna and child… well, sort of."

It was a classic Barbism, and after an especially long day, it gave me a good laugh.

"When I saw your car in the yard, I began to think the absolute worst about my son. Tell me he hasn't screwed up. Wasn't he supposed to be here? Why aren't you at work, anyhow?" I pulled off my sweater and settled into the matching love seat. "Brian always hated this set and I still love it—white wicker with yellow cushions. It doesn't get any more sunporchie than that, does it?"

I looked over at Barb for her reaction, expecting a sarcastic response—but what I saw stopped me cold. Her skin was puffy, red, and splotchy. Tears lay on her cheeks.

"Oh God, I knew it," I moaned. "What has Sam done?"

She wagged a finger at me.

"Shame on you. Relax. Sam hasn't done a thing. He's our Wonder Boy, and how dare you think for even a minute that he's anything less than perfect." Barb blew her nose. "In case you didn't get the memo, those days are over for him."

Barb blew her nose again, this time loudly, dramatically. The sound shocked Lily, who burst into tears. Her mother bent down to pick up her startled daughter.

"Oh, sorry, kiddo. I was going for some comic relief. Didn't mean to freak you out."

Lily stopped crying as soon as she was in her mother's lap. She looked at me and smiled, pushing both chubby cheeks up high. Barb craned her neck to see her daughter's face.

"See, there it is, that little Eskimo thing I was telling you about. Look how her eyes get all deliciously squinty. Isn't that the sweetest baby blob face you ever saw?" Barb's eyes filled with tears, and I couldn't stand it anymore. I slid onto the ottoman.

"Ha! I win, Liliputt, I bet her that you couldn't stay on the love seat if I started crying. What is it with you and tears? It's as if they have some magnetic force that pulls you to them." Barb blew her nose for the third time, this time her approach uncharacteristically ladylike.

I ignored the comment and asked, "What's going on?"

Barb took a long, deep breath and drew Lily even closer.

"Like the good little girl you wanted me to be, I not only made an appointment with Dr. Birchard, but I actually kept it. In fact, I've kept a couple of appointments in the last few weeks. I was surprised at first that you weren't bugging me anymore about going to see her. But then I got to thinking about how well you know me, and I figured that you backed off to make sure I would go. If you had kept on me, you know I wouldn't have gone, just to be stubborn. Am I right or what?"

Barb wiped her eyes and stroked Lily's curly black hair. "Thank God she seems to have her father's hair. At least, I think I remember some curls on his head." She bent down to kiss Lily's head. "No matter, little girl. Just remember that though it wasn't the most memorable twenty-seven minutes in your mother's life, your conception was the best thing to have ever happened to her." She took another deep breath and looked up at me.

"Get this. I have cancer." Barb paused, then added, "No joke."

I sat perfectly still, trying to make meaning of the words I had just heard, words that were roaming around my brain, frantically trying to find a place to land, to take hold, to be real. I took Lily's tiny hand, wishing all the while that I could gather up the mother, whose eyes were filled with terror.

I paused a moment. "Okay, tell me more."

Barb played with a curl at the nape of Lily's neck.

"I went in a couple of weeks ago, and she did a pelvic and ordered an ultrasound. Not the fun kind, like when I was pregnant. It wasn't actually painful, by the way, just weird. I imagine it's what the Martians do when they come to earth and abduct unsuspecting people with low IQs, you know, the probing and all. Anyhow, Dr. Birchard told me not to worry, probably just a minor problem with my uterus—perhaps it wasn't healing correctly. She was very reassuring, and I believed her. I figured I'd tell you when I knew something." She started to cry again. "Well, now I know too much." I reached out to hold hands with Barb and Lily.

"I saw her today, and all the tests had come back. It's some weird uterine cancer that has a tendency to strike older women. Bummer to land in that category, but I digress. Of course, it didn't help that I was fat and pregnant. Three strikes, I guess. Did you know fat cells produce estrogen? That sucks, doesn't it, the older part?" She wiped her eyes again. "Well, I suppose the cancer part sucks even more."

I waited for her to continue, counting my breaths so I would appear calm.

"She wants me to cruise on up to Eugene, immediately no less, to see a specialist for more tests. She says I need a complete hysterectomy, but beyond that, she's not sure—'most probably chemo' was how she put it—but she wants to wait and see what the oncologist says. Chemo! Can you imagine me bald? I'll look like a freakin' sumo wrestler. Poor Lily, look, kiddo, no hair!" Lily smiled at the sound of her mother's voice. "Aren't you just the luckiest girl in the world?"

Barb began to weep. I wrapped my arms around her and held her while the woman I knew best in the world cried and cried.

All the while, Lily seemed surprisingly content to cuddle between the two of us. After what seemed like a very long time, Barb finally whispered, "Baby Pickle in the Middle" and came up for air. She wiped her face and kissed her daughter's hair.

"Oh Lordy, I've leaked all over your sweet baby head."

Lily broke into her Eskimo face and tried to grab her mother's nose. It was as close to playing a game that a five-month-old could muster, and Barb joyfully played right back.

After a few minutes, I asked, "Okay, so when do we go to Eugene?"

"I knew it. I just knew you'd want to tag along on my date with destiny." Barb tried for a laugh but managed only a weak chuckle. "Sorry, that was pathetic." She spoke to her daughter. "Pay up, kid. That's the second bet you've lost today. I told you she'd have to come along for the ride." Looking back at me, she said, "You are so predictable..."

Barb adjusted herself in the chair. "And I am so grateful." She paused, then added, "I have to be there on Thursday. Dr. Birchard is sending up the results of a major body scan she did. Creeped me out, that tubular experience. So, lucky us, we'll know even more then." She blew her nose again. "I hope this cancer adventure isn't as messy as all of this snot."

In a flash, Barb pulled one of her famous 180-degree turns.

"Shit, enough of this Lifetime Channel, movie-of-the-week crap. Forget the cancer; maybe I have a rare case of egoechophobia as well. Ever heard of that?" she wondered. "Aha, stumped you again."

I sat in my chair, overwhelmed by what she was saying but knowing better than to ask any more questions. Barb was back in the driver's seat, determined to shift the focus off herself. It was the time to play by her rules.

"All right, I'll bite," I conceded. "What does egoechophobia mean?"

Barb laughed as she pulled Lily close to her.

"Ha! Gold star for me. Okay, for starters, it's not some strange disease from the Amazon rain forest, just a new word an NPR talk show guy made up, referring to people who don't like to talk about themselves. He's trying to get people to use it enough times so it will eventually be included in Webster's. Egoechophobia, egoechophobia, egoechophobia, egoechophobia—that's four right there. Get the editors on the phone." She looked out the window before going on.

"Sums it up rather nicely, don't you think? Diagnosed today, and I'm already sick of hearing myself talk." Barb looked back at me. "Where was I? That's right, Eugene-bound. Can you think of anything fun to do in that good-old college town? I mean, the sum total of the trip can't be hanging out at the oncologist's. You might as well shoot me now. At first I thought the best thing would be to take Ella out for some great chow, but the truth of the matter is, I don't know if I can fake it well enough to do that."

I nodded in agreement. We were both stalled by the reality of the situation. And with that, the Farmhouse Three slipped into silence. Lily, a thumb sucker from early on, slurped happily on her tiny digit while we stared out at the pond. It was still and glassy. Tiny wildflowers were beginning to sprout around the edges. A small flock of ridiculously plump red robins searched for worms in the evening air. There we sat, holding hands, the two of us lost in the dreadful possibilities of our own thoughts.

It was after midnight when Sam finally came home. Sleepy dog tails thumped a slow greeting as he gingerly closed the kitchen door behind him. I could hear him taking off his boots in the darkness. Listening to his careful, considerate movements, I waited in the dim light of the living room.

"In here, Sam," I quietly called out.

Padding down the hall, he pushed open the door and took a small step into the room, his eyes adjusting to the soft light of the antique reading lamp.

"Can't sleep, huh? Sorry, Mom."

"Hi there. Did you have a good time, whatever it was you were doing tonight? Tell me you were having fun!" I looked at my dear son, wishing I could somehow avoid what was about to happen.

Sam was relieved. "Yeah, actually I had one of the best nights I've had in a long time. Nice people, really good musicians. They're all a little older and wiser than I am, and, just in case you were wondering, they're a very clean-living bunch of vegetarian types."

"How happy I am to say that I wasn't wondering at all." My reassurance seemed to be what he needed. As he relaxed, I dreaded even more what I had to do next, knowing that his life was about to change. "Sit down next to your old mother. We have something to talk about."

Sam listened to the news about Barb, concentrating very hard on what I was telling him. But when he started fidgeting with his sweatshirt zipper, I knew he was about to break. It was a habit he'd had since he was little, and it always preceded a very big cry. I wondered what he would do now that he was all grown-up.

"Mom… " was all he said, and then the tears came. He reached for my hand, then put his head in my lap and began to cry quietly. All I could do was stroke his hair.

Mother and son sat in the shadows for a long time. Butterball,

Sam's seventeen-year-old cat, made her way into the living room and jumped up on the soft sofa to cozy in with Sam. He drew her close and began to pet her. Soon we could both hear her distinct purr. He sat up and blew his nose.

"I tell you, this kind of stuff? It's when Buddhism fails me. I think I'm supposed to say 'challenges me,' but what in the world are we all supposed to learn from this kind of stupid pain?"

He looked at me. "I'm sorry, Mom, I'm such a jerk. Look at you. What can I do to help?"

I looked steadily into my son's beautiful, clear eyes. "It's so odd to have you all grown-up. Do you have any idea how grateful I am for what you are doing with your life? And now, to know I can rely on you for help, that you'll support Barb, take care of Lily with natural talent, fill in for me at the gallery? All of those things will be a huge help."

Right then, our noses filled with an acrid odor. "Oh, Butterball, God that's foul. And talk about lousy timing," I said, fanning the air in front of my nose.

Sam dropped the cat to the floor, saying, "Nothing worse than an old-cat fart, is there." Somehow this struck us both as very funny, and we broke into laughter.

I was the first to regain my composure. "Well, we needed that. Butterball to the rescue, I suppose. Much as I don't want to, we need to return to the task at hand, and that's getting Barb through this." I went on to fill Sam in on what would be happening over the next few days. He immediately volunteered to take care of Lily while we were in Eugene.

"Tom can pick up some shifts at work. He's there most every afternoon anyhow. And sometimes I can have Lily down there with me. It hasn't been that busy. Besides, people love it when she's there. It's a better draw than a cat sleeping in the window like they have over at the Main Street Gallery." He threw his cat a look. "Don't get any ideas, Stink-o. You'd drive the customers out in record time."

I shook my head, laughing. "Right, no public appearances for you," I repeated to Butterball, then turned back to Sam.

"That was my first thought too, that you'd have Lily, but that's not what Barb wants. No, she says she wants to take Lily with us to Eugene because she'll be a great diversion for us. While I think a few diversions would be nice, I can't imagine having the baby there. But this isn't about what I want or need. This is all pretty new, so I think we let Barb sleep on everything and see what she says in the morning. It could all change by then."

"Mom." Sam's voice dropped a full octave. "Barb's going to be okay, right? I mean, I guess hysterectomies aren't exactly easy, and chemo doesn't have a reputation for being a walk in the park. But after all that, she's going to be all right, isn't she?"

I took his hand. "I wish I could answer those questions. We'll know more when we see the oncologist. Until then, I guess I might just have to go back to praying."

Barb didn't change her mind about taking Lily. Two days later, the Farmhouse Three waved good-bye to Sam and headed off down the road.

"He looks kind of pathetic, don't you think?" Barb asked as she craned her neck to look back at Sam. Without waiting for an answer, she rolled down the window and stuck her head out.

"Enough of that shit-ass face. I want one of your famous smiles to send me off!" she yelled.

In the rearview mirror, I could see my son burst into a radiant smile. How far down the road would we be before he started crying? Maybe he could maintain it until the first bend. When I checked the mirror again, he was out of sight. I wished I could have stayed with him, as my need to comfort was split between two people I dearly loved.

"You have such a tender, caring manner," I finally said to Barb.

"Yep, that's me, Queen of the TLC... only right now, I'd kill for a BLT. Is it too early for lunch?"

"You're serious, aren't you?"

"Well, eating beats thinking, and these days I can't seem to stop either. I wonder how many pounds I've gained in the last few days? Great, I'm just a walking estrogen factory on two stubby legs."

We fell into silence and stayed that way for a long time. Soon, both Barb and Lily were dozing, which left me with too much time to think.

I had called Ella with the news the day before to give her the "cheery rendition" Barb had made me promise as we packed things for Lily. "No reason to freak out my beautiful goddaughter, right?"

Barb informed me of our plan. "I've given this a lot of thought, and just so you know, I'm approaching this as our first mother/daughter trip—a tradition that's just been waiting to happen. We'll do a little shopping, stop by the hospital for the requisite medical crapola, go rescue Baby Ella from her cell, and then have a smashing dinner at that Chinese place we like so well, if for no other reason than to have the waitstaff assume I'm one of them as they break into rapid-fire Chinese and I look like a total dumb fuck in response. You'd think they, of all people, could tell a fat Japanese from one of their own tribe."

So that was our schedule: just a little trip to the hospital, a quick visit with the Oncologist of the Year, as Barb had taken to referring to him, and then playtime with our daughters. Some plan. I felt myself beginning to cry and wondered how I was going to pull off my part in this.

The drive was uneventful, for which I was grateful. Although we stopped for lunch, Barb had insisted we fill up on snacks at the mini-mart, buying only food she had the stomach for and that, as she put it, "you don't have the heart to stop me from chowing down on at the moment." Fortunately, Lily was in one of her "angel baby moods," a phase first coined by Sam when he had her at the gallery one afternoon and every time someone came in, Liliputt burst into one of her big smiles and charmed the customer into a sale.

We checked into the motel around three o'clock, dragging suitcases and endless baby paraphernalia into the room. I wondered how one small human could require so much stuff. It would be another two hours until the doctor's appointment.

"Now what are we going to do?" I asked the question both of us had been thinking. "Were you serious about the shopping? I mean, we could go—you know how much I love it!"

Barb laughed. "Ha, shopping for you is right up there with root canals and tax season. Why is that, anyhow, that you have a shopping phobia? Is that something you and Pissant Man ever touch on? And by the way, do you see him anymore? Are you cured?"

I laughed at the barrage of questions. "You have the unique talent of covering more ground in sixty seconds than is humanly possible. And in answer to your questions, number one, it's because I'm six feet tall, and near as I can tell, the world only dresses women up to five eight. As for question number two, the answer is no. To number three, yes, I think so."

Barb stuffed another Cheeto into her mouth, making sure Lily didn't get it first. "Really, you're cured? Could have fooled me!" She tried to keep the orange bits in her mouth as she enjoyed a self-satisfying laugh. In spite of her best efforts, a few crumbs sprayed out on Lily's head. The sight of neon bits on her daughter's jet-black hair was too much for her. She laughed all over again, brushing the debris from Lily's curls. "I am some mother, aren't I?"

When she had managed to clean up most of her mess, she continued. "But really, I've been wanting to ask you about that. I mean, Brian is over all the time, you two never fight, you're both so God-awful cordial these days, well, happy even. Why, I even caught him with his arm around your shoulder the other day. What's up with that? You must be horny as hell by now. Have you done the deed? I hope so—one of us should be getting some these days. And even though I wish I was the lucky winner, tell me, I can take it."

I rolled over on the bed and glared at her. "That's none of your damned business!"

"None of my business? Since when? How long have we known each other? While we're on the subject, I still can't believe you didn't fuck your brains out with Mr. New York—what an opportunity. Tall, dark, handsome, and The Plaza, too? You fool!"

I grabbed the Cheetos. "No more until you promise to lay off. My miserable sex life, or lack thereof, is the last thing I want to think about." I eyed the Cheetos, knowing their fat content would land in my belly like a pair of concrete tennis shoes. I popped one into my mouth, feeling the fat melt all over my tongue. It was disgusting... in a pleasant sort of way.

But I was also giving thought to my friend's predictably invasive and brash inquiries. She was right. Fifty-three and celibate? The thought ran shivers down my spine, which made Cheeto bits and words tumble out of my mouth.

"I mean, really, do you think I'll ever get laid again?"

We looked at each other, my question hanging out there between us, as if asked to God himself. It struck us both as funny, and we were off, ignited, pulled into a glorious, senseless fit of laughter that only women seem to know how to do so well. Lily stared at the two hysterical women on the bed with her for a long moment and then burst into baby giggles, which made us laugh even harder.

Barb kissed her daughter's head. "Oh, you laugh, my sweet! Your day will come, young lady." She realized what she had said only after it was out of her mouth. "Oh God, what a terrible thought, my daughter's sex life, icky, icky, icky, erase, erase. Quick, talk about something else before I throw up all the junk food I've managed to stuff in my gullet within the last three hours."

I patted my friend on the leg and smiled. "Oh, the fun you're going to have—ha, I can hardly wait to see you with a teenage daughter. It will be payback time extraordinaire."

With that, the conversation abruptly stopped, as we realized what we were talking about—the future.

Barb broke the silence. "Short-term memory loss, it's a good thing." She munched down on another Cheeto. "But let's look at this a different way. Maybe missing adolescence isn't such a bad thing."

I threw up my hand to silence her. "You know, you're ornery enough that you're going to suffer a long and miserable motherhood just like the rest of us in this elite club."

Barb snorted like Miss Piggy and threw out, "I should be so lucky."

After listening to what the oncologist reported that afternoon, it was obvious to both of us that Barb was quickly running out of luck.

"I'm very sorry to tell you that your CAT scan shows stage-four cancer. It has metastasized considerably, to your stomach, liver, and lymph nodes as well. After the hysterectomy, we'll put you on an aggressive round of chemo, and it just may be that we can get you stabilized."

Barb was stroking Lily's hair, her face expressionless, her eyes staring at the black curls under her fingers. She was silent, controlled, uncharacteristically focused. The baby sat perfectly still, mesmerized by her mother's touch.

I put my hand on Barb's shoulder and turned to the doctor.

"That's good, isn't it, that you can get her stabilized?"

"Well, yes, that is very good. Once we stop the progression, we can put all our energy into maintaining your current level of health, keeping the pain in check, making sure that your quality of life is everything it can be." He paused for a moment, as if waiting for a reaction. When there was none, he went on. "Ms. Yakamura, I know this isn't what you want to hear, but I believe we will be able to give you a few more years with your beautiful daughter. We'll get the surgery scheduled as soon as possible. Once you have your strength back, we'll begin chemo. It should take about ten to twelve months. Then we'll know much more than we do right now."

Barb finally looked up at the doctor. "You will be able to give me a few more years, right? That's after major surgery, nearly a year of chemo, and then you'll be able to keep my pain in check and my condition maintained. Do I understand you correctly?"

The doctor looked Barb straight in the eye. "Yes, that's what I said."

"And so I'll feel even worse than I already do, there's not much chance I'll ever feel any better, and at best it will be like that for a few more years, right?"

"Right."

"So it would be correct to say that I have terminal cancer, in a few-more-miserable-years kind of way?"

Compassion washed over the doctor's face. "That would be correct," he replied quietly.

We sat silently in the car in the parking lot. Lily tugged away on the bottle I had somehow remembered to bring along. It had begun to rain. The drops slid down the windshield, blurring the outside world into an Impressionist's landscape. Lily finished the bottle and was sucking air for a couple of minutes before I even noticed. I gently pulled the bottle from the baby's mouth, and she reluctantly let go of the nipple.

"Hold up there, baby cakes. You're running on empty. Let's have a go at a burp so you don't get a bad belly."

Throwing a cloth diaper over my shoulder, I put Lily on top of it and began gently patting the baby, as I had done with all my children countless times before. Her back was so tiny. The rhythmic sound of an experienced hand on delicate bird-bone ribs filled the car.

"What'd I tell you?" Barb finally spoke. "Cancer sucks." She fell silent again and then added, "I can't quite wrap my brain around what he said. Ha, maybe it's in my brain too. That might actually be a blessing in disguise, wouldn't it? To not know everything that I know now?" She caught her breath. "Yeah, I vote for that version—complete and total oblivion. Works for me."

Right then, Lily produced a burp befitting a truck driver, so robust even she was surprised. Instinctively, Lily searched the car for her mother, reaching out for her when their eyes met. Barb gathered her up and smiled.

"That's my girl. Why, we'll have you burping the alphabet before preschool. That will wow and zow your unsuspecting teacher. Show and tell just got a whole lot better." Barb hugged her daughter and began to cry.

I reached over and began patting my friend, just as Barb patted her daughter. We sat like this for a long time. There was simply nothing to say.

The sound of my cell phone ringing brought us back into the moment. I checked the number. It was Ella.

"It's your godchild. I'll cancel dinner. I can take you back to the motel and then go talk to her."

"Cancel dinner?" Barb looked up. "Are you nuts? Answer the damn phone, woman. We'll give that child a quick, 'everything is going to be okay' version and then move right on to her life. Come on, I can do anything when I'm surrounded by Peking duck, mu shu pork, and cashew chicken."

The dinner was a surprisingly good thing to do. Ella accepted what her godmother and I had to say about the doctor's visit without question. Although I was relieved, it was sad we were giving her the party line, knowing eventually the other shoe would have to drop. I also had a pang of guilt over the deception, me being the one who practiced honesty above all else. Brian would say the honesty requirement was one of my "things." It had been the very thing that had forced him into telling me about his discontent. And now, here I was, colluding with Barb on issues far more serious than any of us had ever encountered before. I rationalized away the guilt, hoping the little white lies would not keep me from Nirvana for too many lifetimes. The truth would come out when it was the right time.

"Pass the cashew chicken, please." Ella's request brought my attention back to the table.

"Sure, here you go. So, tell me some more about this intramural volleyball you're playing. How tough is it?"

"It's great, Mom, except I'm the team midget. Why didn't you give me growth hormone or something? The women are all like five foot ten, they're Amazons, totally buff, and most of the guys are giants, six five and over. It's pretty hysterical when I'm opposite them on the net, so mostly I play back row, you know, defense, just like in high school. It's okay; it's just fun to be able to play."

Barb had been listening to the two of us. "You know, Ella, some women would kill for your brains!"

The remark caught Ella off guard. She looked over her forkful of vegetable fried rice. "Thanks, Barbie, but where'd that come from?"

"Oh, I was just thinking how screwed up I was at your age. They couldn't have paid me to go play volleyball against giants. I would have been terrified. Not for my physical self, which given the nature of the game should have been my first concern. No, I always avoided anything that could possibly make me look stupid. But not my Baby Ella! You just seem to have your head screwed on straight, and I think that's because you're a brainer."

Ella laughed. "Well, I don't know, but I hope your theory holds true for the biology test I took yesterday. I think I may have tanked it." She gobbled down a mouthful of egg roll. "Don't look at me like that, Mom, I'm just kidding. Dad would kill me if I didn't do well in my science classes. He'd string me up over the pond and let the geese nip at my heels until I promised him I'd study until my brains fell out." She laughed. "I am so happy you had to come up here. Well, you know what I mean. Sorry, that didn't come out right. I just meant that since you had to go somewhere for this, I'm glad I got to see you guys."

Barb nabbed a shrimp off Ella's plate. "Me too, kiddo. You are the best part of this visit, no doubt about it."

When we dropped Ella off at her dorm that night, it was all I could do to keep myself together. Tears pounded against my eyelids. I fought against my need to cry, afraid that if I let loose now, I wouldn't be able to stop.

As Barb hugged Ella good-bye, I finally identified the soft spot I was trying to protect. We were all going to have to say good-bye, forced into a life-altering change that was unfair. The voice in my head screamed out, "Stop it, you pantywaist." I pretended to clear my throat, sucking up air in an attempt to keep the tears at bay. "Pantywaist," now there's an interesting expression. What the hell does it mean, anyhow?

"What Mom, what was that?" Ella asked.

I had actually asked the question out loud, which was even more alarming. Great, now I was really losing my grip.

"Oh, I was just wondering where the expression 'pantywaist' originated from. Weird, huh, how the mind works."

Barb stood with her short fat arms around Ella, smiling at the absurdity of what I had just said. "Or, in this case, how the mind fails to work! Ella, it may be time for you kids to start looking into a home for your mom—sometimes she's a bubble off plumb!" With that, she reached up to park a huge kiss on Ella's peachy cheek and said, "See you around, my precious godchild. Let's go, Wonder Woman, I'm exhausted. Why does Chinese food always do that to me? It doesn't even have turkey in it."

We sank into a gray silence on the way back to the motel. Fortunately, Lily had fallen asleep in the car and slept right through a diaper change, her relaxed limbs slipping easily into the soft fabric of her pajamas. Barb gently kissed her on both cheeks and put her into the crib, pulling the quilt I had made up to her sweet chubby neck. With that, Barb slipped off her clogs, pulled back the covers on her bed, and climbed in, fully clothed.

"You don't think there'll be a bed check tonight, do you? I can see the headline: 'Cancer-Riddled Japanese American Discovered Sleeping in Ducks Sweatshirt; Police Suspect Fowl Mood.'" She turned off her light. "I thought it was pretty sweet of Ella to surprise me with the sweatshirt from 'our' school, her sentiment and all, her wish of good luck. Maybe I'll wear it to every chemo session I have. Man, how bad will it stink by the time that's over?" She fell silent, then added, "Good night, friend. I promise I won't be a bummer for the rest of my life, although the way I feel tonight, that might not be for very long at all."

The drive home the next day was simply awful. Lily's exceptionally good mood of the last week had completely disappeared sometime in the night. She awoke fussy and impossible to please, craning her neck to avoid the breakfast that, just the day before, she couldn't get enough of. Barb's speech seemed to be limited to grunts and monosyllabic words. And, on top of everything else, it had begun to snow.

I maneuvered the Jeep through the unexpected driving hazard. "So much for an early spring," I thought to myself. The visibility was rotten. The truckers on the highway seemed unaware of the icy conditions, racing past us. I hoped we would make it home without having to put on chains. Although I knew how to thread the heavy metal couplings around the freezing tires, that had been one of the jobs Brian had always done, along with bug wrangling, dead animal disposal, and kid-puke clean up. Over the years together, we had managed a certain division of labor, and it wasn't until after he moved out that I realized he had always been stuck with the gross jobs. I had never fully adjusted to having to do them since we separated.

With this insight, I realized I wanted to call him as soon as we got home, trying to figure out how I could sneak over to his place. Because one of the other things he had always done for me, another job that fell to him in our division of labor, was to provide the most comforting shoulder when I needed to cry, and the only thing I knew for sure was that I needed to cry, big-time.

There are those times in life when it feels as though things can't possibly get any worse, but then they do anyhow. For all our optimism, no one was prepared for the results of Barb's surgery ten days later. The doctors had opened her up and found what they described as a "nothing we can do" situation. The cancer had spread far beyond what the CAT scan had indicated.

"What about the chemo?" I had asked.

"It might slow the process some, buy her a little time," her oncologist offered. "But, frankly, chemo would have to be so aggressive, so toxic, I wonder if it would be worth compromising what time she has left."

I sat in silence, trying to comprehend what was being said, grateful that Brian was with me, not only for his strength but also because he had the wherewithal to ask questions that kept getting stuck somewhere inside my head.

Finally, Brian took my hand and asked the question I couldn't bear to speak out loud.

"Is there any way you can make an estimation of how much time she has if she decides against the chemo?"

The surgeon looked very fatigued and, suddenly, very young. He gave off a sense of wanting to disappear right off that spot on the planet rather than answer the question. I stared into his hazel eyes and found myself wondering what kind of kid he must have been like. Then I realized he was talking.

"… hard to say with these kinds of situations, a couple of months, maybe more, maybe less. This one snuck up on everybody, the speed with which it metastasized. I really can't be any more definite than that." He looked briefly at the floor and then back at the two shell-shocked people standing in front of him. "I'm sorry. Believe me, I wish I could tell you something more positive, but I'm afraid this is the situation we're dealing with." He started to walk away. "I'll be back to check in on her in a couple of hours. She'll be in recovery for a while. It would be a good time for you two to grab some dinner." He walked off down the long green hall, disappearing through a set of double doors.

"He must hate his job right now," Brian said, "to have to give people that kind of news. You think he keeps some fifty-year-old whiskey in his desk? I can't imagine doing this for a living."

We both stood frozen in the empty hall, staring at the doors. I imagined how absolutely grand it would be if the kid masquerading as Barb's doctor popped back out and yelled, "April Fool's!" But of course, he didn't.

"Are you hungry?" Brian asked.

"Not hardly." I couldn't imagine eating. "When is Sam due to arrive?" I tried to remember our conversation from the night before. No matter how hard I tried, I couldn't retrieve the details that were buried under the rubble of what I had just heard.

"Seems like he said he'd bring Ella and Lily over about five thirty or so. It must be about that time now, isn't it?" He turned to look at me. "What in the hell are we going to tell him? Tell all the kids?"

I looked at my sort-of-husband and realized I had stopped thinking of him as a "sort of" these last few months. My hand found his.

"I just want you to know how grateful I am that we seem to be back on track, somehow, someway." I watched his eyes as they softened even more with my words. "I don't really know what that means, and now isn't the time for us to stop and figure it out. I just felt so comforted when you said, 'What are we going to tell him?' I can't imagine having to go through this without you."

Brian circled me with his arms. We stood silently in the hall, relying on each other's comfort and familiarity, struggling with how to proceed with our heartbreak.

Within a minute, I could hear Brian's deep voice tenderly, quietly in my ear. "There's our boy, with our girls. Right on time. Four years ago if you'd told me that he'd show up on time, clean, healthy, fully responsible for his little sister, and with a baby in his arms no less, I wouldn't have bet a penny." He held me as I turned to look down the hall. He continued, "Of course, I wouldn't have bet that our dear wacky Barbie Doll was ever going to be in this situation either. So what do you think—is it good we don't know the future, or bad?"

Sam looked at his parents' faces. "It isn't good, is it?" he asked.

I reached out for Lily as Ella made for her father's outstretched arms. "No, sweets, it isn't good. In fact, it's pretty damned bad. Let's go sit down." I led the way down the hall to the waiting area as Brian and Ella fell in step next to Sam.

"But the doctor said the surgery would be the first step," Sam was saying as we walked along.

Brian had his arms around both our children. "It looks like there aren't going to be many steps for Barb. I'm sorry to tell you guys, but the cancer is everywhere, and there's not much the doctors can do."

With that, Ella began quietly sobbing into her father's chest as our strapping man/boy crumbled into his father's arm. "It's not fair. It's not fair," was all he could manage to say. There was something about my children's tears, their raw expression of pain, that broke my resolve. I lowered myself into a cold vinyl chair, buried my face in Lily's neck, and began to cry.

I could not think of a sadder moment in my entire life. Even when we were most heartbroken over Sam, I had always believed that my son would eventually find his way, never losing hope, even when my logical brain said it was hopeless. But as I sat in the quiet of the hospital, the only sound my children's weeping, I finally knew what it was like to be truly hopeless, and it made me cry all the more.

Eventually, I could hear Brian talking, and I realized he was speaking to all of us, even Lily.

"We're going to do whatever it is we need to do to take care of Barb, however it is she wants to proceed. That's what families do: take care of each other. I can move all her things into the den downstairs. We'll just do everything, I mean everything, we need to do." And then his voice cracked, and the four of us cried together. That is, until Lily began to join us. It was her tiny baby sobs that brought all of us back to the moment at hand. Instantly, I started patting the baby, Ella rubbed her foot, Sam made funny noises, and Brian wiped her tiny rosebud nose.

"God, Mom, what about Lily?" asked Sam. "You and Dad have to take her. I would, but believe it or not, I think you two would do a better job of it than I would." He tried for a weak smile. "I can't believe this is happening." He stared at the floor.

Brian put his fatherly paw on his son's knee. "Let's not get ahead of ourselves here. One step at a time. I'm thinking that in spite of what the doctors say, we still have the indomitable spirit of one Ms. Barbara Yakamura with which to contend. Knowing her, all of our tears will be for naught."

I wiped my eyes. "Wouldn't that just be the best thing in the whole wide world?"

I made sure I was with Barb when the doctor gave her the news. Barb listened carefully to what was being said, her expression calm. The questions she asked caught me off guard, as if she wasn't as surprised by the prognosis as the rest of us had been.

"So the value of chemo is negligible?" she was asking.

"Yes," the doctor replied. "Of course, I understand if you want a second opinion." He cleared his throat. "I'm so sorry, Ms. Yakamura. Believe me, I wish I could offer you some clinical trials or miracle drugs. I scoured the medical journals this afternoon. This situation simply doesn't lend itself to any options that I could locate."

Barb straightened herself on the bed. "No shit." She laughed. He remained expressionless. "That was supposed to interject some levity into the scene, you two. Come on, lighten up. It is what it is. What do I do now? I mean, do I just look for the nearest iceberg to climb aboard, or should I plan on being a burden to my friend here for a while? You'll have to walk me through this, doc. I'm a little short on experience with this one."

The young man squared his shoulders. He was back in command. Finally there were questions he could answer.

"I've put in a call to hospice. I imagine you're familiar with their service?" Back in his white coat, doctor mode, he didn't wait for an answer. "One of their staff members will be in to talk to you tomorrow, well, whenever you want. They're waiting to hear from you directly. I encourage you to take full advantage of their services. It's a team approach. The hospice staff and I will work together to make sure you receive the best possible care. I'll be a part of your treatment plan every step of the way. You can expect to have your pain well managed. You will not suffer." The irony of his last words hung in the air. The room suddenly felt dank.

Barb broke the silence. "Hospice, huh? That means less than six months, right? I saw that on *Oprah* or something."

"Yes, that's correct." His discomfort had returned.

"Okeydokey, Doc. I think that's about enough for today!" Barb put out her hand. "Do you like Shakespeare? We're doing *A Midsummer Night's Dream* this season, and it's my professional opinion that you need a few more classic laughs in your life or your wife is going to find herself living with a real pain in the ass. I'll make sure you get the best seats in the house." She put out both her arms, and the slight man awkwardly accepted the hug she was offering. When she had him in her clutches, Barb whispered into his ear, "Doc, it's not your fault." He pulled away from his patient and smiled.

"Thank you. I think a dose of William might be just what the doctor ordered," he said, and he left the room.

I stood by the bed for a moment and then sat down next to my friend, careful not to get too close. Swooping in without an invitation would be the wrong move, and I knew it. I waited. Barb finally spoke.

"So, do you think I'm going to make my exit as a morphine addict? Man, can you believe it? All those years doing drugs, and now they'll be offering up anything I want. Where's the justice in that? Maybe this is some weird kind of payback. I mean, in my twenties I wondered if I was using up my allocated time too quickly, you know, all the sex, drugs, and rock and roll stuff. Now they're going to be giving me stuff on demand and my insurance will pay for it, no less. Really, Oprah said so. Weird, ain't it? Damn weird all the way around."

That's when she began to cry.

"Tell me this isn't really happening, Lee. Tell me I'm going to see my daughter grow up and all of your kids have kids and that I'm going to get to make a shitload of jokes about watching you and Brian live happily ever after. Tell me that my life hasn't fallen headfirst into the crapper."

18

*B*rian and Sam took it upon themselves to create a bedroom in the den for Barb. It had double windows that caught the lusty spring sunsets ("which will be better for her," Brian had noted, "Barb not being a sunrise kind of gal") and framed the occasional storms, bright and thunderous, as they roared up the valley. From her upstairs bedroom, they carried down Barb's hand-painted end table, the mirror framed in theater programs, and the collection of *New Yorker* cartoons she had hanging along the north wall of the bedroom. The new bedroom took shape with each addition of personal whimsy.

But no matter how hard they tried to artfully place Barb's belongings around the room, the rented hospital bed still stood alone, "like the cheese... or Moby's dick," Barb said when she first saw it. We had all shared an uncomfortable laugh.

"Do I really need it?" she asked. "I mean, Bushmen don't have a mechanical bed for their final days. Of course, a grass mat on the dirt doesn't sound too good either, so, okay, the bed stays. But where is my red satin brothel shawl? I think we throw that over the top of the bed, gather up all my mismatched pillows, and call it a done deal." The men scurried away, happy to be able to do something, relieved to escape the thick emotions swirling around each of us as we all tried to dodge the reality that seemed to suck the air out of the room.

Barb turned to me. "You know, this could be a real hoot—seeing all of you fall over each other to take care of me." But then, after inhaling deeply, she spoke slowly and deliberately, with an edge I didn't quite recognize.

"But I'll not have it. From now on, we go heavy into fake-it mode and stay there until the last possible moment. I know that's not your way, but I can't be talking about my feelings twenty-four-seven." She plucked at a long thread hanging from her robe. "No, I'm not an honesty freak like the rest of you. I've lived a happy, but apparently short, life in the land of denial. If you really care about me, we will go on about our business and ignore the knives that are sticking in our hearts until the very last moment." She searched my eyes for agreement.

"Deal?"

"Deal," I reluctantly agreed.

"Oh, and one more thing. I want Brian to move back in. We're going to need him. I've given this a lot of thought. The way I figure it, you're going to be busy taking care of me and Lily, so we have to have someone around to go after the moths and creepy crawlers."

I instantly bristled at her directive. "Hold on one minute. Since when do you get to call the shots in my life? I don't think you're in any position to wear out your welcome the very first day! Brian move back in? Just when we were getting the hang of being friends? I don't know."

Barb rolled her eyes. "That's a bunch of crap and you know it! You two have always been friends. Come on, you've both had your little dillydally phase, though I don't think either one of you took full advantage of your opportunities. No, I think what you've really figured out is how to be good old married folks. Just in the nick of time, I might add. Admit it, you want him back here just as much as the rest of us do." She flashed me one of her "I know better than you" smiles.

I contemplated the arrangement Barb was proposing. It wasn't the first time I'd thought of it. In fact, though I'd never admit it to anyone else, it was something I'd given plenty of consideration, especially during these last few months. But I had never wanted to breathe a word of it, afraid that by saying it out loud, the comfort I had been feeling with Brian would disappear like a frightened fox in an open field.

No, I'd packed it away to the back of my mind, telling myself that it belonged there for the time being because my friend was dying. There had been plenty of those moments when having Brian around held great appeal, but then Barb's situation would slam into me. Sudden flashes of guilt would erase all thoughts of how Brian and I would, or could, resume our marriage. What remained of Barb's life was my first priority. It seemed foolish to take my marriage back. Our current arrangement was not ideal, but nothing in my life was at the moment.

Just then, Brian and Sam arrived with their arms full of pillows. My dear son had thrown the red satin shawl over his head. Barb laughed a belly laugh at the sight. "Sort of a skanky Mary Magdalene kind of thing happening there, kiddo," she said. "Gimme that. You have no taste." She laid the shawl over the glaring white hospital bed.

"There, that's a step in the right direction," she announced. "Now for the pillows. Put the 1942 Yosemite one down first, then the two from the San Diego World's Fair, the twenties I think. Where is the one I got from Mardi Gras? Oh good, that wicked purple satin, lovely in a decadent sort of way, isn't it? Now gently, very gently, put Elvis and all his silver sequins on top. Ha! Graceland, 1997. Hey Sam, did I ever tell you about what happened at that show?" Sam smiled, knowing a bawdy tale was waiting behind her lips. Barb looked at Brian and me and thought better of it. "Wait till the old folks have found something else to do and I'll give you an earful!" Her attention returned to the task at hand.

"Okay, the gold brocade ones with the fringe, from my Parisian holiday, they go to the side of The King. And finally, the one with the black velvet silhouette of Rock Hudson sits on the very top of them, the place of honor, after all."

We all admired the pile of tacky, colorful pillows. Brian was the first to speak.

"Well, what do you think? Anything else we can do for the moment?"

Barb settled herself on the bed, pulling the shawl up around her as she lay back on the pillows. "Do I look like Cleopatra? No my slaves, that will be all for now."

Brian managed a half-hearted bow as he made it to the side of the bed. Surprising everyone, Barb most of all, he threw his arms around her and kissed her on the forehead. "Okay, Your Royal Hiney, I'm off then. I have some papers to correct. How about I grill us up some burgers tonight? Looks like a beautiful evening out there, and we could all use a little animal fat to brighten up the mood. Dinner on the porch and a good sunset. What do you say?"

"Ah, always a man after my own heart. Can we have oven fries too, dripping in that imported extra-virgin olive oil your wife keeps stashed in her epicurean pantry?"

"Yeah, and strawberry shortcake," Sam chimed in. "I'll make the shortcakes while you're gone. Mom, you won't have to do a thing." Slightly stunned, the three of us all turned and looked at Sam.

"I cook, you guys," he replied somewhat defensively. "You don't know half the things I've learned how to do."

Brian gave his son a friendly pat. "I'm beginning to get the idea that you learned quite a few things," he offered. "Okay, it's a deal. I'll get the groceries after I finish the papers, and I'll be back about five thirty." He looked at me. "Is this working for you?"

"Yep, it's working for me," I smiled in return. He hugged me and left. Sam followed him out of the room.

"Anything I can help you with, Sam?" I offered.

"Nope, you ladies just hang out. I've got this covered."

When we were alone, without missing a beat, Barb took up where she had left off. "So, if Brian can move me in an afternoon, I bet he could have all his crap back here in under two hours. I mean, half the stuff he has in the Plastic Palace can't cross this threshold or I won't be the only one facing an early death."

I glowered at her last remark, and she quickly resumed her

campaign. "It's a good plan, you have to agree. Brian moving in, I mean." She waited for me to respond.

"Why mess with what's already working?" I asked.

"Because, dumb shit, and I say this with love in my heart, you and I both know this arrangement, as you so cleverly call it, is no longer a good thing. Honestly, it's for the birds. I hate to admit defeat, but I think your foolish old dog of a husband has actually learned some new tricks. And you, look at what you've managed this last year. You didn't exactly set the world on fire, but I think it's safe to say that you proved you could happily fly solo if you wanted to. But what's that worth in the long run? Naw, be done with the double rent. Save each other from a fate worse than my own. Really, dying alone is the shits. Trust me on that one." She shifted her weight on the bed as her words slammed headlong into both of us. It was unbearable. Barb quickly tried to relieve the tension.

"What's up with that, anyhow? For the birds—why do we say that? This is for the birds. That is for the birds. What the hell does that mean? Why do people have it out for our fine-feathered friends?" She took a deep breath. "Okay, screw the birds. Now, where was I going? Ah yes, I was dishing out my sage advice if I recall correctly, in a self-centered, I-know-more-than-you kind of way. Think about it. Since you two are going to be raising Lily, I need to know that you have patched up for good. I won't have my daughter the child of divorce. Very tacky, especially considering her mother never even got married."

I stared down. Barb had spoken the unspeakable. Lily was to come to us. I tried to shake myself back into my skin, but anguish flooded over my body, and I quickly looked out the window. Bright wildflowers dotted the fresh green pasture. It was odd to see such beauty while feeling such angst. Surely I could manage to keep the tears at bay, no matter how they burned.

Barb reached for my hand, her touch gentle and soft. "Please, I know it's asking a lot. God, you're practically done with your four and I'm asking you to start all over. But you two are the best. You're already her family. She'll grow up always having you as her mother, never knowing any differently." Her voice cracked, and she took a moment before continuing on. "Please think about it."

My vocal chords finally engaged.

"It might not surprise you to know that I already have thought about it. For a while I considered campaigning for Sean and Deb, but I didn't think that would sit very well with anyone but them." Barb rolled her eyes in an exaggerated gesture of agreement. "Then there was that thirty-two-minute phase when I considered Sam, perfect in so many ways and wrong in all the others."

"Wait a minute," Barb interrupted me. "I won't have you say such things about that boy. There was nothing wrong with him. For your information, I actually considered that he might be a better match than you two old coots. But then I figured I couldn't saddle him with a kid, no matter how perfect she is. He's got his entire life ahead of him." She stopped, looking braced for a fight.

I reached over and patted my friend's knee. "Listen to you. Joan of Arc should have had such defenders. It doesn't surprise me that you thought of him—it's amazing, isn't it, how good he is with Lily? Makes me hopeful for the future. No, every time this topic floated through my mind, I always came back to me and Brian. It's a no-brainer, isn't it? And downright weird. We've been roaming around these last couple of years, trying this and that, neither of us wanting to be married, only to discover that being married is what we wanted all along. And now, you offer us your most prized possession."

Barb beamed.

"There, you said it—being married is what you want. I knew it. Okay, all right… so, we can consider it a done deal?"

I moved in quickly for a hug, knowing it was a fleeting opportunity. But Barb hugged me back with a strength that belied her physical condition. We sat this way for a long moment, each of us afraid to speak. Finally, I did what I knew Barb would want and pulled away.

"If you don't mind, I think I'll go call Brian and tell him the good news." The words stumbled awkwardly out of my throat. A tear managed to escape and rolled slowly down my cheek. "Ha, good news in a heartbreaking kind of way." I tried to calm my voice. "Aw, Barb, how can this be happening?"

Barb stiffened. "Don't go there, damn it, not for a minute. You promised me. Quick, it's back to la-la land. Yeah, go call Brian. That poor son of a bitch is going to be so happy he'll wet his pants. You and a baby all in one. By his measure, I don't think it gets any better than that."

Brian and I sat on his faded thrift store sofa in the dark. I found myself wondering why he never fixed up his apartment. He had a real eye for design, color too, yet he'd settled for hand-me-down furnishings and Dollar Store purchases. There were a few photos of the kids, layer upon layer of academic journals, newspapers in the corner, stacked with precision, waiting to be recycled, but there was no real sense of Brian. Was he too befuddled these last few years to create a home for himself? Or did he think all this time that he would eventually be back in the house? How could he? I never expected this outcome, but then, I had never expected to be the one to ultimately decide our separation either.

I kept my hand on his shoulder as he took in what I said. The air was stuffy, stale, and flat. I got up and went to the sliding glass door that opened to the concrete slab, the apartment's "patio" that did nothing more than spit in the eye of nature. Pulling on the worn metal handle, I opened the door a crack. I stood very still in the fresh air for a minute, trying not to think, not to feel. But it wasn't working. I walked back to the couch and snuggled in next to Brian. He turned to gather me up, his strength familiar and comforting. As he wrapped his arms around me, I wiped the tears from his cheek.

"It is too sad. I don't know how we're going to do this," I said.

"Is Barb sure, does she really want us to have Lily? And what about you? I mean, yeah, it's been great, incredible these last few months. I think we've been doing better than ever, but I never figured you'd take me back." He stopped and blew his nose. "I hoped for it, told Pissant I'd do anything to be married to you full-time again, but I honestly thought those days were gone forever." He leaned slightly away from me so he could look me in the eye, then continued.

"Now hear me out." He chose his words carefully.

"I don't want to move back in just because we're both trying to do the right thing for Barb. I mean, of course we're going to do whatever it is she needs. You can count on me to always be a part of Lily's life, you know that." He pulled back even farther until we were no longer touching, as if to create a safety zone. "I guess what I'm trying to say is, would you have me back if we weren't in this damned cataclysmic situation?" His body tightened up, braced for my response.

I considered what he had said. The same questions had rattled around in my brain during the drive to his apartment. Now was not the time for either of us to take the wrong step simply out of our loyalty to Barb and her precious daughter. I knew we could both raise Lily and still live separately. Based on the ease of the last few months, strange as the arrangement was in some ways, I knew it would work. But I also knew that it wasn't what I wanted or needed.

"Brian, look at me." I took his hands. "Honestly? I started thinking about living with you again the day you moved out. I always knew I was taking a huge risk; I knew we both were. But I have to say our separation was one of the best and smartest things I have ever done for myself. I wouldn't trade it for anything." I stopped to brush my hair from my face, wondering what had happened to my snazzy New York trim and not caring in the slightest.

"But I never fully adjusted to being on my own. No… no, that's not right, not right at all. I completely adjusted to being on my own, and there were parts of it I loved, like when the house was still and absolutely silent or when I only had to do laundry once about every ten days, and it was just my dirty clothes, mine and only mine. One of the best things? I could leave my book facedown on the coffee table and you wouldn't come along, determined to tidy up, and make me lose my place."

I leaned back into the lumpy sofa. "There were things I discovered about living alone that I absolutely adored. One week I ate nothing but salad and granola for dinner, every single night, and believe me, if we are back under the same roof full-time, I won't be the only cook in the house anymore! I treasured calling my own shots. I adjusted to that part just fine. But Brian, what I never adjusted to was the loss of your presence in my home, in my life. I remember when I was falling in love with you, that moment when I realized that somehow you had moved right into my heart. It was pure magic, and I wondered how you got there. I wasn't sure how it had happened, but I knew it felt right. And this last year, there were so many things I missed about you, odd things, like making memories with you. Not necessarily the big huge ones but rather the little ones, like when you broke your ankle that summer and we spent hours down by the pond with the kids pouring water on you to cool off, their kindness and your good humor, or when we'd all be down by the pond in the light of a full moon, you gently helping the kids put their marshmallows on the end of sapling sticks you had carefully sharpened, making sure no one dipped their marshmallows into the fire, which of course they always did. All those little moments in a lifetime that are the goodness, the backbone, of a marriage and a family. We stopped making memories together, and that felt like my greatest loss." I paused to gather my thoughts.

"Sometimes during this last year, I'd lie in bed at night and think about how perfect it was to wake up in the middle of the night and always have you right there. Sharing a bed. It's primal, intimate. Brian, I have simply missed so much about your presence in my life." I took a breath. "Here's the truth, Brian, my truth. Since the day we separated, well, I guess, months and years before that, I have never been able to imagine my future without you. Yeah, you were a rat, an award-winning butt, and I was pissed off at you for a very long time. Maybe it's age. Or maybe it's the realization, and acceptance, that I too contributed to our problems. And maybe it's even having Sam back, seeing how he has taken charge of his life. And then again, perhaps it's helplessly standing by as Barb slides uncontrollably down the hill and there's nothing any of us can do to stop her. Whatever the reasons are, there have been so many times these last months when I'd imagine the next path waiting for me, and I could only see the two of us walking along, hand in hand, like always. Pretty corny, really, but honestly? It never struck me as a good idea to start down that path without you."

We sat in silence. Brian leaned away from me again, letting go of my hands, finally speaking.

"Well, I guess we got here by being honest, and, much as I absolutely hate it at times, and I mean hate it, I guess it works." He suddenly looked down. I struggled to hear what he was saying.

"I have to ask you something. Maybe it's not any of my business. Well, I'm sure it's not any of my business considering everything I put you through, but for some warped reason I need to know." He looked me directly in the eyes and cleared his throat.

"It's been awhile now, but Rod Wyeth, remember him, that jerk from Chemistry? He made a crack about seeing you with some good-looking guy at The Peerless, said the guy was all 'spit and polish' and that you had obviously 'traded up.' Thought it was hilarious. Maybe it was. I went a little crazy thinking about you with another man. I know I had absolutely no right to feel that way. I finally asked Tom if he knew who he was, and he told me that you met him in New York. But…"

I flared, throwing up my hand to silence him. The speed of my reaction startled both of us.

"Cut to the chase, Brian. What do you want to know?"

"Aw, shit. See, you're mad. I knew I should have left it alone. I don't know what I want to know, maybe nothing." He rubbed his hand through his hair, and a slow smile came across his face.

"Not as much up there as there used to be, huh?" He took my hand. Surprising both of us, I let him.

"Lee, I've rolled this around more times than you'll ever know. Here it is: some handsome, full-head-of-hair New York art lawyer courting you, or me, the balding nerd with the slowly expanding waist, struggling to save the earth one aluminum can at a time, who thinks an exciting night is building a balsa-wood model of the Golden Gate Bridge? Are you sure you're making the right choice?"

I considered what he was saying, feeling my anger quickly subside. It was odd to have such harsh feelings simply scoot away without any effort. I looked at this man with the thinning hair and the thickening belly and smiled, confident my decision didn't have anything to do with what was on the outside.

My next move was one we'd both laugh about for years to come. I crawled into his lap, both of us very aware that I was no Pekinese. Brian made a gallant effort to embrace my tangle of limbs, as he always did when I moved in for such awkward closeness.

"Brian, we said for better and for worse. We've known a fair amount of both, and right now, we're living the very worst. It's as if this terrible thing has happened to shake us back to our senses. I learned that I'm all right on my own. I ain't bragging, but I could continue with our current situation. I just don't want to. And by the looks of this dump, I'd say you're a bit of a lost cause as a single man. It's staring both of us in the face. I think we've both learned a lot from our folly. What we do the very best is be married. We're not all that bad at raising kids. Overall, we've been a damned good team. That may not be considered a worthwhile, hip and groovy vocation in some circles, but it sure feels like a worthwhile purpose to me. I don't know why else we'd even be on the planet if it weren't to take care of each other and our family."

We sat like this for a long time, melding into each other with a comfort and ease that could only be achieved through experience. He absentmindedly rubbed my toes, and I worried his lap would soon be numb from my weight. But instead of sliding back onto the couch, I rested my head on his chest, feeling the deep, familiar rhythm of his heart. I took a deep breath.

"What?" Brian wanted to know.

"I don't know about you… but I have to tell you that I've never been as horny as I am at this exact moment. How completely sacrilegious would it be for us to go make love right now?"

Brian's laugh was huge, deep, and rich with appreciation. "I'd offer to carry you into the bedroom but those days are over." We kissed, and it was warm and scrumptious.

I broke away first. "I'll race you!"

I hopped to my feet and started dragging Brian behind me, but he threw his arms around me, stopping me in my tracks. We stood facing each other, eye to eye, in the way that felt good.

"Are you sure, sure about our future, sure about what we've both figured out, sure you want to do this?" he wanted to know.

"I am very sure," I said as I took him by the hand and led him into the bedroom.

19

Summer moved along quietly. The day began as all the others had. Each of what Barb now dubbed the Farmhouse Three plus One and Crap, One More slid into his or her respective roles and routines.

Early one morning, after kissing me gently on the forehead, Brian popped up at Lily's first coo, just as he had with our four kids. While stealing a few more precious minutes under the covers, I appreciated the comforting sounds of morning. Brian ambled down the hall to Lily's room, offering her mumbled sweet nothings while he changed her diaper. Then they headed downstairs to see if Barb was awake. (Pain medication made her drowsy in the mornings, but he always, always gave her first crack at Lily cuddles while he prepared the baby's bottle. The house was still, and that meant a deep morning sleep for Barb.) Soft steps carried Brian through the hall to the kitchen, and that was, sadly, my signal to rise and hopefully shine. It was another day.

Pulling on my robe, I headed for the stairs. As I began to make my way down, I could hear Brian talking to Lily.

"What'll it be, sweet cheeks? Hey, I know. I bet you're in the mood for a bottle this fine morning." I pictured her reaction. She'd be playing with his ear as she sucked her thumb, her legs kicking in wild anticipation of food. There would be that desperate grab for the bottle, and she'd begin to suck hungrily as though it was her first meal ever. Brian would then give her his morning forehead kiss. It was just what he did. The image of such tenderness overwhelmed me. I sat down on the stairs, appreciating his gentleness and the strength he was bringing into our lives.

My thoughts were interrupted when I heard Sam enter the kitchen and then his father's welcome.

"You know, Sam, one of the things I can't seem to get used to is that not only do you hear your alarm, but you get up and are showered before anyone else is. Amazing."

I waited for Sam's familiar chuckle, but it never came. The compliment seemed to land hard in the space between them. I made my way down to the end of the hall where I could see them but they could not see me.

What I saw was not reassuring. With Lily in his lap, Sam sat on a stool, his back to his father. He had that bristled posture we had all come to know so well.

Brian popped bagels into the toaster oven and stared out the window. Finally, taking a deep breath, he turned. Speaking to Sam's back, he said, "I'm not sure if you know this or not, but your Mom and I saw a counselor for a while. It took me a hell of a long time to get the hang of what the guy was selling. But right now, I can hear little Pissant Man's weasel voice saying something like, 'There are times when you should not open your mouth until you know exactly what words you want to come out.' This sure seems like one of those times."

Sam offered only silence. I stood frozen, silently willing the dear man on, hoping he'd reach a conclusion I'd come to months before: There are times when there is nothing to lose. And this was one of them. He could fight back as he always had and things would disintegrate even further, or he could risk trying something different.

He finally spoke. "Sam, I'm not exactly sure what just went wrong, but, believe it or not, I was trying to say something nice."

"Really, Dad?" Sam asked. Lily startled at the anger in Sam's voice.

I fought the temptation to make my presence known, to rush in and make it all better. But this was between the two of them.

Sam rubbed Lily's back, trying to soothe her. He finally spoke. "I've been busting my butt for months now, trying to get back into everybody's good graces, and all I get are constant reminders about how different I am. Is anyone ever going to let me forget I was a pain in the ass? Yeah, it was bad. I was bad. But shit, let's move it along, shall we?"

Knowing Brian's zero tolerance for disrespect—especially when it came from one of his children—I held my breath. His jaw muscles clenched as he worked to keep his mouth shut, undoubtedly fighting the urge to turn around and yell at the kid who had caused all of us so much grief. I thought about the worry, the endless fights, the way the other three kids had suffered, how all of us had suffered because of Sam's troubles. For some reason, I recalled the time I had found Sam drunk, passed out in the yard. I had quietly helped the boy up to bed so his father wouldn't find out and we'd be spared even more upset.

My heart broke, watching father and son struggle in silence. I turned to go back upstairs, not wanting to witness what would happen next. But then I heard Brian speak.

"I'm trying real hard here, Sam. You know how crappy I am at stuff like this. All I was meaning to say was it's good, everything you've done to get your life back on track. I sure as hell wasn't trying to rub your nose into the past. That was never my intention, but I can see how you might think that." Turning, I saw him take a stool across from Sam and Lily.

"You and I both know I managed my own share of bad shit in the last couple of years. I've been busting my own ass to get your mother to forgive me. I know the feeling." He offered Sam a mug of coffee and took a sip from his own.

Lily leaned back into Sam's chest and reached up for one of his ears. "What is it with you and ears, Liliputt?" he asked.

With this, I saw Brian make his move.

"I'm sorry, Sam."

Sam looked up at his father for the first time.

"Apology accepted. Me too," he said. "No Barb this morning?"

Oh my God! They made it through! I wanted to jump up and down. Throw confetti into the air. Light some firecrackers for good measure. In their own awkward way, they had managed to maneuver a conflict that previously would have ended miserably. It was nothing short of a miracle.

"No, sounded pretty quiet in there. I heard her in the middle of the night, at least I think I did, or was that you wandering around? It surprised me because usually it's your mother who wakes up." Brian laughed. "You never had a chance sneaking in with your mother's ability to sleep with one ear open, one eye too, I swear. It used to creep me out. Bagel?"

"Naw, in a minute, thanks. Why don't you earn some brownie points and take some coffee up to Mom. I've got L'Put covered."

Suddenly aware that I might get caught, I silently made my way back up the stairs, pulled off my robe, and slid under the covers, hoping against hope that some yoga breathing would calm me in time for Brian's arrival.

I opened one eye as Brian came to my side of the bed and gently sat down.

"There it is, the one-eyed surveillance Sam and I were just discussing." He leaned in for a kiss as he put the coffee on the nightstand. With feigned effort, and silent guilt, I pulled myself up to a sitting position. Brian slid the pillow behind my back.

"Thanks, and coffee too, you're an angel." Now it was my turn for honesty. "It was a terrible night. I spent most of it in the den with Barb."

The information surprised Brian. "When did that happen? I could have sworn you went to bed when I did."

"I was here for about an hour, and then I heard her rustling around so I went down. She was having a lot of pain, but of course instead of talking about that, she volunteered that she'd just killed a spider with Sam's copy of the Dalai Lama's book, *An Open Heart: Practicing Compassion in Everyday Life*, and was worried that Sam, not to mention the Dalai Lama, would think she was an utter failure as a spiritual being. Which of course she admitted she was. With that, she announced that 'drugs and a couple of hands of poker might be a fun way to while away the midnight hours.' Yeah, real fun. You know how good I am at Five Card Stud. I stayed, we played but mostly we talked, and then she'd doze off only to wake up ten minutes later to slap down a card and continue talking. So I slept on the couch for most of the night." I leaned back against the pillows, sipping the hot coffee. "How is she this morning?"

"Don't know. When I checked in on her, she was sleeping hard, so we just went straight to the kitchen. Is her medication really working? I was wondering if we needed to ask hospice about it. Seems like it hasn't been doing the trick these last few days."

I thought about his question.

"Yeah, I guess it is. It either did the trick or she finally had to give way to exhaustion. You know her. She definitely settled down and was able to doze. But it was good-old night-owl Barb last night, kind of fun actually, kicking my butt at poker, of course. I thought our laughing would wake up the entire house at one point." I paused for another sip of coffee. "So why do they call it a royal flush? It can't be what Barb told me."

"Probably not. What'd she say?"

"No, I'll pee my pants if I start thinking about that again." I took his hand. "The hardest part was when she got all serious on me, making me promise what we'd tell Lily about her, what to do with her house and furniture, stuff I thought we'd decided, but it was as if she wanted to make sure I understood all of it. I hate that part of this. She can get so businesslike. It takes everything I have to keep it together, which of course is what she wants. How can two best friends in the world be so completely different?" I took another long sip of coffee, all the while holding Brian's hand.

I looked at my husband. "Have I told you how glad I am to have you back under this roof, back in my bed? Perfect timing, I think."

We heard a soft knock on the doorjamb and looked up to see Sam standing in the doorway. Lily sat happily on his shoulders, milk drops landing on his freshly shampooed hair.

"Sorry to interrupt, but I need to get going here. Who wants Stinky?"

I put down my coffee and reached for Lily. "Is there a particular reason why you seem to have a hundred different nicknames for this child? She's going to be completely confused, Sam. Think of the identity issues you're creating!"

But he was already out of the room and headed down the hall. We could hear him laughing as he went into his bedroom.

I explained to the baby, "I bet that's not a 'with me' laugh but rather an 'at you' kind of chuckle. Lily, that boy thinks we are a couple of weirdos, and in time so will you."

I turned my attention back to Brian. "Thanks for the coffee. We might just hang out here for a little while since I'm not scheduled at the gallery today. What are you up to this fine summer morning?"

"I know I'm lousy when it comes to figuring time, but by my estimation, I have about an hour left on the lake house and then it will be ready to move into. Funny, Barb insists she has no real Japanese roots, but this thing looks a lot like a teahouse if you ask me—well, a teahouse with an Elizabethan market/running of the bulls kind of motif." His brow furrowed at his words. "Lee, do you think she's going to like it?"

"Ah, Bri, she's going to love it. What a gift you've given her, all of us, really." I leaned in for a kiss. "Thank you."

"My pleasure," he replied. Gently rubbing Lily's curls, he kissed the baby on the cheek and made his way out of the room.

I stripped off our pajamas and slipped into the shower with Lily for a quick rinse. It was something I'd discovered about her from the very beginning—this baby loved the water, the more of it the better. She was old enough by now to try scrubbing me, but mostly her tiny hands just slipped off my soapy skin.

The shower over, I dried us off, pulled on shorts and a top, and turned my attention to wrestling a happy baby into a diaper and a T-shirt. It was already too warm for anything else. "It's going to be a hot one, Sweetie," I said to Lily as I tried to pull her plump little arm through the short sleeve. "Aw, come on, give me a break, work with me kiddo, you know the routine." I finally got the sleeve past her elbow when I realized what our little struggle was about. "That's it, isn't it, Stinky? You're old enough now to have a little attitude, an opinion about where you want your arm to go. Ah, growth—it's a wondrous thing." With that, Lily's other arm popped through, and the two of us headed for the kitchen.

20

*B*rian stepped back from the lake house to survey his handiwork. He was pleased with what he saw. Going into this project, he had been doubtful about the final outcome, having felt a terrible pressure from the moment Barb first cornered him on the porch with her idea.

He had been on his way down to the barn to replace a couple of rotten boards in one of the stalls. In the old days, he would have made himself tear out and replace the entire wall. It would have been his definition of the "right way" to solve the problem. He smiled at the thought of having come up with a new definition of "right." It was making his life a whole lot more enjoyable and satisfying.

Heading out the front door, he found Barb resting on the chaise longue. She snagged him by the pant leg.

"Listen, Brian, I've been thinking. I want you to build the lake house before I croak." The blunt delivery stopped him cold in his tracks. "I figure it's the perfect summer project for a professor with time on his hands, especially one who seems to have come home to roost. Since it's going to be my dream house, I better be here to dictate every piece of construction. And I have such few pleasures left—harassing you all summer long sounds like sheer joy!" She laughed and glanced up at him. "Oh Brian, stop your squirming. I'll be easy on you." And then she dropped into that place none of them could get used to and all of them hated. Brian immediately recognized her shifting to a more solemn demeanor. Pissant's work was paying off again. He pulled off his baseball cap and settled into the wicker chair next to her.

She kept her eyes on the pond. "I never got to build my own dream house. It was something I always wanted to do. As a kid, living over my dad's grocery store with my parents, the three of us pinballs in a rattle trap machine, endlessly bouncing around in those four walls, I think it's safe to say it was a little bleak. I vowed a different destiny for myself. Then, when Lily arrived on the scene, I became all the more determined to have a proper home for the two of us." She collected her thoughts, a new trait Brian was having trouble adjusting to, and then plowed on.

"Why, before this crap hit, I had it all planned out. With only a few more years of mortgage payments on my Victorian, I was going to borrow against it and build me a spiffy place right on the edge of town. Had my eye on a lot and everything. It would have been far enough away from the theater that I could get a break but close enough to town that I could walk home if I was too drunk. Good logic, don't you think?" Brian murmured his agreement, and she continued.

"Well, we all know what happened to that plan. So, when Sam came up with the idea of the lake house, I saw an opportunity, a mini dream house. Maybe not for me, but for Lily. Really, it could be her dream house too, a little place where she could hang out and maybe even gather a sense of who her crazy mother was." Barb took a deep breath.

"I hate to ask you, Brian. It seems like you are already doing way too much, but do you think it could happen? Of course, I'd pay you, and naturally, I'd cover all the materials. I wouldn't expect you to do it alone, so whatever help you'd need, that would be included. I just don't want complete strangers doing it. I know the new you hates doing construction, but really, I'm not thinking anything huge." Barb stopped short. "At least think about it, will you?"

The two of them sat in silence for a minute. Then Brian reached over and took her hand.

"Barb, it would be a pleasure and an honor to build you your dream house. Consider it done."

She turned her round face to his and out rolled a classic Barb belly laugh. "Well, I don't know how much pleasure you'll get out of it, so the honor will have to carry you." She grew quiet and then said softly, "Thank you, Brian, from the bottom of my heart."

He squeezed her hand and, knowing how much she hated to stay serious, helped her out of the moment.

"Just promise me we're not talking Bill Gates and forty-two thousand square feet. I'm way too old for that." He pulled her hand up to his face and gave it a gentle kiss. "Where are your plans? I know you must have them or you wouldn't have brought this up."

In the evenings, the two of them pulled out the sketch pad and worked on the design Barb had in mind. It was the closest they had been in all the years of their friendship, heads bent over the paper, questions asked, lines erased. Their final design was a true collaboration. It was very simple, just an eighteen-by-eighteen-foot room. The fourth wall, "like the theater," was to be four recycled French doors, hinged together and capable of completely opening up to the pond. Odd-shaped windows graced the other three walls. There was a window seat for "cozy times" and finally a little balcony Barb insisted on: "What a place for a kid, high above the world. Yeah, Lily has to have that balcony. One of these days, she may feel a little Juliet coursing through her veins, and what will she do without a place to deliver her lines?" It struck Brian's sensibilities as all wrong, but as he worked on the design, the balcony fell right into place.

And now it stood before him. Sam had helped when he could, and between the two of them, they had managed to get the entire place built in a matter of weeks. He looked at the little balcony and thought about Lily up there. Barb was right, that girl would need a balcony. Brian was pleased with all the mismatched windows he had salvaged from the town's recycling center. Barb insisted that he hang them all at different levels, asking, "Don't you think it's unfair that some people stand on tiptoe while others stoop, all to look out the same window? No. In my dream house, anyone who comes for a visit will have a window just right for them, even if they're crawling on their bellies at the end of a long and riotous party."

He glanced up at the monitor, a piece of construction he was especially proud of. A rectangle of multipaned windows, another salvage coup, popped up through the center of the roof. A small-shingled roof sat on top of the windows. From there, the sunlight poured into the building and, at that precise moment, landed directly on a small counter holding a ceramic sink Barb had magically produced one day. He had dutifully plumbed the place for water because she had insisted. "Could be a need for some tasty mud pies or perhaps even a cocktail or two. You just never know who might be entertaining here," she said. Barb had begged him to put in a tiny bar refrigerator, suggesting that he "steal one from the dorms; they'll never miss it." Always the honest guy, he had found one at the end-of-the-year campus auction. For ten dollars, the lake house was complete.

Brian stepped back for a better perspective. He smiled at the funny little cottage, pleased that, with a little landscaping, it would appear to have grown right out of the bank, just as Barb wanted. Two Corinthian columns from one season's *Julius Caesar* stood proudly at the far corners of the redwood deck, connected at the top by narrow remnants of Victorian lattice. It was Lee's idea to string the entire perimeter in Christmas lights, which, when turned on, would bathe the deck and calm waters in festive primary colors. Hot summer evenings by the pond were beginning to seem very inviting.

He could hardly wait to tell Barb that now all it needed was her crazy decorating and it would be done. He cleaned up all his tools, swept the floor, and washed the windows he could reach without a ladder. He wanted the place to look as good as it could before "Barb, the inspector" arrived on site for the final walk-through.

He found her in her room and for a moment thought she was dozing. Turning to leave, he heard her say, "Ah, the last time I had a man sneak into my room, I recall a very good time." He faced her bed.

"Well, I can't promise you that, but I do have some good news for you." He settled down on the edge of her bed.

"I'll be dead by morning?" she shot back. Brian sucked in a chestful of air.

"Barb, I can't stand it when you say things like that. I know that's pretty selfish of me, but I came in here all excited to tell you something that I thought would make you happy, and you have to remind me you're dying." He fell quiet, finally adding, "I'm sorry, Barb, I sound like a real jerk."

Barb reached for his hand. "Aw, shit, Brian. I'm the sorry one." They sat in silence for a moment. Barb was the first to speak.

"But since we're being totally honest, I think I hate the new you, all kind and caring to me. It really throws me off my game. Used to be I could always count on you to disappear at the first sight of anything emotional. It's like we belonged to a secret club of coconspirators, committed to working our disinterested evil against poor sensitive and caring Lee. Geez, how did she ever put up with the two of us?" He smiled as they shared a knowing chuckle. "That's better," Barb continued. "Now what's so damned special that you had to barge in here and interrupt my fifth nap of the day?"

"The lake house is finished and ready to move into. Want to go see it?"

Barb squealed with delight. "Help me into my wheels and let's roll on down to admire your handiwork."

The decorating had taken most of the weekend. None of us had seen such energy and enthusiasm in Barb for weeks. She was giddy, as if back at the theater, directing her crew to perform magic.

There was little painting to do because of all the windows. We painted what walls remained in a few hours, in color choices Barb had asked me to make. "After all," she had said, "you do own a paint store, for God's sake." The combination of warm yellows complemented the window trim, which had already been painted deep burgundy and rich pumpkin, "spicy for those long winter afternoons," as Barb described my somewhat unorthodox selections.

Sam was sent to her storage unit to gather up some belongings she had been saving for the lake house—a walnut rocking chair she had bought in London; a Chinese rug in rich blues, purples, and gold; a small Spanish table "a lesbian dancer sent me after she returned home to Barcelona. Why a table? I'll never know, although after a pitcher of sangria, this broad was known to take to the tabletops," she explained. Finally, Barb had also instructed Sam to bring a number of different boxes, each filled with mementos from different productions.

"Ah, here's the crown from *King Lear* I swiped after we closed. Check out the fake rubies and emeralds. And lest we forget the crimson matador's cape from that terrible one-act play we took a chance on, only to promptly lose our shirts. Remember? It was something like *Tijuana Madness*. Well, it was madness, but I did manage to score an authentic bullfighter's cape." She continued to rummage through the boxes, finally letting out a squeal. "Here it is, here it is, look, Lily, the fake English silver service from that Noël Coward run in the summer of ninety-five. Can't you just see the tea parties you're going to have? You'll be the envy of the first grade!"

The sound of her own words stopped her short. Barb, fully deflated, sank into her wheelchair and began to weep. Our family stood in awkward silence, looking at each other helplessly. I was the first to approach Barb, kneeling at her side and gently putting my arms around her. Brian came up behind her and encircled her thin shoulders. Sam dropped to his knees and grabbed for the only thing left, her legs, allowing Lily, who had been sitting in her mother's lap, to grab at his hair.

In a moment, it was Barb's voice we all heard, coming from deep within the human tangle of arms.

"This takes the cake. A Pickle in the Middle... on Wheels. Okay, everybody, back off and suck it up. I'm in no mood to experience death by suffocation."

One by one, we backed away from Barb, wiping eyes and noses, though Lily refused to let go of Sam's hair. The resulting yelp broke the tension.

"Hey Stinky, let go of me," he called out as her mother tried to pry Lily's tiny fingers from his curls.

"Yeah, come on, little girl," Barb implored, "don't be a barbarian. Let the handsome fellow go." Both mothers were trying to gently pull Sam's hair from the baby's grasp. "It doesn't help that you're laughing, Sam. She thinks it's a game... ah, there we are. You're free. Quick, make your escape."

Sam sat back on his heels, offering Lily his finger to hold instead of his hair. She grasped it tightly.

"Who's hungry?" I asked. "We've been at this all day. Let's get you back up to the house; Brian can start the barbecue and we'll get dinner going." I started to push Barb's chair.

"Hold on! Don't I get a vote?" Barb took a breath and continued. "I want to eat down here. It's a beautiful evening. Come on, you wimps, it won't be that hard. Let's rally for the final assault. Sam, there are two boxes under my bed, the ones that were delivered the other day. It's been driving your mother nuts—Williams-Sonoma boxes, and I wouldn't tell her what was in them. If you bring those down, we'll have plates, glassware, and cutlery for the cottage—a service for twelve. Surprise!"

I laughed, knowing we had been beaten. "You've had this planned for weeks, haven't you? I kept wondering why you insisted that Sam bring your long farmhouse table along with this first load. Never one for delayed gratification, were you? All right, I'm in. I'll take Lily up and change her. Bri, guess you get to haul down the barbecue, and the rest is a snap, although I hate to admit that. Leaves me wide open for some serious gloating from we-know-who."

Barb reached for my hand. "No gloating, just appreciation." She looked around the cottage. Twilight hung in the air. The glow of the Christmas lights was beginning to float on the calm waters of the pond.

"Leave Lily with me, would you? We'll just hang out here and enjoy the view."

It was the best meal any of us had shared in months. The evening breeze was warm and gentle and the food fresh and delicious, with salad greens and tomatoes from the garden, juicy orchard peaches, and rich, creamy vanilla ice cream for dessert. Lily was full of giggles, content as always to be passed from one set of loving arms to another, finally falling asleep in her mother's lap. The evening was drawing to a close, fatigue creeping up on each of us. I knew it was the right time and disappeared into the house, returning with a familiar black case.

"Now, promise me, no laughing. I've been practicing." They were all speechless.

Brian was smiling. "How did you pull this off? I haven't heard a note." Barb and Sam nodded in agreement.

"Well, it's been a challenge, but it was kind of on my list of things to do. I just kept it in my car, and on the way home from the gallery or on my way to do errands, I'd stop and play in some deserted pasture. We have a lot of them out here. I knew I was getting my hands back when the cows stopped running away at the first note." I opened the case. "It's been really good for me to be making music again, and, well, you guys used to say you liked it, so here goes."

I carefully tuned the violin, my head slightly tilted so I could focus on the perfect tone for each string. As I concentrated, my tiny audience settled into what Barb called the best seats in the house. Mother and baby snuggled under the mommy wrap, both cozy on the velvet chaise longue, the final piece of furniture Barb had requested from the house. Before sprawling out on the rug, Sam pulled an afghan over Barb's legs, the fire in the copper pit a mere pile of ashes and glowing coals. Brian took to the armchair on far side of the deck, knowing that the music would carry forth and grace both his senses and the still air of the summer's night.

I began to play, and after the first few notes, it was as if I had never put down my violin. The opening measures of Paganini's Violin Concerto in D floated into the air. Recognizing the piece, one of her favorites, Barb closed her eyes and cradled Lily, who seemed enchanted by the music. Sam sat motionless, unable to take his eyes off his mother's mastery of the delicate instrument. Brian stretched out his legs and sank deeper into the chair, watching with admiration.

I played on, the music surrounding the Farmhouse Three plus One and Crap, One More in a gentle swirl of comforting familiarity.

21

We fell into an odd routine, each of us doing what we could for Barb, all the while trying not to fuss over her. It was an awkward dance at best.

Fortunately, the late-night poker games Barb and I shared became a ritual, since neither of us was sleeping all that well. While most of the time was spent with her crowing over yet another winning hand, these endless hours together proved to be the time when we had some of our most difficult and painful discussions about what was happening.

One night, after throwing down yet *another* full house hand, Barb started rummaging through her nightstand. Finding what she wanted, she tossed an envelope on top of the cards.

"Here, read this while I tally up the damage."

I opened it and unfolded the pages. At the top, she had typed "Barb's Big Bash-A-Roo." Reading the first few lines, I realized she had written, in exacting Barbara Yakamura detail, her own funeral arrangements. I concentrated on not crying.

"Really, Barb? You want me to read this now? For once, I'd actually prefer playing cards."

"Sorry. You had to get the directive sometime. Seems like this is as good a time as any. I mean, either way you lose, right?" She had me, and we both knew it.

I started reading. Her memorial was to be held on "the first Saturday night following my death… or whenever is convenient. You decide since I won't be here to tell you." From decorations to food, Barb had decided everything. No detail was left undone. The lake house was to be decorated with Japanese lanterns and "even more" Christmas lights. A local restaurant would provide the menu—tapas and paella and enough lemon meringue pies—her favorite—for one hundred. (When I relayed this to Brian the next morning, he threw up his hands in disbelief. "Where in the hell are we going to get that many pies? What if somebody's allergic to lemons? Or maybe just hates them? She's nuts." He was at least a little right, which of course was exactly why I had always treasured my friendship with Barb.)

A bar was to be set up, "and make sure it is well stocked," Barb had written. "I may not be Irish, but I insist on a proper wake when it comes to boozing it up." Music was to be provided by a variety of local musicians and singing groups. I did a double take on the inclusion of the Rogue Valley Gospel Choir.

"The gospel choir? Is this really their kind of gig?"

Barb met my question with a laugh. "Pretty good, huh? Okay, maybe it's a bit of a stretch, but you remember how much I love their half-crippled, recovering-alcoholic leader? Surely I told you that story?"

Shaking my head, she continued.

"He was the best clarinet player in the entire Pacific Northwest until the night he was drunk, fell into the orchestra pit, and made a one-point landing on the Rubenesque harpist and her instrument. The woman was unscathed, but neither he nor the harp were ever the same again. Sadly, the rather painful and permanently disabling event sobered him right up, and even sadder still, in my humble opinion, it turned him on to Jesus, so grateful was he that, in spite of his gimpy leg, he still had two good hands for his stick." A belly laugh escaped her fragile frame. "Yes, he and his mighty singers just *have* to be there!"

Appreciating the sound of her laughter, I returned to my reading. "The choir will perform the Beatles' 'Let It Be' and the Ray Charles version of 'Let the Good Times Roll.' They will be fed well and paid handsomely. If they want to stick around for non-religious music, fine," she added. "But if they start cranking out God tunes, show them the door."

"It seems you've thought of everything."

"You're not surprised, are you? But there's more. Read on."

Doing as I was told, I learned that the guests were to be instructed to "bring a blanket to sit on at the pond's edge, come hungry, and plan on staying late." I groaned out loud when I read this, imagining the goodwilled debauchery many of her friends were so well-known for.

"Oh, you're at the part about getting all my drunk friends home after the party? Well, keep going."

I did. Her words were clear and direct: "Screw designated drivers. Take some money from my vast estate, rent a couple of vans, and pay drivers to deliver all of my lush friends to wherever it is they want to go. I know you two won't be happy to find any of them passed out by the pond in the morning."

Winding down, her instructions included: "There is to be no religious crap, period. I don't want some asshole who didn't even know me up there spouting all things Biblical. Besides, can you even begin to imagine me in heaven?"

She closed with one final thing for good measure. "And none of this 'let's all talk about how great Barb was' now that she's long gone. What a waste of time."

Reading this last decree proved to be too much for me. Picking my words carefully, I tried to explain myself.

"Please, give this some thought. It's natural for most people to want to share something, to talk about what they are feeling. I know, I know, that sounds like the most unnatural thing in the world to you, but try to understand. As selfish as this may sound, your bash isn't just about you."

My logic was met with a groan. "Great, my own funeral, and I have to think of others. Holy shit, I thought I'd at least get to call the shots this one last time."

We both fell silent under the weight of reality. Try as I might, I couldn't bear it and broke first.

"I'm sorry. I'll try to do everything exactly as you want. What are friends for? But just know that I'm not making any promises."

She dealt each of us five new cards. "Fair enough. Give it your best shot. Now, can we please get back to the more important business at hand? Watch out. I'm on a roll."

Over the next few days, I tried to digest what Barb was asking us to do. It wasn't easy. I'd begin to contemplate her wishes, but the pain would quickly become intolerable. I'd scramble to shift gears, move away from the feelings, do something, anything else. I simply couldn't reconcile her instructions with what I imagined the reality of that point in time to be. How would I possibly pull off throwing this "party," as Barb liked to call it? Broken hearts don't go to parties.

As our nightly poker games continued, I realized there was another significant detail Barb had, not surprisingly, failed to address. Knowing her history, I dared not second-guess her on this emotionally charged detail. But, much as I loathed bringing up this particular topic, I knew there was no escaping it.

My opportunity came one night after she had clobbered me seven hands in a row.

I took the chance. "You're in a pretty good mood now, right? Creaming my butt with your bluff-of-all-bluff style of poker annihilation. I want to ask you something."

Barb stared at the cards. "Ask away. You can't throw me off this winning streak, no matter what you want to know."

"I'm actually not so sure of that. There's something I need to understand. I want to make sure I do the right thing."

Barb groaned, "No, no Porta Potties at the memorial! I know you guys are all organic and everything, but that's where I draw the line. Let my crazy bastard friends at least come in the house and use the downstairs john!"

I paused and took a deep breath, refusing to let her joke throw me off course.

"What do you want me to say to your folks? I mean, I don't even have their phone number let alone know how you want me to tell them."

Barb flicked the cards in her hand with a practiced, syncopated rhythm: one, two, three-four-five. Her eyes shifted from her cards to the chips and back again. She appeared to be calculating her next move, but I knew better. No, my friend was calculating her response to this, the most difficult of questions. Finally, without taking her eyes from the pile of chips, she spoke.

"Lee, I really don't think there's any point in your telling them anything. You can't possibly have forgotten my last conversation with my father. Remember right after Lily was born? I was drowning in that swirl of a hormonal tsunami, and I called them. If you don't remember that third-act climax, it means you're demented and I'm revoking your guardianship to my daughter. Think about how that seven-second conversation went. Don't you remember? I said something like, 'This is your daughter,' and I believe my dear father said something like 'Our daughter is dead' and hung up the phone. Didn't miss a beat." Barb inspected her hand again. "Classic Yakamura. Shit, just thinking about that last conversation with my dear old dad I'm breaking out in a sweat. Yeah, you go ahead and call him, but you'll only be delivering old news."

With that, Barb threw down a card and announced, "Hit me." I tossed her a ragged playing card. It glided smoothly to a spot right in front of my poker buddy, who slid the card into place and reevaluated her hand.

"Honestly? And I know how much you like honesty. I don't want you to say anything to them. Why would you, except to make them feel terribly guilty." She paused, considering her last words. "Now that may potentially be a worthwhile endeavor. However, since I won't even be around to relish it, save your breath." She stopped and inhaled deeply.

"Besides, gambling woman that I am, I'm hedging my bets that there is a God who is all forgiving and suffers from short-term memory loss who might actually give me a pass through the pearly gates. Best not to show up on the heels of something so completely mean-spirited, don't you think?"

The silence that followed was brutal.

"Call," she announced, and the conversation was over, her winning hand the only thing Barb was willing to focus on. I knew better than to pursue the topic any further.

That was our last poker night. After that evening, Barb hid out in her room, rarely asking for anything at all. After dinner, I'd offer myself up for poker abuse, but she'd gruffly wave me away, telling me she was too tired or that she wanted to read. At night I could hear her below me in the quiet house, moving awkwardly, painfully through her self-imposed isolation. The cool distance between us was all wrong. We were wasting precious time. I hated it, and one night, I decided I'd had enough.

It was time for an over-the-moon approach. Going to the kitchen, I surveyed the possibilities for my bribe, Barb's favorite foods. Though her appetite was off these days, she hadn't lost her emotional attachment to food. Keeping it simple, I filled a bowl with strawberries, added a bit of sugar to mascarpone cheese, and put the tea kettle on to boil. As a crowning touch, I even poured her a bit of her sickeningly sweet port.

Laying out my best china, I set a tray befitting a queen, right down to linen napkins and my grandmother's silver. When the water was ready, I filled the teapot. Carefully walking down the hall to her room, I worried the entire way. Would Barb would let me in? Tapping on her door, I waited for her answer.

"It's kind of late. What do you want?"

"I wondered if you might share a midnight snack with me?"

It seemed to take forever for her to answer. "It depends on what you've got."

Were these the first words of a truce making their way under the door? If nothing more, I figured it was about as good an invitation to come in as I was going to get. Turning the knob, I pushed the door open with my hip and took a small step into the room. Barb lay in bed, Lily snuggled cozily into her chest. I offered up my tray while keeping my gaze directly on the crystal stemware holding the port.

I could hear a smile in Barb's next words. "If that's Burmester you have in that glass, it's safe to come in."

We shared our food in near silence, but it didn't matter. Simply being together again was what both of us needed. Midway through our bedside picnic, Barb handed sleeping Lily over to me. I believe this was her ultimate peace offering.

The summer moved slowly. Days melted together, with some far better for Barb than others. When the days were good, we took full advantage. As a measure of just how different things were, Barb seemed happiest sitting out on the porch, enjoying the shade, content to simply savor the peaceful countryside.

I was grateful we were back on track, having been so saddened by our brief estrangement. No matter what, I knew I didn't want to risk anything like that again, even though I also knew there was one final detail Barb had failed to address. To be honest, I almost felt relieved that I didn't have to confront this last bit of painful planning, because… how in the world does a friend ask another what she wants done with her ashes? Every time I thought about this, my heart ached, and I was reminded of how impossible it was for all of us to be living this tragedy.

Silly me. I should have known that Barb would eventually get to this painful detail on her own.

We had been sitting on the porch watching Brian and Sam plant shrubs down by the pond. Lily crawled between the two men, alternately putting dirt into her mouth and spitting it out.

Her mother observed: "Do you think she's going to figure it out that maybe dirt isn't the best-tasting thing going? Right now she's not looking like the smartest kid in the county, which we know her to be."

"Oh, she'll get it," I reassured her, "but at this rate, it will only be because of a terrible case of parasites." I called down to the pond, "Hey guys, would one of you do something with Lily so that she doesn't consume every ounce of shoreline we have?"

The two men looked up at me and then back at Lily. She beamed through her muddy cheeks. Brian scooped her up, wiping her face off with his sleeve.

"Oh, great, that'll help. His filthy shirt sleeve adding to the muck." We laughed.

"Ah, well, it can't hurt her all that much," Barb said. "I read somewhere that there's a tribe in Africa that eats dirt on a daily basis. Some fancy-pants scientists determined that it was the only way they could get a certain mineral into their diet. Who knows, maybe Lily descended from that branch of the family tree." She smiled at her grimy daughter. "Speaking of trees, I know what I want you to do with my ashes."

I sucked in my breath.

"You know, Barb, a little segue would be nice now and then, to alert me that we're about to descend into something oh, let me think, heartbreaking?" I kept my eyes on the pond so that Barb wouldn't see the tears.

"You're such a wussy. All right, if you insist. Take a couple of deep breaths. We're going in." Barb fell silent for a short moment. "Ready now? I've been thinking a lot about this ashes business. I've never been a big cemetery gal, all of those boxes underground and then drawers full of people aboveground—the Trump Towers for the Dead, zoned for multiple dwelling. Too weird. And the idea of being sprinkled into the sea? Well, fish food doesn't feel like the best final resting place either, except, of course, if you could find a lobster farm somewhere. Then I imagined getting dumped from a plane over some forest, and you know me, not exactly Nature Girl."

I wondered where she was headed.

"Okay, I'm listening, Barb. Drop the bomb."

"Hold on, I'm getting there. It just came to me a couple of nights ago, right after we finished that incredibly delicious cherry pie you made. I took my last bite and said it might be the one thing on earth better than sex."

I interrupted her. "For as long as I've known you, you've said that about pretty much anything that arrived in front of you on a plate."

"Okay, busted, but really, your cherry pie is different, made right from the yard and all, so fresh. That combo of sweet and tart you somehow manage. Amazing. Remember, I actually said it was otherworldly? That's when it hit me. How about this? You guys get another cherry tree to plant during my bash, and when you're throwing in the dirt, toss me in as well."

I was speechless. Of all the things I had envisioned Barb wanting, this wasn't one of them. I stared at the pond, trying to imagine how it would feel having my best friend's ashes as part of my garden.

"Come on, Lee, don't you think that's the best? I mean, then from here on out, you guys can let those plump, delicious cherries roll around in your mouth and think of me!" The vivid image hung in the air between us. "Ohhhhhh, shit. That's gross, isn't it? Oh yuck, and creepy too! Forget I said that. Let me put it another way, my goofy yoga friend: I just want to be one with a cherry pie tree."

"Is that even legal?"

"Legal? Since when has legality ever been one of my driving concerns? Besides, who has to know? You'll notice I haven't invited anyone from Jefferson County Public Health to come to my party. And Lord knows my friends aren't going to breathe a word. The more illicit the better for them. What do you think? It's perfect, right?"

I wasn't so sure of the perfection of Barb's plan. It struck me as far too sad to look out at the pond year after year and see a tree that held my best friend's soul.

"Let me give it some thought. I'm going to have to get used to the idea."

It didn't take me much time at all to recognize that the edge of the pond truly was the perfect final resting spot for my best friend. Where else should she be but that close to her one true family? However, as hard as we all tried, Barb included, none of us could make the leap between her ashes and cherry pies of the future. Eventually I suggested we plant a Japanese dogwood, another one of her favorite trees that lined the pond. When it had last been in full bloom she'd even said it was "her" tree, "You know, it grows low to the ground, and it's so round."

22

*B*arb died exactly five months from the day she moved into the farm-house den. No one expected it, and no one was ready for it. Unlike her life, her death was quiet and calm. She simply passed away one night when the house was silent and the moon was full, a detail not lost on me.

Peeking in on her, as he did each morning, Brian was the one to discover Barb's lifeless form. He broke the news to me as I sat in the middle of our bed, cuddling with Lily. All I could do was gently rock the baby back and forth, struggling to keep silent through the tears flooding my cheeks. Brian held us both until we heard our son coming down the hall. He stood up quickly and walked out to meet Sam, dreading the task at hand. I could barely see Sam's face as he stood perfectly still, listening. Consumed by deep sobs, he crumbled into his father's arms like the tender five-year-old he once was.

I had been watching them through my own grief. When I heard Sam's cries muffled in his father's chest, I grabbed Lily and rushed into the hall. The two of us surrounded our two children. It was the saddest Pickle in the Middle any of us had ever known.

That afternoon, after Barb's body had been taken to the mortuary and Lily was down for her nap, we gathered in the kitchen for some-thing akin to lunch. Anything that looked remotely appealing was pulled from the cupboards and fridge and put on the table. In spite of the many choices, we only picked at the assorted items in front of us.

I stirred my tea endlessly until I said, "Okay, boys, I'm still stuck on the girls. I noticed none of us tried to call them yet." Ella and Sophia had managed to squeeze in one last backpacking trip to the California redwoods before they had to return to school. They were scheduled to be back the following day.

"I was thinking," Brian said carefully, "even though they have their cell phones, maybe we should wait until they get back to tell them. I can't imagine them hearing this on the phone."

"Yeah," added Sam, the dark circles under his eyes reminiscent of his former days, "and what if the reception is bad? I can hear it now, you yelling into the phone and all they hear is 'I'm sor... to ell you ut arb ied... terday.' And them cracking up, giggling, 'Dad, I can't understand a word you're saying. Was it, 'I'm sore to yell you, put carb fried yesterday?'"

We all contemplated the painful folly of that possible conversation.

"Naw," Sam asserted, "I vote you wait until they get home. Anyhow, this is too crappy to hear on the phone, only so they can cry all the way back over Highway 199? You know the way they drive. We don't need that worry on top of everything else."

I took a sip of my tea, which was lukewarm and sour. I looked at my son, touched that he had included himself in the worry normally reserved for parents.

"I think you're right, Sam," I told him. It's not the best, but I go with you guys. They'll have plenty of time for their broken hearts when they get home to us."

The sun sat low in the sky when Ella and Sophia finally arrived home. Brian and I were on the porch, spent from a day of making arrangements for Barb's "bash." The girls bolted from the little red Toyota pickup that had been their wheels since high school. They waved at us, tiny little girls with their big hearty greeting that had long been their trademark. Filthy from their ancient forest adventures, they were full of pristine youthful spirit.

I could tell from the way they bolted for the porch that they were brimming with stories to share about their adventures. But within minutes, our daughters sat crumpled in tears on the wooden porch, holding each other as we held them. Their sobs skipped off the pond and disappeared into the failing light of the evening.

The days that followed were long and bleak. Each of us moved through time with a great heaviness. I wondered how we would ever complete the preparations for the memorial. But, with a nod to Barb's planning, the service came off without a hitch. Midway through, I surveyed the motley crew of guests and concluded that it was just the kind of party she would have approved of—heavy on the laughter and light on the tears, including a stream of gut-splitting stories expertly delivered, many actually performed with a practiced dramatic touch. The alcohol flowed nonstop, and a loud cheer went up when the thirty lemon meringue pies were paraded down from the house to feed the nearly two hundred people who had showed up.

The roughest moment for everyone was when we buried Barb's ashes with a Japanese cornel dogwood. Brian and Sam started digging the hole, but the girls decided they should have a hand in it as well. Sean was next to ask for the shovel. In the end, it truly was a family effort. We had decided in advance that we couldn't bring ourselves to literally throw in the ashes; I think that was the only detail that had never been finalized with Barb. Instead, we decided that Barb should have a "home away from home," as Sam had put it, opting to place her ashes in an exquisite piece of pottery from the gallery, raku-fired in deep blues, maroon, and purple, with a carved maple lid.

Each of the family members took a turn holding the clay pot. Both of the girls simply wept when it was their turn. Sean said a silent prayer. Sam, who was holding Lily, hugged both mother and daughter tightly and then whispered to his new baby sister, "wave bye-bye." Lily did, with her mother's trademark Yakamura enthusiasm, her tiny hand fluttering through the still afternoon air. It was a gesture that made the gathered friends cry and laugh at the same time. Finally, Sam handed the ashes to his father, who gently kissed the lid and passed it over to me.

Taking it into my hands, I stood tall and silent for a long time, feeling the cool clay against my chest. Staring at the pond in the distance, I wondered why it had all happened, why one of the most generous, loyal, creative, crazy, fun people I had ever known would come to rest in a ceramic pot. None of it made sense; none of it seemed right. I wept openly, then quickly realized that Barb would not approve of my unbridled display of emotion. The thought brought a smile to my face. Finally, I whispered her farewell, kissed the lid, and gently placed the jar into the hole. It was done. Barb, the dogwood tree, and her one true family, together for eternity.

———————————◆———————————

When I woke up the morning after the memorial, the first sounds that registered were nonsense words being sung slightly off-key. They floated up the stairwell, greeting me in a wonderfully natural way. A smile came to my face as I realized it was Brian singing to Lily in the kitchen below me. Then, right on the heels of this lovely moment, the events of the previous day slammed into my brain. I began to cry, selfishly wishing I could have magically been greeted by an entirely different day.

I've always thought that one of the strangest things about death is that life goes on. There we were, in the shadow of utter heartbreak, and Brian was singing to his new baby daughter. I caught my breath, knowing that life was just going to be like this, utterly juxtaposed, for a long while. I'd have given anything for a fast-forward button, something that could propel me through the unavoidable grief. But no. I knew what was to happen. I would be up, I would be down, and somehow I'd move forward until the day finally arrived when I wouldn't cry. Then there would be two days, then three, and eventually the grief would settle into a tiny corner of my heart, where it would mostly, but not always, live quietly for the rest of my life.

And so it was. As those difficult days passed, I watched each of the MacPhearsons, in his or her own unique way, try to get on with the business of living. I hadn't been surprised that Sean made a quick departure soon after the memorial. Knowing him as I did, it was a move I entirely understood. Better for him to throw himself into preparations for the coming school year than to muck around in the loss. And though I sent him off with my blessing, I secretly hoped the day would come when he could face these wicked things called emotions and not pack them around like the burden he had allowed them to become.

Fortunately, we had a few more weeks with the girls before they had to return to school. It was a bittersweet, tender time. They seemed most content to lose themselves in Lily's care, often playing with her in the waning summer days, making up songs about the "three sisters." When it finally came time for each of them to return to school, our good-byes were especially touching. None of us wanted to let go. Somehow we did. Though they returned to their familiar surroundings of friends and school, they each made their share of teary phone calls home. Young souls, they questioned why such a terrible thing had to happen to Barb, to Lily, to all of us. Ella seemed to struggle the most, and it broke my heart, so helpless was I to make things better.

Predictably, Sam disappeared into long hours of helping at home and down at the gallery, all the while reassuring us he "was fine." I waited, knowing he was anything but fine, wondering when his private dam would burst. It happened weeks later, during dinner, when I passed him a plate of pickled beets. How was it that such a simple act could carry such a roundhouse punch of heartache? He left the table in tears, and Brian quietly followed. With that, Lily erupted with her own upset. Gratefully trusting that the father was best suited to comfort the son, I pulled my daughter from her high chair, comforting her as any mother would do.

A month later, in early November, Sam announced he would be moving out. A room in a house full of friends had become available, and he was going to take it, saying it was time to move on. He also, somewhat sheepishly, offered that he would begin studying for his GED, since he'd need a high school diploma to be able to register for a few classes at the community college the following semester. Telling me how much he appreciated his "day job," he hoped I would "please" keep him on. I'm sure he could read the pride his parent's faces. It was a precious moment for Brian and me. Sam was on his way, ready to fully reclaim his own life. For the first time in months, we had something to truly smile about. We popped open some sparkling apple cider and toasted his success.

With only Lily to care for, Brian and I began the business of living as the couple we once were and the better couple we had become. The comfort of knowing each other so well was soothing. Gone were the assumptions, the second-guessing, and our indifferent responses of days gone by. Naturally, we had bumps. Some were real doozies. And to be perfectly honest, it was tempting to slide back into those familiar habits that had once split us apart. (I think it's safe to say both of us also discovered that self-righteous indignation can be hard to shake!) No, instead of pushing the friction away, hiding ourselves in the demands of daily living, we faced difficulties head-on. It wasn't easy, but more often than not, we were rewarded for our efforts. Of course, given everything we had been through, it helped that we both shared a new perspective on life, understanding and believing in that worn out cliché "the small things really are small." Yes, even though the weather outside grew increasingly cold, life inside the farmhouse felt reassuringly warm.

One day, as I drove over the back road to town, my focus on the icy pavement and thick snowbanks blocking my view of the next curve, I wondered why this, of all winters, would have to be the one to drag on. Hadn't we had enough gloom? I was hungry for spring and sunny skies. The glare off the snow was hard on my eyes, and I questioned my decision to venture out into this weather for my yoga class. Brian sounded concerned but knew better than to try and stop me, something he certainly would have done in our old marriage. As I pulled on my coat and scarf, I kissed him, then Lily, and reminded him that I knew the roads "like the back of my hand." He couldn't possibly understand all that yoga had become to me.

Not many people could. I recalled Barb's reaction when I had decided to try number six on my "Ten things I'd like to do before I'm too old to remember my name" list. Barb had jumped up out of her chair, no easy feat for a pregnant woman.

"You want to spend even more time each week with your yoganites? Careful, girl, I hear they're like some religious cult. Sure, it all begins innocently enough: a simple cat pose here, downward-facing dog there. Be aware. Nay, be vigilant! You know there's something wrong with people who are all so calm, so limber. Shit, most of them live on tofu and sprouts. It's mind control, I tell you. Watch your back."

My yoganites had been anything but that. In fact, they were the most comforting, accepting group of middle-aged and downright old women I had ever known. They had surrounded me with compassion and support throughout Barb's illness and after her death, bringing casseroles and fresh flowers for days after Barb died. And now, months later, my time stretching, twisting, contemplating, feeling, laughing, and sharing with this these women was one of the highlights of my week.

"No," I thought to myself, "a little snow will never stop me from time with my yoganites!"

I parked the car in the nearly empty lot and hurried into the church's community room. I held the door for Dotty, who at seventy-six was the oldest member of our group. We chatted about the weather, laughed at our muscles stiff from the cold, and wondered when we might get the first hint of spring.

"Hummmmm," said Dotty, her flat New England accent obvious even when simply pondering. "We're not exactly living in the moment, are we dear, pining away for spring. Ah, well, I think there are worse things than being human, don't you?" The older woman sat on the bench and slid off her sweat pants to reveal hot-pink yoga pants.

"Indeed, Dotty, far worse things than being human."

We joined the other women, who had already laid out their brightly colored mats. Our teacher was leading a warm-up of simple stretches and gentle twists. Talk flowed easily and happily. Rosemary was beaming with news about her first grandchild, a healthy baby boy who "is truly the most beautiful baby in the world, I kid you not." At sixty-three, Dolores had made the decision to go back to school for her master's degree in music, and the women applauded her announcement. Victoria, the newest member of the group, shared a recent success with her very difficult supervisor, and we cheered loudly, having coached her through a series of difficult communications. Jennifer, the quietest member of the group, hemmed and hawed until Marie, the most forceful among us, finally lost her patience. "Out with it, Jen, before I come over there and twist you into submission." She finally told us that she had been on her third date with "the most handsome, kindest baker I've ever met." There were a few catcalls over this one, but it was deadpan Dotty who asked, "Just how many bakers have you known in your lifetime, dear?" We all dissolved into giggles.

After a few minutes, the teacher had us begin to massage our feet with bright green tennis balls. It was one of my favorite experiences when, one at a time, we would roll each foot over the warm, fuzzy surface of the ball. The first time I tried it, I had been surprised that something so simple could feel so good—wrapping my toes over the edge, pressing my arch against the firm curve of the ball. My feet had melted into the experience, and today was no different. We all worked our feet, some lost in the movement while others chatted quietly. I heard their murmurs in the background but concentrated on the beautiful sensations my feet were experiencing. In the moment, I felt completely at ease, at peace, somehow at home. I smiled at my revelations and wondered what Barb would say. That thought made me smile even more, and my mind filled with her bright, clear laughter.

Suddenly, the tennis ball rolled away from my foot. It was something that happened to all of us at some time or another, a random ball of fuzz making its way to someplace else. I watched it travel silently over the old wooden floor, rolling forward to the center of the room. As if guided by an unseen hand, the tennis ball came to rest between the candle and the tiny brass Buddha that always graced our class. I looked at the three objects in perfect alignment and registered the wonder of their position to one another. It was then that I heard Barb's voice: "Oh that's rich, my friend, a Tennis Ball Epiphany." I felt tears in my eyes and a quiet smile on my face.

And in that moment, I finally trusted that the MacPhearson family was going to be just fine.

Acknowledgments

My heartfelt gratitude to my agent, April Eberhardt. How was it that our stars aligned themselves so perfectly? Your knowledge, experience, enthusiasm, and unfailing humor have brought me to this point. I look forward to many more adventures with you.

I have lived long enough to know that success in any pursuit takes nothing less than a ton of hard work and, often, the talents of others. So, while I may have written this book, breathing life into it took the combined efforts of many gifted professionals. My sincere thanks to my publisher, Brooke Warner, and all of the wonderful people at She Writes Press who have made this project a truly positive experience. How happy I was to work with Barrett Briske; know that you are a writer's dream editor. And what is a book without its cover? Kudos to Rebecca Pollock, who transformed my vision into an alluring reflection of my manuscript.

Finally, to my dear children, Taylor, Davis, and Evan, my thanks to each of you for the family we have.

About the Author

photo © Maia Cheli-Colando

*T*racey Barnes Priestley holds a master's degree in Community Counseling Psychology and spent many years as a therapist before moving into the field of personal coaching. An award-winning syndicated columnist for fourteen years (*Juggling Jobs and Kids*), Tracey currently writes and blogs about issues she, and countless others, face in the second half of life at www.thesecondhalfonline.com. An amateur singer and performer, she finally earned a percentage of the box office when, inspired by her print column, she co-wrote, produced, and starred in a one-act musical, "The Second Half: A Lively Look at Life after Fifty." Married for thirty-five years and the mother of three, Tracey lives among the redwoods of northern California with her recently retired husband and their loyal mutt, Bella von Doodle.

www.ingramcontent.com/pod-product-compliance
Lightning Source LLC
Chambersburg PA
CBHW030205221224
19326CB00002B/22

9 781938 314247